Praise for
THE ULTRA-FABULOUS GLITTER SQUADRON SAVES THE WORLD AGAIN

"The squadron is a gang of gender outlaws who take on the universe's toughest jobs and come through without chipping a nail. They find solidarity, sisterhood (with an asterisk for drag queen Butch and gender-eschewing M), and courage, as well as a greater understanding of self, as they face off against evil and triumph in style…. This groundbreaking collection will leave readers breathless with delight."

—PUBLISHERS WEEKLY, STARRED REVIEW

"I didn't realize how much I needed these women and their stories in my life until I started reading, at which point I found it very difficult to stop. Thank you, A. C. Wise!"

—JIM HINES, HUGO AWARD WINNING AUTHOR OF THE MAGIC EX LIBRIS BOOKS

the
Ultra Fabulous
Glitter Squadron
Saves the World Again

A.C. Wise

LETHE PRESS
MAPLE SHADE, NEW JERSEY

Published by Lethe Press
118 Heritage Ave, Maple Shade, NJ 08052
lethepressbooks.com

ISBN 9781590214343

'Doctor Blood and the Ultra Fabulous Glitter Squadron' first appeared in Ideomancer, Vol. 12, Issue 2 (2013)

'How Bunny Came To Be' first appeared in Shimmer, Issue 17 (2013)

Library of Congress Cataloging-in-Publication Data

Wise, A. C.
The Ultra Fabulous Glitter Squadron saves the world again / A.C. Wise.
pages cm
ISBN 978-1-59021-434-3 (pbk. : alk. paper)
1. Women heroes--Fiction. I. Title.
PS3623.I823U58 2015
813'.6--dc23
2015027764

Cover design
by Staven Andersen

Interior design
by Inkspiral Design

FOR MY FAMILY, BY BIRTH
AND BY CHOICE,
AND FOR ALL THOSE WHO GLITTER,
INSIDE AND OUT.

TABLE O[F

ONTENTS

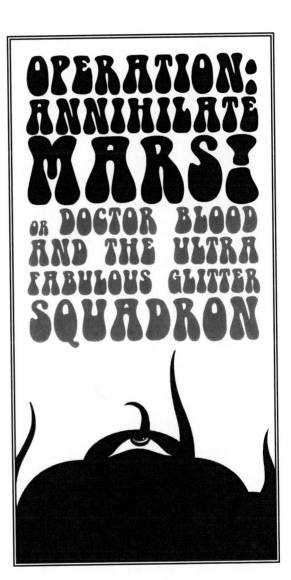

MARS NEEDS MEN!

But the Ultra Fabulous Glitter Squadron will have to do. At least one of them self-identifies as male, Butch in all his spangled glory. He tucks proudly, or sometimes not at all, and fuck you very much if you don't like it.

By night, they work at clubs with names like Diamond Lil's, the Lil' Diamond, and Exclusively Lime Green. Every Thursday, they bowl. In between, when they're not bowling, or dancing, or singing on stage, they kick ass harder than you've seen ass kicked before. And they do it all in silver lamé and high heels.

This is Bunny, their leader, born Phillip Howard Craft the Third. At the moment, she is up in the recruiter's face, waving a poster of Uncle Sam under the aforementioned tag line, a floating head against a backdrop of Martian red. Her nails are manicured perfection, each painted a different metallic shade, all the colors of the rainbow, and then some. Her hair is piled in a frosted bouffant so high it barely fit through the recruiter's door. Despite the anger written in every line of her body, she doesn't raise her voice.

"Your sign says you need volunteers. We're volunteering, and since I don't see your waiting room clogged with other candidates, dare I suggest: We're all you've got."

"I can't...I won't..." The recruiter turns bright red. He takes a deep breath, faces Bunny, and almost, but not quite, manages to look her in the eye.

"I can't just let a bunch of..."

Bunny's eyes, tinted violet today, shine cold steel. They stop the words in the recruiter's throat, hard enough that he looks like he might actually choke. Her tone matches her eyes.

"Think carefully, General. If the next word out of your mouth is anything but 'civilians' I will dismember you myself. You won't live long enough to worry about an invasion from Mars."

The general's jaw tightens. A vein in his forehead bulges.

"The Glitter Squadron's record speaks for itself, General." Bunny's voice is level. She places the poster on his desk. "Cleaner than yours, I'll dare say. And—" Bunny smirks, and points to the general's medals—"our bling is better."

Rage twists the general's features, but his shoulders slump all the same.

"Fine," he says. "The damned mission is yours. Add a little more red to the planet, if you want it so badly."

Bunny smiles, teeth gleaming diamond bright. "I promise you,

General, the Ultra Fabulous Glitter Squadron is more than up to the task."

★

THEY ARE LOADED INTO A ROCKET BY CLEAN-CUT SCIENTISTS WITH white coats and strong values, men and women who believe glitter is for little girls' birthday cards as long as they're under six years old, and leather is for wallets and briefcases.

"Some people have no imagination," Starlight stage-whispers as they climb the gangplank. Starlight was born Walter Adams Kennett. Her mirror-ball-inspired outfit forces the good, moral scientists to look away as light breaks against her and scatters throughout the room.

Starlight pauses at the airlock door, looking up at the floodlit rocket, all sleek length, studded with rounded windows, and tipped at the base in fins. "Well, maybe not *no* imagination." And she climbs aboard.

Bunny reads over a brief as they hurtle between the stars.

"Imagine the outfit I could make from one of those," Starlight whispers, pointing to the stars pricking the vast dark.

"Hush." Esmeralda , born Christina Joanne Garcia Layton, elbows her.

"Our target is Doctor Blood," Bunny says, rolling her eyes.

She flips a page in the neatly-stapled file, scans, while the twelve other bodies crammed into the rocket lean forward in anticipation.

"The least they could have done was give us champagne. We are off to save the world, after all. And this seating…"

No one answers Starlight this time. She's young; they hear the nerves in her voice, and excuse her incessant giggling and talking. Today they are twelve; they are together and strong, operating like a smoothly oiled machine. But they have all at various times been afraid and alone, less perfect than they are now. And they will be again. Their numbers may fluctuate, members coming and going, but always they are this: The Glitter Squadron. And they are fabulous.

For this mission they've chosen strictly retro-future, which means skin-tight silver, boots that come nearer to the knee than their skirts, bubble-barreled ray-guns, frosted white lipstick and, of course, big hair. CeCe the Velvet Underground Drag King called in sick with the flu, so it's lamé all the way.

Each member of the Squadron has added their own touch, as usual. Starlight's peek-a-boo cutout dress, which is really more skin than fabric, is studded with mirrors. Esmeralda wears a wide belt with faux gems, green to match her name. Bunny is wearing her namesake animal's ears, peeking out from her enormous coif.

M is the only exception to all the brightness and dazzle. M wears leather, head-to-toe. Think Michelle Pfeiffer as Catwoman—erratic, angry stitches joining found leather so close to the body there's no chance for the flesh underneath to breathe. Only it isn't like that at all. There is a whip hanging at M's side, and plenty of other toys as well. Only eyes and lips show through M's mask, and their gender is indeterminate. No one knows M's birth name, and it will stay that way.

Bunny clears her throat. "Doctor Blood, born Richard Carnacki Utley, is a brilliant scientist. He was working on splicing human and animal DNA as a way to cure cancer, or building better rocket fuel using radioactive spiders and black holes. Blah, blah, blah, the usual. We've all seen the movies, right?"

Esmeralda smiles soft approval. Bunny goes on.

"He caught his wife cheating with his lab partner, or his brother, or his best friend. He tried to burn them to death, or blow them up, or turn them into evil monkey robots, and horribly disfigured himself in the process. So he did the only sensible thing, and shot himself into space where he built a gigantic impenetrable fortress on Mars. Now he's threatening to invade Earth, or shoot it to pieces with a space laser if the United Nations doesn't surrender all of Earth's gold."

"Can they *do* that?" Esmeralda asks.

Starlight mutters, "No imagination at all," and shakes her head, sending bits of light whirling around the rocket.

"That's where we come in," Bunny says. "We take down Doctor Blood, easy-peasy lemon squeezy, and we're home in time for tea."

"Ooh, make mine with brandy!" Starlight says. Someone elbows her in the tight space, and she falls silent.

Bunny rolls her eyes again. "Look sharp, we're almost there."

PENNY IS THE WEAPONS EXPERT. BORN PENELOPE JEAN HARTRAUB, she is the only member of the Glitter Squadron who has actually seen war. Her minidress has a faint coppery sheen, befitting her name. She stands at the bottom of the gangplank, distributing extra ammo and back-up weapons as eleven pairs of chunky heels and M's flat boots kick up the red dirt of Mars.

She keeps the best gun for herself, not just a laser pistol, but an honest to goodness Big Fucking Gun. It has rings that light up and it makes a woo-woo sound when it's fired and everything. Fashion-wise, it may be *so* last year, but it'll get the job done. As they leave the rocket behind, heading towards the ridiculously oversized fortress, all done up in phallic towers and bubble domes, Penny takes the lead.

They encounter guards, dressed oh-so-predictably in uniforms purchased from the discount bin at Nazis-R-Us.

"Boring." Starlight buffs her nails to a high shine against a rare patch of fabric on her dress.

She delivers a high kick, catching the first guard in the throat with the bruising force of her extra-chunky, mirror-studded heel. If she had her druthers she'd be in roller skates, but she doesn't quite trust the uneven Martian soil.

Esmeralda uses her belt instead of the gun tucked into it, because it's more fun. She wraps it around the second guard's throat and neatly throttles him into submission before returning it to her waist.

The second wave of guards approaches with more caution. Penny singles out a man with a nasty grin, the one most likely to cause trouble. He reaches for her. She surprises him with her speed and uses his momentum to bring him crashing down. He springs up.

"I won't make this easy on you, girly," he says, or something equally cliché.

Penny ignores him and goes in for a blow to the ribs. But it doesn't land. This time he's the one to surprise her with his speed. He catches her and spins her around, pinning her. She swears he tries to cop a feel, and his breath stinks of alcohol when he speaks close to her ear.

"You like that? You want a *real* man to show you how it's done?"

No imagination, she imagines Starlight saying, and smashes her head back against his, hoping it will break his nose. At the very least it breaks his concentration. She slips free. The BFG is too good for this one.

He comes at her fast and hard, excitement clear in his eyes. She can see from their shine just what he thinks he'll do to her when he bests her, how he'll make her beg, and how she'll like it. She sweeps his legs out from under him; there's a satisfying crack as his head hits the floor. Even dazed, he grins up at her, blood between his teeth as she stands over him. She knows exactly what he's thinking: So, you like it rough, girly? Me, too. I like a girl who knows how to play.

Disgusting.

Fashion be damned. She pulls out a battered old 9-mm pistol. "Fetishize this, asshole." And she puts a single bullet in his brain.

THERE ARE GORILLA MEN—OF COURSE THERE ARE—ALL SPLICED DNA, dragging knuckles and swinging hairy arms. Bunny makes short work of them. There are radioactive zombies, slavering, pawing, glowing green and dropping chunks of unnamable rot in their wake. Esmeralda handles them with grace and aplomb. There are even spiders, which sends Starlight into a fit of giggles, before she takes them out, singing Bowie at the top of her lungs.

There are two female guards in the whole sprawling expanse of the base, both wearing bikinis, chests heaving before they've even thought to pick a fight.

"Oh, how progressive!" Starlight claps her hands in mock rapture. "I suppose there's a mud pit just behind that door?"

The girls in bikinis exchange glances; this is outside their training.

"Look, honey. Honeys," Sapphire, who has just helped to take out a trio of genetically-altered snake creatures, says. "Let me explain something to you. Supervillains pay crap. And there's no such thing as an Evil League of Evil healthcare plan."

One of the women takes a questioning step forward. Sapphire holds up a hand.

"I won't make some grandiose speech about the fate of the world, or doing it for the children you'll probably never have, but I will say this—killing bad guys is a heck of a lot of fun. And we pay overtime."

And the forces of might and justice and looking damned fine in knee-high high heels swells to fourteen.

M IS THE ONE TO FIND DOCTOR BLOOD, DEEP IN HIS UNDERGROUND lair. He stands at a curved control panel, raised on a catwalk above an artificial canal, which more likely than not is filled with genetically enhanced Martian piranhas.

He screams profanities, his voice just as high-pitched with mania as you might imagine. He's wearing a lab coat, shredded and scorched, as though he has just this moment stepped out of the fire that destroyed his sanity and nearly ended his life. To his credit, the scars covering half his face are pink and shiny, stretched tight, weeping clear fluid tinged pale red when he screams. His finger hovers over a big red button, the kind that ends the world.

M approaches with measured steps. The profanities roll off the leather; the imprecations and threats don't penetrate between the thick, jagged stitches. Doctor Blood runs out of words and breath. He looks at M, wild-eyed, and meets only curiosity in the leather-framed stare. Oddly, he can't tell what color the eyes looking back at him are. They might be every color at once, or just one color that no one has thought up a name for yet.

His voice turns harsh, broken, raw. The weeping sores are joined by real tears—salt in the wound.

"I'll make you pay. All of you. Nobody ever believed in me. I'll show them all. They'll love me now. Everyone will."

It comes out as one long barely distinguished string of words.

M puts a hand on the sobbing scientist's shoulder. M understands pain, every kind there is. M understands when someone needs to be hurt, to be pushed to the very edge before they can come out on the other side of whatever darkness they've blundered into. And M knows when someone has had enough, too. When there's no pain in the world greater than simply living inside their own skin, and all the hurting in the world won't bring them anything.

Doctor Blood's words trail off, incoherent for the sobs. "Daddy never…I'm sorry mommy…"

And M does an unexpected thing, a thing M has never done before. M steps close and folds the doctor in leather-clad arms, patting his back and letting him cry.

FIFTEEN BODIES CROWD THE ROCKET SHIP HURTLING BACK TOWARD Earth—just like Bunny promised, home in time for tea.

Starlight fogs the window with her breath, looking out at all that glittering black. Esmeralda discusses wardrobe options with the women in bikinis.

The others talk among themselves, comparing notes, telling stories of battles won, the tales growing with each new telling. Ruby and Sapphire, the twins who aren't twins and couldn't look more opposite if they tried, single-handedly took down an entire legion of Martian lizardmen, to hear them tell the tale. Mistress Minerva knocked out a guard with her clever killer perfume spray and rescued a bevy of Martian princes who couldn't wait to express their gratitude. Butch swam across a canal filled with radioactive Martian alligators in all his glittering, untucked glory. And Empress Zatar, who was born for this mission and didn't even get a single moment of screen time, fought off three Grons and a Torlac with nothing more than a nail file.

And so the stories go.

Penny cleans her guns and her blades, humming softly to herself as she does, an old military tune.

Bunny uses an honest to goodness pen and makes notes in a real paper journal.

Doctor Blood's head is bowed. His shoulders hitch every now and then.

M sits straight and silent, staring ahead with leather-framed eyes, and holds Doctor Blood's hand.

All together, they tumble through the fabulous, glittering dark. They are heading back home to claim their heroes' welcome, even though every one of them knows this moment, right here, surrounded by so many glorious stars it hurts, is all the thanks they will ever get for saving the world. Again.

THIS IS BUNNY. THIS IS BUNNY BEFORE SHE WAS BUNNY, BACK WHEN he was Phillip Howard Craft, working as a lifeguard at Sun Haven Beach Resort by day and slinging drinks in the resort bar by night. Back before the Ultra Fabulous Glitter Squadron saved the world from Mars, or fought the lizards from the center of the earth, or kept Air Force One from exploding with nothing more than a jeweled hairpin and a wad of peach-flavored chewing gum.

This is Bunny back when he was a bronzed god rather than a curvy goddess. His legs already go on for miles but he doesn't shave them yet, though he does wax his chest until it gleams in the sun. Even before the Ultra Fabulous Glitter Squadron, Phillip knew the importance of a good beauty regimen.

Nearly the entire female population of Sun Haven Beach swoons over Phillip, from the giggly teenage girls barely out of braces and only just filling in their brand new bikinis to the lifers who have been coming to the resort every year, their skin tanned leather orange and stitched together with so many surgeries they either can't smile, or can do nothing but.

More than a few of the men swoon over Phillip, too, though they're less obvious in their attentions. There are more covert glances, more suggestions of after-work pick-up games where teams are divided into shirts versus skins and Phillip is inevitably shunted to the team forced to take their shirts off than outright ploys for his affection. Except for one very sweet invitation to dinner from a boy named Billy who works the day shift at the resort pool, delivering sweating tropical drinks to guests and picking up their used towels. The invitation came in the form of a note smelling of honeysuckle, tied with a silk ribbon around a bouquet of a dozen pale purple roses.

Phillip politely declined the invitation. As he has declined every invitation for the past few months. He barely notices the furtive glances tossed his way, or even the outright stares. It's not that he isn't flattered, and maybe even a little tempted from time to time, but he's been restless lately, distracted.

More than once he's caught himself staring at the horizon from his perch atop the lifeguard station, unable to tear his gaze away from the hazy line where the ocean meets the sky. Something is coming. He can't put his finger on it, but he's certain things are about to change. There's something just under the surface of the ocean's skin, and it terrifies him.

So while Phillip isn't rude to his suitors, while he still flashes the dazzling smile that makes anyone he turns it on feel like the world has shrunken to include only the two of them, he spends his nights alone.

Now, for instance, in the rare moments of solitude between sunset and twilight, Phillip is walking the beach. Most of the resort's guests have retreated to their rooms, putting on new skins and new faces to meet the night, which will be filled with Vegas-style shows, foam parties at the disco, flashing lights in the casino accompanied by the clatter of coins, bar-hopping, and bed-hopping—all fueled by sweet-sugary drinks topped with little paper parasols. This used to be Phillip's life, too, even though there is a never-enforced resort rule against staff fraternizing with guests. But that mask has worn thin.

So Phillip walks. Alone.

A few scattered lovers snuggle together on blankets. A jogger or two dares the edge of the sand where the ocean laps the shore. One lone figure tosses a Frisbee for a delighted golden retriever who bounds after it into the waves.

Phillip watches the sky bruise as the first stars pin-prick the dark, and lets the waves erase his footsteps. Sometimes he thinks about walking away from Sun Haven, shedding his skin entirely to leave Phillip Howard Craft behind. He thinks about the impermanence of his footprints, devoured by the tide. Why shouldn't his whole life be that way? There has to be something else out there, further down the road, something more.

As he thinks this he keeps part of his attention on the horizon. It's harder to see the divide between water and sky at dusk, but somewhere in that charcoal smudgy distance the sense of waiting remains. The world is holding its breath, and Phillip holds his breath with it.

Between his thoughts and the sky, he doesn't notice the Frisbee sailing his way until it strikes him in the chest.

"Sorry about that. Little help?" The man shouts to be heard over the crashing surf and points at the Frisbee now lying at Phillip's feet. The dog barks, bouncing in anticipation of a new player joining the game.

Phillip picks up the Frisbee, but rather than throwing it, he stares at it. Something in its shape, the perfect roundness, brings the unsettled feeling to the surface of his skin and leaves it prickling. He thinks of the moon. He thinks of an eye.

"Hey, buddy? You okay?" The man jogs up to Phillip, reaching for the Frisbee.

Phillip says, "Your dog." And at the same moment, the sea opens.

The waves heave, and something vast and dripping lurches upward. A tentacle, almost the same slick greeny-grey as the water, and thicker than Phillip's body thrusts into the sky, framed for a moment before it crashes to the sand. The man is knocked off his feet. Phillip jumps back, but his legs lock him in place there and refuse to move any farther.

Another tentacle emerges from the sea, its tapered end almost graceful as it slithers over the sand.

"No!" Phillip cries out as the creature catches hold of the dog bounding towards its master, who is just now picking himself up and brushing off the sand.

The dog lets out a yelp as the tentacle wraps around its body. The tentacle lashes, whipping the terrified dog over Phillip's head. He stretches his arms but they're not as long as they used to be, fear-stunted, and the tips of his fingers barely brush the dog's feathery golden tail.

There is a roar and it might be the monster or it might be the ocean. Water pours from skin now flushing greeny-black as the thing rises, but it doesn't surface all the way. A vortex opens, lined with teeth, and this time there is no doubt that it is the monster bellowing.

Two tentacles meet and as Phillip watches in horror, the monster tears the dog in half. Hot blood splashes his face, his chest. The sea monster drops the two halves of the dog into its jagged maw before sinking back beneath the waves. Water surges around their feet. Phillip's pulse trip-hammers, chest too tight to breathe.

"My dog!" The man pushes Phillip out of the way, and he stumbles to one side.

"Wait!" Phillip finds his voice, but it's hoarse, weak. He wants to run after the man, but doing so would mean moving closer to those retreating tentacles. He's saved people from drowning, pulled them out of tides determined to sweep them away, but this is something different.

The foam surges around his legs, pink with blood.

Bile burns Phillip's throat. The dog's owner charges into the waves, screaming obscenities. Phillip's legs finally unlock, but they remain rubbery, numb. Even though the water is only around his ankles he feels like it's waist deep, pushing back at him, keeping him from reaching the man.

"Wait," Phillip says again and it's barely a whisper.

He reaches the man, touches his shoulder, and the man whirls on him, eyes red and face contorted.

"Get the fuck off me!" the man screams.

He shoves Phillip. Hard. His hand lands square in the middle of Phillip's bronzed chest. It leaves a bloody handprint, the perfect impression of five fingers and a thumb.

Phillip's stomach turns. He bends over, vomits into the waves, sees the dog again behind his closed eyes. The man splashes away ahead of him and Phillip looks up just in time to see one of the tentacles crack the air like a whip as it disappears.

It's a casual gesture, without malice or intent, a cat flicking its tail. But it catches the bereaved man across the side of his head, sending him spinning. He falls; the waves roll him. The monster disappears and the man lies still. He doesn't get up, doesn't scream again for his dog. He doesn't do anything at all.

"Oh. God." The moan brings another wave of sickness. Phillip's stomach clenches but there's nothing left to vomit.

He staggers towards the man, crashes to his knees and rolls the man over. Half the man's face is gone. The exposed eyeball glares, too round, from white bone and red muscle. The jaw, shattered, is still clenched in rage.

"No. Oh, no." Phillip buries his face in his hands, and while the tide rushes around him, washing the dead man like a sea-smoothed stone, he sobs.

AFTER THE POLICE FINISH QUESTIONING HIM, AFTER HE HAS TOLD his story over and over again, vomited it all up to an endless series of notepads and tape recorders, the sea of interchangeable people finally retreats and leaves Phillip alone. In his small room in the staff wing of the resort he strips out of his swim trunks and the thermal blanket the police gave him. His skin is still tacky with blood.

He can't stop shaking.

He climbs into the shower and turns the water on full force, as hot as he can stand it, and hotter still. He scrubs and scrubs until his skin is raw, until he's sure blisters will rise from his heat or the skin itself will slough from his bones. He wishes it would. No more Phillip. No more useless bronzed god who stood by in terror and watched a man and his dog die. He wants to be someone else, anyone else.

He towels his burned-raw skin until he can't stand it anymore. He can't bear to get dressed. None of his clothes are right. They aren't him anymore. Or rather, they are too much him, and that's not who he wants to be.

Instead, he pulls the sheet from his bed and wraps it around his body like a toga, and goes out into the balmy evening air.

Tomorrow he will quit. Tomorrow he'll pack his bags and get as far from Sun Haven as he can. He'll go to the Arctic, the Amazon, the moon, somewhere, anywhere. Anywhere but here.

But for now he can't stand to be inside. The walls are too close. His life is caving in. He goes to the pool, empty now that all the guests are in the restaurants, or at one of the shows, or under the swirling mirror ball of the disco. Blue-green lights set in the pool's cement walls cast everything in an unearthly glow. Phillip sits on one of the long, plastic chairs surrounding the pool, puts his head in his hands, and tries to breathe without sobbing.

He hasn't eaten anything, but still his stomach roils, alternately clenching in pain and growling against its emptiness. The thought of putting food in his mouth, chewing it, grinding it between his teeth…

"Are you okay?"

Phillip looks up. Billy clutches the towel he's holding tighter in his hands.

"Sorry. I didn't mean to scare you. And I know you're not okay. I heard what happened. Is there anything I can do?"

He says it so earnestly, like he's afraid Phillip will shatter at any minute, like he'll bolt, or lash out in anger.

But Phillip doesn't do any of these things. He is so exhausted that he wants to sink right down on the concrete and go to sleep. Or better yet, sink into the pool, lie on the bottom and breathe water and never come up again.

"No, I don't think so. Thank you." Phillip's jaw aches from clenching it so hard.

He hears Billy shifting from foot to foot, but Phillip doesn't look up again. He doesn't want to see the concern in Billy's eyes. He doesn't want to be reminded of anything good, or innocent, anything human right now.

After a moment, Billy perches on the chair opposite Phillip's, close but not touching. He doesn't say anything, and Phillip finally raises his head. Then words spill out of him, words he never intended to say. He tells Billy everything, and feels the terror come back as he describes it, crawling over his skin and drawing a cold sweat, leaving him shaking.

"I want to be strong," Phillip says, finally. "I want to be the kind of person who saves people, not the kind of person who stands by and watches them die. I'm a lifeguard, for fuck's sake. And the dog... And the man. I didn't do anything, I just stood there."

Billy is silent for so long Phillip is afraid he'll get up and leave. Even though he didn't want the company, now he's terrified of being alone.

"So do it," Billy says, his voice soft, almost a whisper.

Phillip stares at Billy, trying to understand what he's saying. Billy takes a deep breath and licks his lips.

"Be strong. Be a hero. You just have to find something that makes you strong, you know? Like armor, like a good luck charm, something that protects you from the world."

Motion beyond the low fence surrounding the pool catches Phillip's eye—three dancers from the resort's Carnival-themed show. Feathers surround their heads like halos, ostrich, peacock, and parrot. Their skin-tight costumes shimmer, throwing off darting fragments of light like scales. Their impossibly high, impossibly thin heels clatter, hooves on the concrete. They don't even notice Billy and Phillip in the dark. They don't pause—a herd of fierce, chimerical creatures, devouring the night.

Phillip sucks in a breath. It's like the man striking him in the chest again, but instead of leaving him tight and unable to breathe, something opens inside him.

"Yes," Phillip says. Yes, he thinks. Strong.

THIS IS BUNNY, WHO IS NOT QUITE BUNNY YET, BUT WILL BE VERY soon: six foot two standing flat, six six in heels. The heels in question are silver, tapered thin, glittering every bit as bright as Dorothy's ever did in Oz. Her dress is silver, too, spangled, spaghetti-strapped, cut low in a V almost to her navel, revealing a perfect, bronzed chest. The skirt brushes her thighs, somewhere between crotch and knee. It flares when she twirls, which she does just once to see how it feels. Her hair is frosted almost white, piled in a bouffant atop her head. Her lips are the reddest red that ever was and her nails match. Red as blood. Her lashes are spider-leg long and above them, her eyelids are smeared with silver to match her dress.

It's not make-up, it's war paint. It isn't clothing, it's armor.

This is Bunny and she is so very strong.

"Wow," Billy says.

Bunny lifts her arms slightly, turns.

"That's not what I was expecting, but wow. You look…great." He blushes and Bunny smiles. "But it's still missing something."

"What?" Bunny says. Her stomach clenches, fear trying to break its way out of her brand new skin.

But Billy still smiles and that smile never wavers as he rummages in a drawer and comes up with a pair of white rabbit ears attached to a wide, rhinestone-studded headband.

"From Halloween," Billy says by way of explanation.

His cheeks color ever so slightly as he places the ears reverently atop of Bunny's bouffant.

"For luck," Billy says.

"I thought that was supposed to be the feet." But Bunny smiles.

She raises a hand and touches one velvet soft ear with the tip of her finger. Electricity courses down her spine. Yes, she thinks—strong.

"So what happens now?" Billy asks.

"Now," Bunny says, "now I go fight a sea monster. Now I save the world."

"Are you…you know…serious?" Billy's eyes are wide. He looks a little bit in awe of Bunny, and a little bit afraid, too.

She sees herself in Billy's eyes. She *is* a warrior. She *is* beautiful. She is strong, and even though she is still afraid, all the fear is on the inside, hidden under glamour and shine. She can do this thing. She has to. Otherwise she'll spend the rest of her life afraid. Besides, the world needs heroes.

"Yes, I am," Bunny says. She meets Billy eye, letting him know she means it.

Doubt flickers across Billy's face. She can tell he wants to ask her how, or what business she has fighting sea monsters, all questions she can't answer. Instead, Billy nods once and sets his mouth in a firm line.

"Okay," Billy says.

"Okay." Bunny lets out a breath she wasn't aware of holding, then manages a grin she hopes doesn't reveal her nerves. "How about a kiss for luck? Just in case."

With the heels, she has to lean down to make the kiss work, but she does, and it does. Billy smells like honeysuckle, and he tastes like light, summer wine. Bunny steps back, smoothing her dress, and Billy touches his lipstick-smeared mouth, dazed. She doesn't say anything else, because what else is there to say? Bunny turns and marches out to save the world.

THE BEACH HAS BEEN CLOSED OFF SINCE THE ATTACK. YELLOW POLICE tape flutters in the wind but Bunny ducks under it. It's harder than she anticipated walking in high heels on sand but she's determined. She wobbles as she makes her way down to the shore, and stands facing the waves while the wind tugs at her hair.

This is it, she thinks. Now it's time to see what she's made of under the glitter and glam, whether her charm works, whether her new skin is more than just a disguise. Underneath the sparkle and shine, this is who she is, who she wants to be—a fighter of monsters, someone who doesn't back down. And if she's afraid, which she is deep down, then she wants to be the kind of person who doesn't let fear stop her, who takes it in stride and uses it as a weapon against the world.

Bunny flashes her teeth, bright in the newly-risen sun. She hefts a harpoon, borrowed from the wall of the resort's nautical-themed bar.

"Okay, motherfucker," she tells the waves. "Come and get me."

She can feel it, the sense of waiting, the monster just beneath the ocean's skin. It's toying with her, not rising yet, but staying safe under the waves. Even in her short dress, Bunny sweats. She grips the harpoon harder, hoping her damp palms won't betray her. Blood-red nails dig into her skin.

"I can wait all day," she says. "Can you?"

A small crowd has gathered behind her, just beyond the police tape. She can hear them murmuring, but she doesn't turn. What if one of them calls the police? What if they have her arrested? A child shrieks, slipping from its mother's grip and dashes toward the shore, eager to play in the waves, oblivious to the warning tape and the waiting doom.

Bunny sees the child from the corner of her eye, toffee-colored curls bouncing.

"No!" She snatches the child, swinging him up into the air.

At the same moment, the water heaves. A tentacle rises, dripping, and smashes down on the sand, spraying grit and salt water but narrowly missing Bunny. Only the points of her heels, dug deep in the sand, keep her from falling. The child's mother dashes forward and grabs the boy out of Bunny's hands, hugging him close.

Another woman runs onto the sand. "Maria!"

"Go!" Bunny yells at both of them, grabbing her harpoon from the sand and whirling to where the tentacle is rising again. It is joined by a second and a third.

The woman called Maria runs, sheltering her son. The other woman hesitates just a moment, and it is a moment too long. One tentacle lashes downward. Bunny drives up with her harpoon, sinking the point deep into the creature's flesh. Black blood like ink gushes from the wound, salty as the sea water across her red lips, stinging her eyes and covering her in gore.

As the woman begins to run farther up the beach, a second tentacle whips around her ankle, dragging her back toward the waves.

"Oh, no you don't!" Bunny wrenches the harpoon, twisting it and pulling it free. Blisters rise on her sweat-slick and blood-wet palms where they rub against the harpoon's smooth, wooden handle. One day, they will be calluses. If she lives that long. The sea monster writhes. It shrieks. It pounds the sand. But it doesn't let go. Bunny stabs at the tentacle wrapped around the woman's leg as the woman claws frantically at the sand. Bunny hacks, fierce, fueled with rage, seeing the dead man with his missing face and the dog ripped in two again and again.

It all comes out of her like a primal scream, but not as a sound. It comes out as the harpoon's point, stabbing until the sea monster finally lets go. Bunny staggers back, blinks, stiletto heels sinking deep in the sand. Her pulse trips, adrenaline making her tremble. Is it over? It can't be over. She blinks again, forcing herself to move.

"Come on. Let's get you out of here." Bunny reaches to help the woman up. Her voice quavers too; the aching muscles in her arms might never stop shaking.

They are both splattered with blood, drenched with sea water. The hand gripping Bunny's wrist is slicked in ichor. She hauls the woman up, but the woman doesn't let go right away. She stares at Bunny, wide-eyed, mascara running to mingle with the gore on her skin, dark hair plastered to her shoulders, her sun dress—dark blue covered in a riot of bright pink and yellow flowers—clinging to her.

"Go on," Bunny says, trying to push the woman toward the shore.

The woman blinks. "What about you?"

"Just go!" Bunny says. It's not over. Of course it isn't over. She can feel the thing beneath the ocean gathering to strike again, bunched tight like a swimmer's muscles the moment before he launches his body into the waves. It's wounded, but not dead. It's angry. As angry as she is, and it too can be fueled by rage.

"But what…" The woman never finishes her sentence.

Water sweeps around them, knocking them both off their feet. The dripping, bleeding bulk of the sea monster looms over them, a paler green-grey now that it's lost so much blood. It screams, a high-pitched, terrible sound, showing rings of teeth receding back into its throat. One eye, yellow, slitted like a cat's, glares at them.

"Get out of here!" Bunny yells at the woman.

Somehow, she's managed to keep hold of her harpoon. She struggles to stand, slipping in the waves, the sand treacherous beneath her. She raises her weapon, but her balance is off, and the monster is quicker, angrier. A tentacle whips out and snaps her harpoon in two. Bunny drops to her knees.

She scrambles after the broken harpoon pieces but the tide snatches them away, sucking them hungrily beyond her reach. The sea monster screams again and it takes all of Bunny's will not to clap her hands over her ears.

She squeezes her eyes shut for just a moment. She takes a deep breath. Forces herself to stand. Then she looks the monster in the eye.

If sea monsters can laugh, she swears this one does, and it's laughing at her. Something inside Bunny clenches tight, making it hard to breathe. The monster is trying to make her feel small again, powerless, afraid. For a moment, she lets it. She shrinks inside her armor, heart beating too hard. She feels her war paint running. What was she thinking? She's no hero.

The monster feints, snaps a tentacle in the air next to Bunny's head, close but not touching. Bunny reels back. Her heels catch in the sand, tripping her. She lands hard, twists, and tries to scramble away from her traitor shoes. A tentacle thuds down, blocking her, a cat toying with a mouse.

The woman, who did not run away when Bunny told her to, darts in, dodging coils of tentacle. She snatches Bunny's fallen shoe and pushes it into Bunny's hand. Bunny stares for a moment, gaping incomprehension before understanding dawns.

"Thank you." She gives the woman a shaky smile, grabs her other shoe, and pushes herself upright, whirling to face the monster. Wielding a shoe in each hand, heels pointed outward like blades, she remembers: She is Bunny. She is a warrior. She is strong.

The sea monster lunges towards her, a falling mass of stinking flesh, determined to crush her and make her into a meal.

"Oh no." Bunny grits her teeth. "Not today, you big, ugly fucker."

The sea monster screams, and Bunny screams right back. As the monster falls toward her, maw wide, Bunny leaps up, colliding, driving both points of her high heels deep into the monster's eye.

Aqueous humor spurts from the wound, slicking Bunny's arms. The monster's scream turns to a sound of pain. It thrashes and heaves beneath her and Bunny jumps back, landing in the sand and somehow keeping her feet under her. Tentacles whip the air, the monster tearing at its eye, trying to rid itself of the shoes. The sound it makes is piteous now, mewling, almost a sob. For a moment, Bunny almost feels bad.

"You shouldn't have eaten the dog," she murmurs.

The monster sinks into the ocean, limbs still thrashing, but weakly now. Water surges around Bunny, up to her waist, and then retreats, rushing to fill the spot where the monster disappeared. The silver dress clings to Bunny's thighs. Her frosted-white hair is askew. She can't even begin to imagine what her make-up must look like. But she's alive.

"Is it dead?" someone calls from the shore.

The woman beside Bunny is the one to answer. "I think so."

The woman touches Bunny's arm, and Bunny starts. "Are you okay?" The woman's dark eyes are full of concern, but wonder too. Admiration for what Bunny has done.

"I think so," Bunny says. "But look at me," she adds after a long moment. "And look at you."

"We could both use a shower." The woman grins, nerves and relief. Bunny sees now that she's shaking, too.

"And after that, I'm going to sleep for a week," Bunny says.

They lapse into silence, and the woman's expression grows serious again. "That was incredible, what you did. Saving my nephew. Saving me. Thank you."

"I did what anyone would do," Bunny says, shrugging, uncomfortable now and looking away. Deep down, she knows her words aren't true.

The woman's hand tightens on her arm. "No. Not anyone. I could never do something like that…"

Bunny hears the longing in the woman's voice. It goes all the way through her, kicks at her heart, and makes her breath catch. What has she lost? What makes her afraid? She turns and looks at the woman, really sees her—gore-covered, soaking wet, skin goose-pimpled. But there's a hero there somewhere inside her, too.

"Well, no, not in those clothes at least." Bunny allows herself a slow smile. It feels good.

"You mean…?"

"Uh huh." Bunny's smile widens, becomes a grin. "Saving the world is hard work. You had my back, just now, with the shoes. It would be nice to have a hand now and then, you know, on a semi-permanent basis."

The woman shakes her head. "I could never do what you do."

Bunny feels the woman's pulse, jumping in her fingertips.

"You already proved you can. And the right wardrobe will do wonders for you, I promise. I'm Bunny. What's your name?"

The woman opens her mouth, closes it again; Bunny sees when she starts to say one thing and changes her mind. The woman straightens, her eyes, dark brown with just the faintest hint of green, glint with mischief, and the beginning of a smile lifts the edge of her mouth.

"You can call me Esmeralda."

"Esmeralda." Bunny takes Esmeralda's hand and shakes it firmly. "Welcome to the team."

The White Velvet Rabbit

2 ozs vodka, chilled

1 oz heavy cream

1 oz white chocolate

½ oz Grand Marnier

Juice from 1 freshly-squeezed

orange

Grated dark chocolate(80%

or higher)for garnish

Orange zest for garnish

Put the white chocolate and the cream in a small bowl and microwave on low power until the chocolate melts; stir until smooth. Place chocolate mixture, vodka, Grand Marnier, and orange juice in a shaker with plenty of ice and shake well; strain the mixture into a martini glass, dusted with dark chocolate, and garnish with orange zest.

This drink is a natural fit for Bunny—one of my easiest creations ever! It's smooth and sweet, but there's a bite in the orange, the vodka, and in the dark chocolate rim, underlying the sweetness. This drink —like its namesake—looks beautiful, but it will sneak up on you and kick your ass before you even have a chance to compliment its dazzling smile.

It's funny, since she used to be a bartender, I figured Bunny would have some of her own recipes to share. I've tried to get her to talk shop, trade secrets, but she's always got some excuse or another. When it isn't excuses, it's flattery. *But you're so good at it, Sapphire. I couldn't possibly compete with you.* She's a master at deflection. You know what I think? I think Bunny wants to forget she ever had a life before this one. Believe me, I understand, it just surprises me. Out of all of us, I figured she would know that the name you're born with has nothing to do with who you are. Of course, just because someone always seems to have it all together doesn't mean they do. Bunny is only human after all. Fearless leaders should be allowed to be afraid every now and then and know their team has their back. I hope Bunny does, because we do.

ROLLER GIRLS HAVE MORE FUN

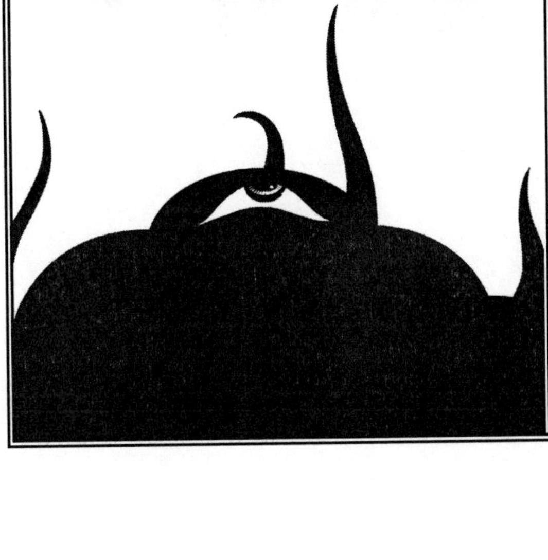

STARLIGHT HAS ALWAYS BEEN A ROLLER GIRL. EVEN WHEN SHE WAS little, when her mama still called her Walter, she knew what she would grow up to be.

When Cindy Williams passed out glittery pink invitations in the shape of cupcakes, inviting the whole class to her birthday party at the roller rink, Walter dragged his mother to the mall, pointed at the prettiest, sparkliest, pinkest tutu that ever was and said, "Mama, I want to wear that."

Walter's mama glanced at the price tag, pressed her lips into a line, then said, "Okay, baby, but just know, the other kids are gonna make fun of you."

Then Walter's mama knelt down, put her hands on her son's shoulders, and looked deep into his eyes. She didn't quite sigh, but he saw a little flicker of pain and larger flicker of determination in her gaze. She squeezed Walter's shoulders just a touch harder.

"And just know it doesn't matter one bit," she said. "Deep down in their hearts, they're gonna be jealous of you wearing something so pretty. But don't you pay them any mind. Ever. You're gonna be the belle of the ball."

The moment they got home from the mall, Walter pulled the tutu out of the bag and slipped it on. Looking at himself in the mirror, he smiled and whispered the name he'd secretly been hugging tight to his chest for weeks, mouthing it silently in the dark as he fell asleep, holding it like a perfect, round marble on his tongue.

"Starlight."

He hadn't told anyone about his real name yet, not even his mama. He'd gotten it from a princess in a cartoon. She rode a unicorn and wore a bright, shiny tiara, and Walter always imagined she smelled like strawberries. He hadn't dared say the name aloud yet. But now, it finally felt right.

And so Starlight went to Cindy Williams' party wearing the pinkest tutu that ever was, and when everyone gathered to play whip-crack, Starlight got to be the end of the chain. And when everyone skated in line, so fast that whoever was on the end of the chain had no control, Starlight understood in the moment before Brent Davies let go of her hand just what her mama had been talking about.

Her pink tutu survived. But Starlight's nose was broken that day. She skinned her knee, too; the barrier surrounding the Moonlight Madness Roller Disco rink was notoriously unforgiving.

To her credit, Starlight didn't cry. She picked herself up, but didn't skate back to the line of seven year olds laughing at the boy in his tutu.

She lifted her chin, took her skates off, and handed them to the bored-looking attendant half-slumbering at his desk. Whether Cindy Williams' mother never noticed there was one less child at the party by the end or whether she was simply relieved to be rid of Walter-in-a-tutu, Starlight never knew.

With a quarter tucked into one of her shoes, Starlight called her mother from a pay phone outside the Moonlight Madness Roller Rink. She didn't mention the bloody nose or the skinned knee. She pretended her stomach hurt from too much cake and ice cream and asked if Mama could please come and take her home.

Mama didn't say anything about the busted nose or the skinned knee as Starlight climbed into their beat-up Chevrolet—more rust than powder-blue paint by now. Instead, Mama handed over a tissue and drove back home.

Starlight's daddy wasn't the understanding kind, and though she never said it, Starlight suspected Mama was just as glad he'd left before he'd ever had a chance to disown his son. There were bruises Starlight wasn't supposed to know about, proving just what daddy thought of women and men and their places in the world. And he'd have been mighty sore at Mama for being so proud of her son.

ON HER EIGHTEENTH BIRTHDAY, STARLIGHT'S MAMA GAVE HER A brand new pair of roller skates.

"I was thinking you could maybe get a job at the new Moon Dust

RollerRama off I-10," she said.

She didn't look Starlight in the eye. Starlight was prettier than her, had been for a while, and she was afraid her girl must be ashamed of having a mama so plain. She should have done better by her, brought her up right. She should have taken Starlight to the best salons for hair and nails, bought her the fanciest dresses, but what did she know with her bleached-up hair, turquoise eye shadow, and three-kitten grey t-shirt over worn-thin black stretch pants?

Starlight's mama fidgeted. She looked at her cigarette. She turned her lighter over and over in her hands. Starlight, her beautiful daughter, startled her by planting a kiss on her cheek.

"Thank you, Mama. They're perfect."

Starlight took the skates to her room. She set them on her dresser, lined with Stop n' Save cosmetics. She'd told her mama the truth: They were perfect. White leather, red wheels, laces aching for her fingers. But how much had they cost? Starlight chewed her lip.

She lifted one skate, spinning the bright red wheel. If she followed Mama's advice and got a job, she could help with the bills. Starlight picked up the other skate. Something rattled. She dug in the boot. Buried in the toe was one last present—a compact of pink lip gloss the rosy color of fireworks bursting over the lake on the Fourth of July.

STARLIGHT GLIDES EFFORTLESSLY AROUND THE EDGE OF THE RINK, palm upturned, fingers splayed, balancing a tray of frosty milkshakes.

Her uniform is regulation spotless; her hair and make-up are her own. Today her teased-up do is silver-threaded with old tinsel salvaged from Christmas decorations, and her lipstick is seashell pink, studded with the most kissable glitter imaginable.

She barely breaks stride handing out each drink, collecting payment with a smile and a perfect pirouette spin. She never gets an order wrong, and everyone at the Moon Dust loves her. She shows up early, not just on time, and she even had her own skates when she applied for the job. Tony, the RollerRama's manager, hired her before she even opened her mouth to say her name.

The RollerRama isn't just a job for Starlight; it's freedom. Gliding round and round under the spin of colored lights feels like love. The music thumps in time with her blood. When she's skating, everything is perfect for just a little while. Starlight doesn't have to worry about most of her paycheck going to help Mama with the bills and how it's barely enough. She doesn't have to worry about Mama working her second job, or that nasty cough she can't shake.

And while those are part of the reason Starlight took the RollerRama job, when she's skating, they're not what she thinks about. No, it's all about the wheels. Her favorite times are the brief moments when the RollerRama is closing and all the customers have gone home. Alone except for Tony and the other employees, Starlight takes center stage, executing the most perfect twirl under the disco ball just before the lights go off for the night. Glints of silver fly around her like the universe holding her in its arms and dancing. For that one moment everything is perfect; she doesn't have any worries at all.

When she doesn't have orders to fill, Starlight glides around the edges of the rink, watching the customers: couples on first dates, holding hands as they twirl under the lights; children fighting to get their wobbly fawn legs under control; teenagers in their black leather jackets gathered on the fringes, too cool to skate, judging and watching, hunters on the prowl.

Starlight keeps an eye on the last ones, the popped-collar hyenas. She watches out for their prey, too, the sad boys and girls skating alone, reaching desperately after the freedom of the glide but so unhappy inside their skins. She is ever vigilant, ready to swoop in and intervene.

On this particular night, Starlight marks them, the predators. Dean, Eddie, and Vic. They remember Starlight back when she was called Walter. She remembers when they were Theodore and Victor, and Dean wore cloudy-lensed glasses with thick, black rims. They've forgotten this, and their names, but they remember the whip-crack kid crashing into the wall at Cindy Williams' birthday party, laughing so hard they almost wet themselves. Starlight has grown up; they haven't.

They're watching a girl with frizzy red hair and glasses almost as thick as Dean's used to be. She can't be more than fifteen, wearing a bulky sweater to hide the fact her breasts haven't come in yet. She also wears thick tights over knobby knees her coltish legs haven't grown into, afraid to smile because her braces only came off last week. Her name is Debra; Starlight knows because she's been paying attention.

Debra has come to the RollerRama just about every weekend for the past three months, watching the grace some lucky boys and girls have found in their bodies. She never joins their formations on the polished floorboards. Debra is a good skater but she's afraid. She doesn't trust her body, doesn't trust that if the girls and boys she watches so avidly ever catch sight of her they won't make her the end of the whip-crack line.

She makes herself small, gliding on the periphery, trying not to be seen. On the periphery, she doesn't see Dean, Vic, and Eddie, watching. But Starlight watches for her. She sees Dean pull a wad of gum from his mouth as Debra prepares to skate past, ready to drop it into her frizzy hair.

Starlight is quicker, cutting in front of Debra without cutting her off, making it look like an accident until she reaches Dean and grabs his wrist.

"Don't even think about it," she says, twisting Dean's wrist hard.

He drops the wad of gum.

Dean's mouth opens, and Starlight flashes him her sweetest smile. She gives him an almost-curtsey, retrieving the dropped gum in a napkin before anyone can skate over it, getting it tangled in their wheels. Dean is still sputtering as Starlight glides away.

As she passes the trash can, dropping the gum-filled napkin, Starlight notices someone else watching tonight, too.

The woman stands at the back of the bleachers surrounding the RollerRama's ring. Her hair is copper, teased high and smoothed into a bouffant dome. Her dress matches her hair, the color of a new penny, short and tight over chunky high-heel boots of soft, dark green leather reaching well past her knees. Her jacket matches her boots.

Arms crossed, she watches Dean, Eddie, and Vic intently. Starlight slows. She's never seen the woman here before, never seen her at all around town. Feeling herself watched, the woman turns toward Starlight. The edge of her mouth creeps up in something that can't quite be called a smile.

Starlight blushes, spinning away. Luckily, the light pops up on the other side of the ring indicating an order ready to be collected. She loads her tray with milkshakes cold enough to frost their glasses. Then Starlight glides across the rink, her tray perfectly balanced.

She isn't expecting it when Dean swoops in. He criss-crosses his skates, making them hum as he whirs past. His hand flicks out so fast he's already gone before the tray clatters to the ground, shattering glass and splattering chocolate and strawberry.

"Watch where you're going, faggot!"

Hyena-laughter trails behind Vic and Eddie, following in their leader's wake. The three of them glide past her, and Starlight promises herself she won't cry, even though her eyes sting as she wipes at the mess soaking her uniform. She blinks false eyelashes hard and fast until the tears retreat. She won't give them the satisfaction. Instead, she pastes on a smile, bigger and brighter than before as she gathers the tray and broken glass.

"Hey." Tony, the RollerRama's owner, comes down from the observation booth above the rink and touches Starlight's shoulder. "You don't have to do that. We'll get someone else to clean it up."

Starlight straightens; she has to fight tears all over again at the look on Tony's face.

"You say the word, and those guys are banned for life." Tony has a smile that peeks out of one side of his mouth.

"It's fine," Starlight says, smoothing her skirt. She notices one of her perfect, shell-pink nails is broken.

"You can take off early," Tony offers.

"No. I want to finish my shift." Starlight squares her shoulders.

"Okay then. But don't worry about this." Tony gestures at the glass, then snaps his fingers. "Hey, Courtney. Grab a mop and broom, will ya? I'm gonna clean this up."

Starlight is almost shaking with gratitude, hoping it doesn't show as she glides across the rink. She doesn't dare look back, afraid the basset-hound sadness of Tony's eyes will break her. Maybe she never had a daddy growing up, but she found one here at the RollerRama, and it hurts every time she sees him worrying about her.

SHIFT OVER, STARLIGHT WALKS TO HER CAR WITH HER SKATES SLUNG over her shoulder. She's still wearing her uniform, even though it smells like strawberry and chocolate and sugary whipped cream. Her feet hurt. She's tired, and she just wants to go home. One of her wheels isn't quite right. Something slipped out of alignment during the incident, and she finished out her shift with a wobble.

Moths circle parking lot lights shining the color of faded bruises. Her car—a beat-up Volkswagen Rabbit, just as rusty as her mama's Chevy ever was—is one of the last left. Except for a forest-green Mustang just outside the glow of the lights. The hairs on the back of Starlight's neck prickle. Dean, Vic, and Eddie are still here, waiting.

"What'd we tell you about watching yourself, faggot?" Vic pushes away from the car, a scrap of darkness separating from a larger clot of shadow. "We don't want your kind 'round here."

Dean says nothing, smacking fist against palm, grinning. Their eyes are bright, shining in a way Starlight associates with fevers.

She is tired. So very tired.

It's not just the milkshakes. It's whip-crack, and Cindy Williams' birthday party, and being told she didn't belong in either the girl's bathroom or the boy's bathroom, her mama's thin cheeks and ugly cough. It's everything weighing on her shoulders since she was seven years old.

Starlight doesn't think. She slings the roller skates from her shoulder, holding their knotted string and whipping them around so fast they blur. They catch Vic in the jaw.

Eddie and Dean stare at her. Starlight's keys are in her hand, threaded between her fingers. She lashes out like they're claws. Dean screams; he trips, turning, before rising to scramble away. Then only Eddie is left standing.

Starlight drops her voice to a growl. "Show me what you got, motherfucker." She's never spoken such foul words before. Her mama raised her right, but Starlight is angry, smelling of spilled milkshakes, her chest heaving with all the hurt ever done to her.

Eddie must see the shape of Starlight's pain, even if he doesn't understand why Starlight is hurt. The pain is jagged, the edges turned outward, ready to draw blood. Eddie is an idiot, but he is wise enough to run. Starlight watches him flee the parking lot, and slowly lowers her hand, keys jangling as she does.

"Nice work."

Starlight whirls, ready to attack again. It's the woman from the RollerRama, the one who'd watched her earlier. The sodium-bruise lights shine off her dress. Shame floods through Starlight. She looks at Vic, still rolling on the ground, clutching his jaw.

Shock sets in; she trembles. Starlight will never be able to look Mama in the eye again after what she's done. Her knees threaten to buckle, everything tilting sideways.

"Hey, relax, kid." A corner of the woman's mouth lifts, but her eyes— the same copper-gold as her dress and her hair, too beautiful to be real— remain hard. "I'm here to offer you a job."

"I'm still not sure I understand." Starlight twists the hem of her skirt, keeping her gaze locked on her hands.

She's never felt this shabby in her uniform before; she can't stop noticing how her shell-pink polish is chipped, how one broken nail is ragged. It takes all of her will to keep from biting it.

She risks a glance upward, and just as quickly looks back down again. It's impossible not to be intimidated by the woman who introduced herself as Bunny, even though she's nothing but patient smiles and encouragement. The copper woman—Penny—isn't helping either, with her arms crossed and her jaw set. Starlight can't help feeling Penny is judging her every word and motion.

"Penny, get this girl something stronger to drink, will you?" Bunny turns her attention to Penny, who frowns.

"I'm not..." Starlight starts to say *of age*, but Bunny's hand covers hers, stilling Starlight's nervous fingers.

Starlight looks up, and Bunny smiles. It's a gentle thing, coupled with a look that speaks volumes. Buried deep within Bunny's violet eyes is a hint of fear. Once upon a time Bunny was scared, too, but she learned how to be strong. Starlight's mouth drops open, and she closes it against as quickly as she can.

She releases the hem of her stained uniform. Penny returns, and Starlight takes the sugar-rimmed glass pressed into her hand.

"I had Sapphire check into the kids from the parking lot." Penny addresses Bunny, but Starlight's stomach does a little flip, knowing the words are for her. "No real damage done, just bruises and scratches. No broken bones and everyone still has both eyes."

Penny turns her attention to Starlight, showing hard eyes, a wry smile, and something Starlight thinks might even be admiration.

"They're not pressing charges," Penny says. "I think they're embarrassed at being beaten up…by a girl."

She turns, leaving them alone. Relief washes through Starlight, but it's only a veneer over the jangle of nerves. Her body buzzes, still wired on adrenaline. Should she send flowers to Vic and Dean by way of apologizing? Or would they think she was making fun? Maybe something for Dean's car? She has no idea what kind of thing boys like Dean and Vic and Eddie enjoy, other than tormenting people. But after what she's done, is she any better? She sips too fast and nearly chokes at the sting of alcohol.

"Esmeralda makes a mean Lime Rickey," Bunny says, tactfully ignoring Starlight's sputtering cough. "We always keep a pitcher on hand in case of celebration. Which brings us back to the matter at hand. Do you want to help us save the world?"

★

"So it's like the army?" Starlight's mama taps ash from her cigarette, her other hand picking at a loose thread on the arm of the chair.

"Not exactly, Mama. It's more like the Justice League. Or the X-Men." Starlight looks away; trying to explain Bunny's offer aloud, the whole thing sounds preposterous.

The night up until now seems far away and getting farther. The sky is already edging back toward light. It was past two a.m. when she got in, but there was Mama, tucked into her housecoat and slippers, her book open on her lap and her head listing into the light spilling over her favorite chair. Starlight hopes her mother can't smell the Lime Rickey on her breath.

"What about college?" Mama asks. "I know we...talked about putting it off for a while, but you still want to go someday, don't you?"

Starlight flinches. Even though Mama is doing her best, she can't quite hide her shame. There's no money for college; they both know it but they both pretend.

"Sure, Mama."

Starlight digs her nails into her palm, wincing as her mother reaches for the pack of cigarettes and lights one. Part of her thinks she has no business playing hero. She should focus on work, saving whatever money she can, and maybe taking a class or two at the education center.

But the other part, the stronger part, *knows* this is the right decision.

Her grades aren't good enough for a scholarship, and she doesn't want to work at the RollerRama for the rest of her life, as much as she loves Tony.

Bunny was coy about finances, vaguely mentioning an aunt—Sapphire's—who made her fortune with a line of women's sportswear, and hinting that for clients who can afford to pay, saving the world is a mercenary affair. Whatever the case, joining the Glitter Squadron means room and board, and regular pay. Starlight can still save up, still help her mama out with the bills. She tells herself this over and over to quell the guilt.

Besides, she's always wanted to travel, and this way she can help people, too. She can keep her mama safe.

"Is it dangerous?" Mama coughs, reaching for the cigarette balanced on the edge of the ashtray.

Starlight covers her mama's hand, and Mama draws back, letting the cigarette burn.

"No. Yes. But the other women will take care of me, Mama. They'll teach me. I'll be safe."

Starlight tries to make her expression convincing, but from the way her mama is searching her face, the worried look in her worn-out eyes, Starlight knows she's failing.

"I'm doing this for you, Mama," she says softly. "To protect you. If anything bad happened..." Starlight bites her lip, tasting pink lemonade lip gloss.

Her mama doesn't say anything, and after a moment, Starlight digs in her purse.

"Um...Bunny gave me her card. I told her you'd be worried, and she said that if you ever have any questions, you can call her any time of the day or night. She'll take good care of me, Mama. I promise."

Mama looks at the silver lettering on the shimmery pale purple background, and raises an eyebrow. "The Ultra Fabulous Glitter Squadron?"

Starlight's cheeks warm. "That's what they call themselves. We. Call ourselves."

Starlight peeks at her mama from beneath her eyelashes. Mama tucks the card into the pocket of her worn robe and lights a cigarette to replace the one that's burned out. Starlight ignores the coughing, just like she ignores the veins in Mama's hands and the circles under her eyes.

Doubt lingers in Mama's expression, but underneath it, there's something else. Is it possible that a tiny part of her is relieved that there'll be one less mouth to feed, with all the attendant guilt of her own for thinking it? Starlight's heart turns over, aching so hard, but there are no words.

"One condition." Mama points with the fingers holding her cigarette, smoke trailing a line of emphasis. "You're home every Sunday night for dinner at six .p.m. sharp, so I know you're safe. You're one minute late, and I'll be having more than words with this Bunny person myself."

"I promise, Mama." Starlight manages a grin, but her stomach flutters; she hopes she's made the right decision. She hopes she'll make her mama proud.

★

"Here?" Starlight's voice breaks. She hates the way it sounds, but if Bunny notices, she does a good job of pretending otherwise.

"That's what our intelligence indicates."

"Real aliens? Like from outer space? Why would aliens land here? I mean there's nothing…"

"Natural resources," Penny says from the doorway. "Oil. Minerals. Who knows what aliens want. But whatever it is, it seems pretty clear these ones have no intention of asking politely. They destroyed several large asteroids and a small moon on their way here. Nothing vital, but still."

Starlight twists in her chair. There's another woman standing behind Penny, dressed all in green, with long, dark hair.

"If we had more time, we'd train you properly, but I'm afraid that isn't an option. So if you want to sit this one out…"

Starlight turns back to Bunny, who lets her words hang. Starlight thinks of her mama, and lifts her chin.

"I'm in," she says.

"You can do this," Bunny says. "We wouldn't have picked you otherwise."

Starlight stands, wiping damp palms on her skirt. If she doesn't leave the room now, she's afraid she'll do something stupid like burst into tears and then her make-up will run.

"Oh, and honey?" Bunny looks like she's fighting a smile. "Now that you're an official member of the Glitter Squadron, you're going to need something far more *fabulous* to wear."

Starlight freezes, fresh panic blooming. How can she tell Bunny she doesn't have money for new clothes?

"Esmeralda will help you. She's a whiz with a sewing machine. Don't worry, you're in good hands."

The woman in green reaches for Starlight, and. as they walk down the hall, Esmeralda squeezes Starlight's fingers. "I was nervous as hell my first day, too."

WHEN ESMERALDA THROWS OPEN THE DOUBLE DOORS OF THE ULTRA Fabulous Glitter Squadron's official wardrobe, Starlight can't help a gasp. It's not just a closet; it's an entire room, ready-made dresses hanging on one side, bolts of fabric lined up on the other. The back wall is dominated by a three-way mirror, and on either side of it racks and racks of boots and shoes.

"It's bigger than my bedroom," Starlight says.

"See anything you like?" When Starlight hesitates, Esmeralda nudges her gently. "Go on."

Starlight takes a hesitant step forward, then another. She's always been a roller girl, but she never imagined clothes like these. They're like something the first Starlight, the princess from the cartoon, would wear. She runs her fingers over velvet, silk, lamé, sequins. Then, *oh*. Starlight stops, stares, barely daring to touch the fabric. It's *her*.

Sequins like mirrored glass, as big around as nickels, cover a shimmery material the color of mist surrounding a rainbow. It's so fine Starlight imagines that without the sequins, she could pull it through the eye of a needle. She lifts the bolt from the shelf, and holds it out to Esmeralda.

"Could you make me something out of this?"

Esmeralda smiles. "I think I can whip up something. Let's get you measured."

★

"CLOSE YOUR EYES. KEEP THEM CLOSED. NO PEEKING." ESMERALDA grasps Starlight's hand and guides her to step into the dress.

Starlight holds her breath as Esmeralda tugs the fabric up, and slips the straps over her shoulders, before zipping her in. Her cheeks warm at the thought of her bony hips, the worn state of her bought-in-packs-of-six underwear. But Esmeralda is a professional, hands sure, and the dress covers it all in no time.

"Okay, open your eyes."

Starlight's eyes open, and so does her mouth. The disco ball above her RollerRama stares back at her. The straps are spaghetti thin, studded in rhinestones; the bodice is heart-shaped, clinging smooth all the way down to a flattering waist. The skirt flares, giving Starlight the illusion of hips where she has none. But her legs, peeking out under the hem, are sleek and long, muscled from years of skating.

"Do you like it?" Esmeralda asks, fussing, adjusting, her eyes glowing with pride.

"It's perfect."

"Go ahead," Esmeralda says. "Twirl."

Starlight does. She puts her arms out to the side and the fabric spins with her, lifting from her thighs and sending light whirling around the room. For just a moment, the universe is all around her, and she's flying through it so fast that nothing can stop her. Tears spring to Starlight's eyes, and this time, she does nothing to stop them.

"Thank you," she says, breathless, throwing her arms around Esmeralda's neck.

"You look lovely." Bunny's voice startles her, and Starlight steps back.

Bunny's long, elegant frame leans in the doorway, her arms crossed, a gentle smile on her lips. Her eyes are blue today, shading toward green, an impossible jewel color that makes Starlight think of tropical seas. She feels plain and awkward again, uncertain what to do with her hands.

"There's just one thing missing," Bunny says, and holds out her hand, adding, "Come on, I won't bite," when Starlight hesitates.

Hand in Bunny's, Starlight is sharply aware of her bitten nails where she couldn't hold back her nerves any longer. She lets Bunny lead her to the vanity just outside the closet, Esmeralda trailing behind to observe. With gentle pressure on her shoulders, Bunny guides Starlight to sit on the plush seat facing a mirror surrounded in soft, rose-colored bulbs.

"Scoot back a bit." Bunny adjusts her so there's room between the table and Starlight, then opens what looks like a tackle box.

It unfolds and unfolds and unfolds, revealing rows of glittering, shimmering, silky make-up. Compacts and brushes and tubes of lipstick, more than Starlight has ever seen, putting her own dollar-store cosmetic collection to shame. Starlight's eyes prickle again, and she shakes her head.

"I couldn't…"

"Shh," Bunny says. "Trust me."

Obediently, Starlight closes her eyes, holding very still. Her body aches with the lack of motion, a sudden fear that the dream will vanish around her, the Glitter Squadron will send her back home. A soft brush traces the contours of cheekbones, feather-light, layering foundation and power. Her eyes come next, and Starlight fights the urge to bite her lip. Bunny works from the inside corner of Starlight's eyes outward, lining, tracing, blending. Starlight never knew there were so many kinds of make-up, or ways it could be so complicated and subtle, fierce and simple all at once.

Her lips come last, and when it's all done, she feels Bunny step back, examining her critically, an artist at her canvas. Starlight is afraid to open her eyes.

"What do you think, Es?" Bunny asks.

"A masterpiece."

"You're going to have to open your eyes eventually, sweetie," Bunny says. "It's hard to save the world with them closed."

Starlight lets out a breath, eyes flying open. She barely recognizes the girl in the mirror. A roller girl. A stardust creature made of cosmic glitter from the beginning of the world. A princess.

"I... Oh." Words fail her. Bunny squeezes her shoulder, watching their reflections side by side in the mirror.

A wild thought spins through Starlight's head that maybe, one day, she'll grow up to be as poised and as perfect as Bunny.

"What about shoes?" Esmeralda asks. "I'm sure we can find something in your size. What are you, a ten? Eleven?"

Starlight shakes her head; she would cry again, but it would ruin her make-up. Instead, she grins, thinking of white boots, freshly-repaired red wheels, and crisp new laces.

"It's okay, I brought my own."

THIS IS THE ULTRA FABULOUS GLITTER SQUADRON, AND THEY'RE here to save the world.

Bunny is in front, wearing chunky, silver-heeled boots that reach thigh-high, real diamonds winking in the soft, white rabbit ears peeking from her blonde bouffant. Penny and Esmeralda flank her, in copper and green. Behind them are Ruby and Sapphire, the not-so-twin-twins. The Squadron's jewel-tones glow bright, and Starlight circles them all, spinning like a disco-ball in her roller skates, keeping in constant motion so the panic doesn't set in.

Bunny carries, of all things, a harpoon. It's custom-made, with rabbits going at it in the manner rabbits do carved all along the wooden shaft.

Esmeralda carries what looks to Starlight a lot like Wonder Woman's lariat of truth crossed with Indiana Jones' whip, a giant faux-emerald topping the handle. It's currently coiled at her hip but it looks to Starlight like a cobra, waiting to strike.

Penny carries more weapons than Starlight has ever seen, pistols, knives, and what Penny fondly refers to as a Big Fucking Gun, even brass knuckles and a set of throwing stars.

"She's a black belt in every form of martial arts there is," Esmeralda whispers when she catches Starlight staring. "Black sash, too."

Starlight swallows hard. She can't tell from Esmeralda's deadpan expression whether she's joking, and she doesn't want to find out. There are no weapons visible on Ruby or Sapphire, but looking at them, she's relatively sure either one of them could kill her with their bare hands.

She feels woefully under-prepared, even though Bunny assured her that the Glitter Squadron had been watching her for much longer than the one night she saw Penny. That was just the first time she'd noticed. "You've been protecting the kids at the RollerRama ever since you took the job." Bunny had told her. "You can do this."

Starlight wants to believe in Bunny's pep talk, but she isn't sure she does. Her mama has an old hunting rifle but Starlight was emphatic growing up she had no interest in learning how to shoot. She'd always trusted Mama to protect her, but now it's her turn and Starlight is on the front lines, the one expected to help save the day.

"It's this way." Penny points, waving a hand-held device with light-up buttons and a glowing screen. An antenna protrudes from the top, and every now and then it makes a soft beeping sound.

They round the corner and Starlight's breath catches. She's been so focused on not throwing up, or tripping, or finding some other way to ruin everything, she hasn't been paying attention to her surroundings.

"That's the RollerRama." It glows softly, and Starlight's heart squinches.

"Maybe the aliens are here to steal our disco music," Sapphire says.

"It's not what's in the RollerRama, it's what's under it." Penny pokes at the device in her hand, frowning, the tone of its beeping more urgent now. "There are old mining tunnels leading straight here, but there was a major collapse in the fifties and the whole operation was shut down. There's are major untapped deposits of—"

But whatever Penny was about say is cut off, lost in the B-movie, science-fiction woo-woo-woo noise of three saucer-shaped spaceships dropping from the sky.

Starlight tries to scramble back, forgetting for a moment she's on wheels. Her skates nearly go out from under her, but Esmeralda is there, keeping her upright.

Even with her feet firmly under her, Starlight can't move. She can only gape at the spinning ships. The multicolored lights ringing them spark off Starlight's dress, bouncing and refracting until she really does look like a disco ball. All at once she's back at Cindy Williams' birthday party, just a boy in a tutu, spinning out of control at the end of a line of seven-year old children intent on hurting her.

Starlight's knees knock together, something she thought only happened in Scooby Doo cartoons. "I can't do this," she thinks, maybe even mouths, but it all comes out as a wheeze of air with barely any words at all.

The door of the lead spaceship opens. The bubble domes topping them are tinted dark, hiding the interior so no one expects what emerges.

"Fucking space eels." Penny draws a pistol, but doesn't fire, waiting on Bunny's signal.

"Let's give them a chance to talk." Bunny holds her hand up, nails winking in the multicolored lights.

She steps forward, grip tight on her harpoon. Starlight watches open-mouthed. Bunny's legs aren't shaking; her head is held high. The leader of the Ultra Fabulous Glitter Squadron doesn't show the slightest sign of fear, as though a trio of six-foot-long floating eels, crackling with blue and purple electricity, is no more of a big deal than running out of cereal.

Bunny's voice rings over the woo-woo of the spaceships and the electric crackle of the eels.

"We are the Ultra Fabulous Glitter Squadron. If you come to this planet in peace, consider us your official welcoming committee. If you're here to do harm, then I suggest you turn your squirmy bodies right back around, get in your spaceships, and go the fuck home."

The eels pulse, rills of energy shifting from blue to purple and back again. Tiny specks of light, like minnows, dart around the eels, clustering around first one then the other, forming patterns than might be words. One eel glides slightly ahead of the others, opening its mouth to show vicious, needle teeth, but otherwise makes no response.

Bunny grips her harpoon so tight Starlight can see the white of her knucklebones straining the skin.

"All right. You had your chance." Bunny hefts the harpoon, spinning it deftly before pointing it at the eels. "Oh, and a word of warning—we fight like girls."

Bunny lets the harpoon fly. A cheer rises in Starlight's throat, but before it can break free, several things happen simultaneously. The lead eel whips around, Bunny's harpoon sails past it harmlessly, and its tail catches Bunny with a casual flick, sending her flying backward. The world goes violet-tinted white, searing the air with the scent of lightning, and Starlight is temporarily blinded. Penny yells, and as Starlight blinks away the afterimage of Bunny flying through the air, Penny fires her pistol, charging forward.

The firefly lights swarm Penny and she whirls and whirls, fighting them off. Esmeralda kneels, touching Bunny's throat. Her kohl lined eyes are stricken and wide, but she nods at Starlight.

"She's breathing. Go help Penny."

Ruby and Sapphire have already launched into action. Despite the height disparity, they move in perfect synchronicity. Sapphire dodges every move the eel in front of her makes, her lithe body moving like liquid. The eel lunges, showing teeth, growing more agitated. Bolts of electricity sear the ground, but none touch Sapphire. And while Sapphire holds the creature's attention, Ruby slips up silently, and the next time Sapphire glides out of the way, she's waiting.

Ruby brings her hands together with a sound like a thunderclap. The eel's skull, caught between them, crumples like a paper bag. Its body twitches once, the sinuous length of it going stiff for a moment, snapping straight out like a wind-caught flag, before it coils uselessly to the ground. Ruby parts her palms and grins, blowing delicately on her smoking skin.

Starlight gapes. All of this happens incredibly fast and incredibly slow, and she still hasn't moved. Penny is forcing a second eel back, despite the darting minnow lights surrounding her. A gliding motion, a shadow pouring itself through the air catches Starlight's attention. The first eel, the one that knocked Bunny down is ribboning its way to her fallen form.

A warning shout freezes in Starlight's throat. Blind panic slams her heart against her ribs. A sound escapes her, more whimper than shout, but the eel whips around to face her. For a moment its eyes lock on her, gleaming malevolent light. It drops its jaw, showing wicked teeth in what Starlight can only assume is a grin. It darts toward her, and before she can react beyond throwing her arms up to shield her face, it's past her.

Stunned, Starlight pirouettes on her wheels. The eel is ignoring her, ignoring the rest of the Glitter Squadron, and heading straight for the RollerRama, *her* RollerRama. Starlight's throat unlocks all at once, with a wordless cry of rage.

She pushes off, wheels humming, gathering speed. She grabs the eel by the tail, ignoring the kick of electricity spiking up her arm. The eel thrashes, teeth snapping. Starlight's momentum carries her, dragging the eel in her wake. The teeth miss her by feet as she yanks hard; the eel's head jerks around with the force.

A glittering swarm of minnows breaks away from Penny, whirling around Starlight. They whine their distress, darting, nipping. Stars, Starlight thinks, ignoring the pain. Just like the disco ball. Just like the universe holding her in its arms. She knows just what to do. She spins.

The lights whirl around her and Starlight stretches her arms straight out in front of her, still holding onto the eel. Centrifugal force spins them, so fast she almost loses control. Everything blurs—the night, the pulsing lights of the spaceship, the firefly minnows swarming around her. The electric surge of the eel crackles through her, igniting her bones, but it's growing weaker. The blood rushes from her head, pressure building with the spin force. Meteors streak in the corner of her vision, and just when she's about to black out, Starlight lets go.

The eel goes flying, crashing into the nearest of the three spaceships. There's a sickening crunch. The ship wobbles, knocked off course, the woo-woo turning into a high-pitched whine. Smoke sizzles from beneath the edges of the darkened dome. As if responding to some primal programming, the other two craft edge away.

The spaceship's wobble gets worse, the craft struggling to right itself. Then, boom! A whump of displaced air, a shower of sparks, and a smell like burning seaweed. Starlight throws her arms over her face, her body heaving with exertion. Chunks of burning shrapnel rain down, barely missing her. One lands by the toe of her skate, smoking. When she lowers her arms, the ship is nothing but a puff of smoke and the other two are rising rapidly, the woo-woo of their engines sped to a panicked sound-the-retreat alarm.

Silence. The rush of Starlight's blood fills her ears. She stares after the retreating multicolored lights until they vanish. A ragged cheer goes up and Penny, Ruby, and Sapphire swarm her, slapping her on the back and hugging her. Trembling shakes her from head to toe and won't stop. Her knees fold, but Ruby is there to catch her, lowering her gently to the ground.

"Easy there, hon." Ruby grins. Starlight stares up at them, the ring of three faces looking down at her. Ruby and Sapphire smile openly, their eyes shining. Penny lifts just the corner of her mouth, keeping her arms crossed.

"You did good, kid," Penny says finally when Ruby digs an elbow into her ribs.

To Starlight's left, Esmeralda helps Bunny sit up. Bunny pats her hair, smoothing frosted blonde strands back into place and checking her ears. She shakes herself once, like a dog shedding water.

"We did it?" Starlight asks. Her voice sounds strange and far away.

"We did it," Bunny says. "You did it."

Esmeralda leaves Bunny, who is climbing to her feet, and crouches beside Starlight. "Think you can stand up, sweetie?"

Starlight, still dazed, lets Esmeralda help her stand. Ruby hovers nearby, ready to catch her if she falls again. As soon as she's up, Bunny surprises Starlight with a hug that nearly lifts her off her feet.

"Welcome to the team," she whispers.

"Really?" Starlight asks as Bunny eases off and steps back to give her space. "You mean it?" Starlight glances at Penny, and Penny shrugs.

"Congratulations," Esmeralda says, her smile relieved and genuine. Sapphire squeezes her shoulder, and Ruby punches Starlight's upper arm as gently as she can, which still causes Starlight to stagger on her wheels.

"But I panicked." The words rush out of Starlight before she can stop them. "I almost got you killed. And what if they come back? What if they're angry?"

Starlight struggles not to hyperventilate. She blinks her long lashes so fast the ring of Glitter Squadron faces surrounding her blur. Any moment now, Bunny will realize she made a huge mistake, and it will be back to trays full of strawberry milkshakes and Dean and his crew hurling insults at her.

Bunny puts an arm around Starlight's shoulders in a way that reminds her of her mama—a bit stronger, where her mama's coughing fits have left her weak, and smelling of lilac instead of cigarettes. For a moment, Starlight feels like a traitor for even thinking it. Everything is different now. She can never go home, not really. She's fought space eels; she is a princess and a cosmic roller girl. Her mama's trailer and the RollerRama will feel so small now. Bunny gives Starlight's shoulder a squeeze, bringing her back, and Starlight manages a smile. It's different, but her mama will always be her mama, and the more time she spends with the Glitter Squadron, the stronger Starlight will get, and the better she'll be at keeping her mama safe. The world *is* different now, but Bunny's arm around her shoulders still feels like home.

"If that happens," Bunny says, "then you're guaranteed job security."

The Blushing Rosebud

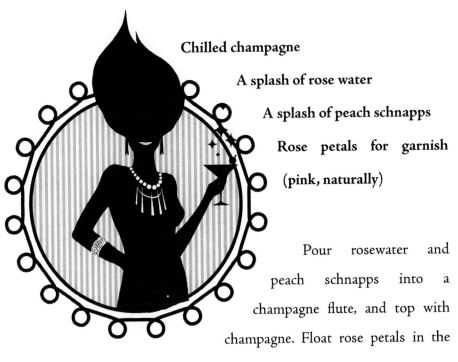

Chilled champagne

A splash of rose water

A splash of peach schnapps

Rose petals for garnish (pink, naturally)

Pour rosewater and peach schnapps into a champagne flute, and top with champagne. Float rose petals in the glass to garnish.

This drink is sweet, inoffensive, and sparkly, just like our Starlight. Honestly, I was tempted to make her drink a virgin. Oh, that's catty, isn't it? She's a sweet kid, I love her, but sometimes she's so naïve. If she just learned to step up and assert herself... Well, she *is* learning. She's got a bit of hero worship when it comes to Bunny, and it's doing her a world of good, if you ask me. Maybe for both of them. Bunny needs someone to look out for, to take under her wig. Oops, I mean wing. Oh, I'm bad, aren't I?

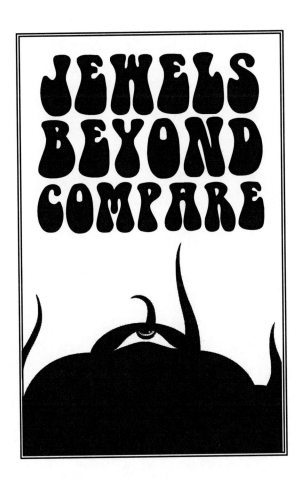

THE GRILL HAS BEEN OFF FOR OVER AN HOUR BUT THE NARROW GALLEY-style kitchen still stinks of grease, strong enough for Ruby to feel it at the back of her throat. Every minute or so she has to stop scrubbing and wipe sweat from her forehead with her uniform sleeve. Under the grease is the scent of bleach from the freshly-mopped floors, just now drying under her aching feet. All the other girls are gone. Somehow, once again, she drew the short straw and got stuck doing an extra hour's cleaning, when it would take them less than half the time if they all pitched in.

It's Friday night, and of course Layla and Jenny assumed she had nothing better to do. What else could the fat girl possibly have planned besides watching *The Amazing Race* and *Real Housewives of Orange County* and *Wipeout* on television while eating a pint of ice cream? Which, when Ruby thinks about it, sounds killer next to Jenny's plan of letting her going-nowhere loser boyfriend feel her up in the back of a darkened movie theater, even though she hates reality television. Or Layla's plan to spend a few hours in a seedy roadside motel with the sweaty, grunting man who is using her to cheat on his wife.

"Darlene. Hey, Darlene!"

Ruby clenches her jaw and doesn't answer. Her white plastic name tag clearly says Ruby, and it's the only name she's answered to for years. Only her grandparents were allowed to call her Darlene, no other exceptions. But Harv Salmetti has told her repeatedly that as long as she cashes his checks, made out to Darlene Shickley, he can call her whatever he damned well pleases. If she doesn't like it, she can take her job and stuff it.

One of these days she's going to take him up on the offer. And she has a very clear idea of where she'll localize that stuffing.

"You giving me the silent treatment, or what?" Mr. Salmetti slides past her; there's ample room, but he makes a point of brushing against her as he does.

He leans against the refrigerator, blocking her path to the sink. There's no point in trying to step around him. Ruby sets aside the steel wool, raising her chin.

"Is there something I can do for you, Mr. Salmetti?" She refuses to call him Harv to his face; they are not friends.

He stares pointedly at her chest. "No hot date tonight?"

Ruby doesn't cross her arms or look away. Those aren't the things that require self-control; it's not kicking her boss in the shins that takes all her willpower.

"You know how the cleaning shifts are divided," she says, keeping her voice as even as she can. "We draw straws. I guess I have bad luck."

"Are you sure? Or were you maybe feeling a little lonely? We could keep each other company."

He steps closer. He smells worse than the grill. On him the fried scent is mixed with too-sweet pipe tobacco, reminding her of carsickness.

Mr. Salmetti leans in, stopping just short of touching her. Ruby balls her fists in the stained apron about her waist. She mentally counts the stains, an exercise to hold her calm. Bitter coffee. Too-sweet cherry pie. Smears of grease. Her arms tremble, but it's the only thing keeping her from gut-punching her boss and bringing a lawsuit on top of a lost job.

She made the mistake of letting him touch her once. And he expected—still expects—her to be grateful. "A girl like you doesn't have many options," he's told her more than once.

Ruby wasn't grateful then, and she isn't grateful now. What she was, at the time, was drunk and filled with the kind of ennui only fake plastic wreaths and tinsel strung up around a diner can bring on. Mr. Salmetti had been even drunker, and the truth was she felt sorry for him. She knew he didn't have anyone to go home to after the staff holiday party.

So she didn't push him away immediately when he'd sloppily kissed her cheek, using the excuse of the mistletoe strung over the door between the diner and his office. Or when he'd moved from her cheek to her neck. She'd even let him squeeze her breast, but she didn't follow him into his office, and stopped him when he tried to hike up her skirt. She didn't slap him either, which seemed like a kindness at the time, but ever since has felt like a huge mistake.

"No thank you, Mr. Salmetti." Ruby makes each word precise, firm as the shove that ended the holiday party, hoping he'll finally get the message.

For a moment, Mr. Salmetti seems genuinely confused, unable to comprehend why she would turn him down. She *should* be grateful, after all. Just like she *shouldn't* have plans other than TV and ice cream, because doesn't the skin, the shape, the body, define all of a person? When Ruby doesn't let her expression falter, a muscle twitches in Mr. Salmetti's jaw. Slowly and deliberately he knocks over the bucket of greasy water and scrapings from the grill.

"I guess you'll have to stay even later than you thought."

His grin is smug, predatory. He's only an inch or two taller than her, and under his fat he's soft. Ruby could break him in half if she wanted to. He crosses his arms again, waiting for her move.

Maybe he expects Ruby to cry. Maybe he expects her to apologize, or take him up on his offer after all, like a bucket of greasy slop water is the key to getting her libido going. Ruby feels sorry for him all over again. But her sympathy only goes so far. He's a shitbag, and she's sick of his bullying. He's nothing to her other than a paycheck and fuck it—she'll deal with the loss of that tomorrow.

Ruby unties her apron and folds it into a neat square. She unpins her white plastic name tag and shoves both into Mr. Salmetti's stunned hands.

"Clean it yourself, asshole."

She slams the diner door on the way out, so hard the glass shatters. It is the most beautiful sound in the world.

THE TREMBLING DOESN'T SET IN UNTIL RUBY GETS HOME. SHE LEANS over the bathroom sink, fighting the urge to vomit as the adrenaline fades.

"What the fuck am I going to do now?" she asks her reflection. Scared-wide eyes stare back at her.

She lives paycheck to paycheck in the bungalow her grandparents left her. Who knows how long it'll take her to find another job. Mr. Salmetti will tell his friends about her. Warn them. She can picture him lying, saying he caught her stealing from the register or some other bullshit. And retail and customer service are all she's qualified for.

Bitter laughter-that-is-panic shakes her, tears of hilarity smudging her make-up. "Maybe I should run away and join the circus." It's an old joke, one she'd used to deflect her friends when they were all getting their college acceptance letters. She couldn't afford the tuition and she'd failed utterly to qualify for any scholarships.

"I'm going to run away and join the circus. Everyone loves a clown."

She even looks the part now—sad Pierrot eyes lined in jagged streaks of mascara, cheeks alternately flushed too-red and shocked pale, lipstick smeared from slurping water against the imaginary taste of bile. As abruptly as it started, the laughter stops. Ruby lets out a breath, grips the edge of the sink, and straightens.

"Fuck it." She's not a quitter. Of all the stupid ideas she's ever had, joining the circus is not her worst plan.

RUBY SURVEYS THE ITEMS LAID OUT ON HER BED: A SLINKY DRESS, cut low, slit high, slithering with sequins the color of her name; bright red cowboy boots with white stitching; three dyed-red ostrich feathers; glittery eyelashes, a good half-inch long, and sparkly lipstick like fresh-spilled blood. The last item she bought is a bus ticket. Together, they ate her paycheck whole. After this, she's fucked.

She dons the clothing, applies the make-up, and sets the ostrich feathers in her carefully curled hair. Bus ticket clutched in her sweaty hand, she steps out the door.

Ruby ignores the stares, the whispers, as she walks to the bus station. She continues to ignore them as she boards the bus. She keeps her hands folded in her lap, staring straight ahead, pretending she's the only person in the world through the jouncing two hour ride. From the end of the line, Ruby walks. Cars whiz by, and even though she's separated from them by the railing of the pedestrian walkway, the hum of the tires seeps up through her boots and wind buffets her as she crosses the bridge.

Sun beats on the back of her neck, exposed by her feather-topped updo. It's almost impossible not to feel wilted, with sweat gathering at the small of her back and the blistery rub of her brand new boots. She feels ridiculous. Until she reaches the midpoint of the bridge and the circus comes into view, taking her breath away.

Tents bloom in a rainbow of color, like a colony of poisonous mushrooms covering the tiny private island that used to belong to a local convent. The central part of the island is now a bird sanctuary, but the circus obtained special permission to use the outskirts while they're in town. Her heart swells as Ruby forgets everything but the memory of sawdust and cotton candy, walking between her grandparents and holding their hands, looking at everything with wide-eyed six-year-old wonder. It takes everything Ruby has not to break into a run.

Yet this circus smells nothing like the one she remembers. She sniffs the air, breathes deep but cannot identify the dry, neutral scent, touched ever so faintly with plastic from the tents dotting the fairway. She can see them all beyond the gate, but the pimple-faced kid doesn't want to let her in. She has no money for a ticket, and besides the circus doesn't open to the public until tomorrow.

Ruby draws herself up to the fullness of her less-than-impressive height, and smiles her sweetest smile. She has an appointment. An audition, really, with the circus manager, Mr. Forsythe. If she didn't, why would she be dressed this way? The kid rings Forsythe's office, receives no answer, and finally shrugs her through, bored. He directs her to a trailer at the back of the grounds.

Ruby pauses outside the trailer, checking her make-up in a small hand-held mirror. She wipes her palms and the back of her neck with a wad of crumpled napkins from the diner, and shoves everything back into her purse. Ruby knocks. The grumbled response is inarticulate, but she hasn't come this far to quit. She eases the door open, poking her head inside.

"Hello?"

A cloud of cigar smoke envelops her. Somewhere within the blue fog is a squat man behind a desk—an incongruous thing of heavy oak that has no place inside the tin-can of a trailer.

"The hell you want?" The man's brows draw together, shaggy caterpillars engaged in making love. Or war.

"Sir, my name is Ruby—"

He plucks the cigar from thick lips with thick fingers, scowling. "You lost?"

"No, sir, I'm here—"

"Well you shouldn't be. Get out. And close the door. You're letting in the air." He replaces the cigar, still scowling, and turns his attention back to the pile of receipts covering his desk.

Ruby notes the lack of computer. There are only paper-swollen folders and an adding machine with smoke-yellowed keys. She resists the urge to draw another deep breath, afraid of pulling more blue smoke into her lungs and choking to death. She speaks as fast as she can, getting the words out before he can interrupt her again.

"Sir, my name is Ruby and I'm here to apply for a job."

Mr. Forsythe freezes, cigar halfway between mouth and ashtray. A chunk of ash drops to the desk and he blots the papers with unnecessary force to prevent the whole thing going up in an inferno.

Taking advantage of his distraction, Ruby squeezes her way into the trailer. There's no chair on this side of Forsythe's desk, so she plants herself firmly in front of it.

"A job?" Forsythe sets his cigar aside, lips pulling up unattractively on one side. "We've already got a fat lady. You're wasting your time."

Ruby opens her mouth, but Forsythe holds up his hand, sneer deepening.

"Not that you couldn't give her a run for her money. How much do you weigh, sweetheart?" When Ruby opens her mouth again, he waves dismissively. "Doesn't matter. No one wants to pay money to see a queen-size queen. Get lost."

Ruby's lip threatens to tremble, but she raises her head. She's spent years dealing with Harv Salmetti and putting up with all manner of shit from the customers at his diner; this is nothing.

"I don't want to be your Fat Lady. I want the Strong Woman job," Ruby says. "I've done my research. You don't have one."

The man pauses in mid-reach for his cigar, mouth hanging, then bursts forth with an exaggerated "haw," slapping both palms flat on his desk, scattering receipts. The laughter turns into a coughing fit, shaking his entire body. Ruby waits it out, refusing to let her heart sink, digging her nails into her palms. Forsythe wipes his eyes.

"Lady, you are some special kind of crazy." He pauses to wheeze, then goes on. "Only thing people want to see less than a queen-sized queen is a queen-sized queen giving herself a heart attack trying to lift a dumbbell. You think I want the trouble of hauling your sorry, tarted-up corpse out of my circus when you keel over from what's probably the only bit of exercise you've ever done in your life?"

He goes on, his lips moving like an exaggerated parody of speech in a silent film, but the words are lost in the roar of blood in Ruby's head. Her cheeks flush hot, but when her voice emerges, it's perfectly even and calm.

"I've changed my mind. I don't want the job. But just so you know what you're missing, consider this my audition."

Ruby steps forward, moving her body, yet floating somewhere just beyond her right shoulder, watching. Her hands—are they hers?—grip the edge of Forsythe's heavy desk. The ostrich feathers in her hair bob as she yanks the desk forward, and with barely a grunt of effort, flips it over.

The trailer shakes. Forsythe lurches back, narrowly avoiding getting his feet crushed. A blizzard of receipts fill the air, and in their midst, Ruby turns on her heel and walks out the door.

She's deep in the maze of tents, blooming all around her like a wild garden, when it strikes her. She crashes back into her body and her knees buckle, dropping her to the ground next to a tent striped blue and gold. A sob breaks free. She has no job, nowhere to go, and she spent the last of her money on the stupid dress and the stupid bus ticket and she has nothing to show for it.

Ignoring the pain, Ruby rips the false eyelashes from her lids. She digs in her purse for a napkin, but she used the last one to dry her sweaty palms. The contents of her bag clatter as she up-ends it, pawing through them as they tumble into the dust.

"Here you go, honey."

Ruby starts, her head snapping up. A hand holds out a tissue.

The tissue and the hand belong to one of the tallest women Ruby has ever seen. Her skin is dark and flawless; her hair straightened to a silky black ponytail hanging halfway down her back. She's also wearing one of the skimpiest outfits Ruby's encountered outside of a beach or swimming pool. In fact, if it weren't covered in dark blue sequins, Ruby might have mistaken it for a bathing suit, with high-cut sides, a peek-a-boo diamond revealing the woman's belly button, and a heart-shaped bodice. The outfit is complemented by a choker around the woman's throat, dripping with blue teardrop beading and a single peacock feather.

In the face of the woman's elegance, Ruby's tears do something complicated, her sobs turning into a kind of strangled laughter as she accepts the tissue.

"I must look like a raccoon rooting in garbage."

"Not especially." The woman's voice is throaty—velvet and smoke. "You look like someone in an awful lot of pain. What happened?"

"The manager..." Ruby waves in the direction of the trailer. "Mr. Forsythe..."

"Oh. He's an asshole. Speaking of, I have to do a set to impress said asshole's investors, but I can sneak you in if you want to watch the show. After I'm done, we can get coffee." She offers a smile. "Or something stronger. You look like you could use a good talk."

The woman extends her hand; her grip is surprisingly callused for the smoothness of her skin.

"Oof." She grunts as she helps Ruby to her feet, then offers a wry smile, looking Ruby up and down.

"My name's Sapphire, by the way."

"Ruby."

"Well look at us. Twin gems." Sapphire parts the tent flap, ducking through.

Ruby follows, thoughts racing to catch up. Twin gems. The words echo, warming Ruby's cheeks, her belly, spreading outward. It lessens some of the ache, makes her not care about the feathers wilting in her hair, or her smudged make-up, or how she's going to pay for groceries. Or anything else, for that matter.

The tent flap drops closed, encasing them in dusky twilight. Ruby follows Sapphire through the narrow space behind a tiered row of bleachers.

"Sit anywhere you like. If anyone gives you any trouble, you tell them you're my special guest." Sapphire pauses long enough to squeeze Ruby's hand before hurrying off.

The strength and warmth in Sapphire's grip sends a fresh spike of heat through Ruby's body. She's never had a friend—acquaintances, co-workers, people from high school she sees occasionally when they come home to visit their families—but no real friends. And even though they've only just met, Sapphire feels like a friend.

Spotlights swing over the ring in the center of the tent, leaving the seats in darkness. Ruby slips into the first available spot. One of the lights snaps upward, illuminating a swing. Then all the lights go out, plunging the tent into darkness.

When the lights return, they're trained on the swing. Sapphire perches on the narrow bar, a train of peacock feathers trailing behind her. The very picture of royalty, Ruby thinks, if royalty was prone to wearing skimpy almost-bikinis. She stifles a giggle.

The giggle turns into a gasp as Sapphire flips backward, her knees catching the swing and the peacock feathers flaring in a halo behind her. Ruby's heart lurches, then soars, linked to Sapphire by an invisible thread. Utterly rapt, Ruby forgets about everything beyond the circle of spotlights and Sapphire moving above her like liquid grace. She drops, glides, swings, trades the swing for lengths of silken cloth she weaves around her body like a spider. She is a bird, an angel, a chimerical creature.

When the show ends, Ruby is on her feet, thundering applause before she even realizes it. There's a small knot of men in suits, presumably the investors, and one of them glances her way. She slips outside before anyone can question her.

"That was amazing," Ruby says when Sapphire emerges, dressed in loose, flowing pants, a light blouse, and heavy leather sandals. Only the jeweled choker remains around her throat, a reminder of her performance.

"I was afraid you wouldn't stay." Sapphire smiles, and Ruby's cheeks warm again. "You looked like a flight risk for a good while there." Sapphire takes Ruby's arm, ignoring the height difference between them and leads her away from the tent. "Coffee or something stronger? I know a place that does both."

"I don't really drink," Ruby says.

"I can cover that for both of us."

"What on earth is that?" Ruby gapes at the drink the waiter sets in front of Sapphire.

The café is cozy, with pressed-tin ceilings holding in warm amber light. Nooks piled with cushions are lit by flickering candles and decorated with hookahs with curling pipes.

"My own creation." Sapphire takes a sip before leaning back with a contented sigh. "Bombay Sapphire gin, tonic, gin-soaked juniper berries, crushed ice, and a swirl of blueberry liqueur."

Ruby wraps her hand around her mug, afraid to take a sip. She let Sapphire talk her into an apple tea, which she was instructed to pour over cubes of raw brown sugar and stir with a stick of cinnamon. She usually drinks Tetley with milk, or Folgers with the same, and she's afraid of embarrassing herself in comparison to Sapphire's sophisticated palate.

"It won't bite you." Sapphire gestures at the tea.

Ruby takes a tiny sip, surprised and delighted. "It's good."

"This is perfect. We were destined to meet today."

Ruby glances around; just looking at the hookahs makes her feel light-headed and giddy. "What do you mean?"

"When my astrologer did my chart last month, she said I would meet someone who would change my life when the moon was in the third phase."

"You have an astrologer?"

Sapphire waves the question away and leans forward. "Now, I want you to tell me everything that happened with Old Toad Face Forsythe."

Ruby's stomach lurches.

Sapphire pats her hand reassuringly, and Ruby takes a deep breath. To her amazement, her voice doesn't break. When she dares to glance at Sapphire, she sees her rolling her eyes at the circus manager's behavior, and when Ruby comes to the part about flipping his desk, Sapphire claps her hands.

"You really did that?"

Ruby allows herself a grin.

"Ye gods and little fishes! You must be strong."

"Little what?"

"Fishes. Something my grandmother used to say," Sapphire says. "Seriously, how much can you bench press?"

Ruby shrugs. "I never really thought about it." She toys with her empty mug for a moment before getting up the courage to ask Sapphire about herself.

"What about you? Why do you work for Toad...I mean, why do you stay with the circus if you hate Forsythe so much?"

"All my life I kept hearing I was too tall to be a gymnast—from

teachers, coaches, my parents. Everyone wanted me to play basketball."
Sapphire smirks a bit. "When I started looking for a job, it was the same
thing all over again. They said the only place for me was in a nightclub,
but I wanted to fly. Toad Face gave me a job, so I put up with his shit.
Besides, I kind of like the way he trots me out for his investors like a prize
pet bird. I keep waiting for one of them to storm off in disgust or accuse
him of setting them up, but so far they've all eaten up my performances.
I guess I give them a kinky little thrill, make them feel like they're being
dangerous and edgy."

"What do you mean?" Something jolts inside Ruby, confusion that
makes her feel stupid, unworldly.

"Oh, honey." Sapphire's eyes widen. "I thought you knew."

Sapphire undoes the choker around her neck, revealing her Adam's
apple.

"Oh. I didn't… I'm sorry. You must think I'm such an idiot." Ruby
stands quickly, almost knocking over Sapphire's drink.

Sapphire deftly catches her glass with one hand, and catches Ruby's
wrist with the other.

"Sit your ass back down." She tugs lightly, and Ruby relents.

She watches out of the corner of her eye as Sapphire replaces her
choker, unsure what to do with her hands. Is Sapphire laughing at her?
No, her expression is wistful, almost pained.

"I feel like an idiot," Ruby murmurs.

"Don't. I'll take it as a compliment." There's a faint hitch in Sapphire's
voice; her half smile doesn't quite touch her eyes.

"But your costume, how do you…" Ruby stops herself, blushing even more furiously. She sounds like such a rube.

Sapphire winks. "I'm a master at tucking. The feathers help."

"I just… I'm sorry."

"Honey, if you apologize one more time, *I'm* going to get up and walk out. Relax." Sapphire signals the waiter, and whispers something in his ear before sending him away and addressing Ruby. "Trust me."

Ruby's stomach flutters, then does an outright flip when the waiter returns with another blue-laced drink for Sapphire, and something red in a martini glass, which he sets in front of Ruby.

"What is it?" Ruby asks.

"I think I'll call it a Ruby Crush. Cranberry vodka, blood orange juice, ruby grapefruit juice and just a hint of champagne, shaken, over crushed ice. Pablo is a doll about mixing up my recipes. I'm going to open my own place one day—each room with a different theme—retro-disco nostalgia, afro-future funkadelic, roaring twenties speakeasy glam, and a fabulous feathered aviary. I'm going to hire Pablo right out from under Terry's nose." Sapphire gestures toward the bar, then points one glittering nail at the drink. "Give it a try."

Ruby lifts the glass, afraid of spilling. It's tart, and the alcohol is stronger than she expected. She does her best not to cough.

"It's good," she manages to say.

Sapphire nods her approval. "Good. Now let it do its work. And speaking of, what are you going to do now?"

"I don't know." Ruby takes another sip before she realizes what she's doing. At least her eyes don't water this time. "Look for another job, I guess. I can't go back to the diner. I ended that just about as badly as my interview with Forsythe."

"Sometimes I wish I had the guts to up and quit," Sapphire says. "Make a real dramatic exit, you know?"

"Why don't you?"

Sapphire looks up, surprised. Ruby takes another swallow of her drink to hide her nerves. It warms her more surely than the tea, a fizzy rush through her blood. It occurs to her briefly that she skipped lunch, and putting alcohol on an empty stomach probably isn't a good idea. But then her mouth is moving, words tumbling out and running away with her.

"You're beautiful, you could do anything. You're too good for Toad Face."

"You really think so?" Sapphire looks as though she's never considered the possibility, which surprises Ruby.

But doubt flickers in Sapphire's eyes.

Ruby continues, emboldened by the alcohol and the hint of humanity peeking through Sapphire's flawless armor. "Sure. We could go into business together."

"What did you have in mind?" Sapphire purses her lips.

"Cat burglary!" The words slip out before Ruby can stop them. She giggles, then puts a hand over her mouth. "Sorry."

She begins to push the martini glass away, but Sapphire stops her, edging it back to Ruby's side of the table.

"Hang on. It's not the world's worst idea."

"I was just kidding, I..."

Sapphire holds up a hand. She leans forward, her voice conspiratorial and low. "Forsythe has a whole stash of treasure up in the old convent house. Stuff that should be in a museum. Half of it was probably stolen by his great grandpappy or something. Anyway, he always travels with at least part of his collection, something else to trot out for the big-wig investors. Honey, you should see the way he puffs up when he's showing it off. Just like a..."

"Toad?"

"Exactly!" Sapphire strikes the table with both hands, then glances around and drops her voice again. "But think about it, your strength, my agility—we could be in and out and gone before Forsythe could say 'ribbit.'"

"I don't think toads say 'ribbit,'" Ruby says.

"We could go anywhere! Mexico! Paris! Rome!"

"Shh."

"Sorry. But really. Ruby and Sapphire, international jewel thieves." Sapphire catches both of Ruby's hands, squeezing.

"Seriously?"

The room swims, not just Ruby's head. But she can picture it, both of them dressed in fine silk, drinking champagne under the Eiffel Tower, each wearing a jewel the size of an egg, matching their names.

"It's crazy." Ruby shakes her head, trying to pull her hands away, but Sapphire grips harder.

"That's exactly why we should do it. *Tonight*. Forsythe is hosting a private dinner in the big top. It's perfect."

"I don't think..."

"Oh, Ruby. Say yes?" The excitement of the moment makes Sapphire glow from within. Ruby is glowing too, from the alcohol and the pressure of Sapphire's fingers.

"Yes?"

"Wonderful." Sapphire signals the waiter for another round.

Somehow, the glass at Ruby's elbow is empty, and despite her trepidation the second drink goes down easier than the first.

It's well past sunset when Ruby and Sapphire leave the café. Sugar and alcohol sing through Ruby's veins. She's floating, warm and giddy. "What time is Toad Face's party?" She takes extra care pronouncing each word.

"Oh, honey, I shouldn't have let you drink so much," Sapphire says by way of response.

Even as she does, one of her sandals catches on an uneven bit of sidewalk and she stumbles. Ruby puts an arm around Sapphire's waist; she doesn't take it away as Sapphire regains her balance.

"That was the pavement." Sapphire frowns. "And eight o'clock. We have plenty of time."

At the far end the bridge, circus tents bloom against the dark, strung with lights. Beyond the tents, the old convent house's windows glow. The bridge is longer than Ruby remembers. The open grating and the dark water make her uneasy.

"Oof, not so tight. Are you scared of heights?"

Ruby lets go of Sapphire's waist with a guilty start.

"A little, I guess. Sorry." Goosebumps rise and she wishes she was wearing something more practical than the slinky red dress.

At the far end of the bridge, Sapphire takes Ruby's hand as she wobbles, helping her down the last steps from the walkway. The stars are very bright. Ruby squints, letting everything blur; she tries to picture the man behind Sapphire's high, sharp cheekbones, but she can't do it. He isn't there. Sapphire isn't handsome, she's beautiful.

What would it feel like to kiss Sapphire? Heat flashes through her at the thought, and horrified, she pushes it away. But it creeps back, insidious, and her body tingles. Just because Sapphire is being so nice to her doesn't mean... And besides, she isn't like that. Or is she? Maybe it doesn't matter, because people are just people, not one thing or another.

The thoughts race and clang inside Ruby's dizzy head. She hears her voice, words out before she can stop them.

"Maybe you don't even like girls." As soon as the words are out, Ruby clamps her mouth shut, mortified.

Sapphire's eyes widen. Ruby's blood thumps. What will she do if Sapphire does like girls? If she likes *Ruby*...

But she sees the answer in Sapphire's eyes, and Ruby's heart drops, even though she hasn't even sorted out what she feels. She tries to pull her hand away, but Sapphire grips it tighter.

"I'm sorry, honey." She shakes her head. "But I would love to be your friend. If that's okay?"

There's a shadow under Sapphire's skin, the same hint of pain Ruby saw in the café. The starlight isn't as quick to dissolve it as the warm lights of the café. That look in Sapphire's eyes is the only thing that keeps

Ruby's tears from starting. Relief and terror and pity flood her, all tangled up. Sapphire's expression changes, the pain not quite disappearing, but softening into something else. Regret, maybe.

"I don't know if this will make it better or worse," Sapphire says. "But if it makes it worse, you have my permission to break one of my bones."

So quickly Ruby barely realizes what's happening, Sapphire leans down and kisses her. It's both the most and least sexual kiss Ruby has ever experienced, and she's so stunned she doesn't even know whether she's responded before it's over.

"Oh." Ruby exhales, breathless. She looks up at Sapphire, so many questions crowding her tongue she can't shape the first one. Sapphire gives her a tentative smile, and because Ruby can't think of a single thing to say, what comes out is, "Thank you?"

Sapphire's smile widens; she lets go of Ruby's hand.

"Come on." Sapphire turns on her heel. "We've got burglary to do."

"Isn't there a security system?" Even though she's whispering, Ruby feels like she's shouting.

Crickets sing; laughter and music drift up from the big top. The circus glows behind them, each tent lit a different color.

"Why bother? Most of the time this place is empty. It would cost more to rewire than anything that's usually in there is worth. There's one security guard, but he must be ninety if he's a day."

Ruby wipes damp palms against her dress, making the sequins rasp.

Now that the alcohol is starting to wear off, she feels foolish and a little sick.

"Do you think we should…"

But Sapphire is already taking her sandals off, hiding them under a bush. Ruby's not going to back down, not if Sapphire doesn't first.

Nobody will think you're cool if you chicken out. The taunt comes back, sudden and sharp and Ruby freezes, one foot bare, the other half out of her boot. She can actually feel the worms wriggling between her fingers, see the circle of bright, eager faces standing around her. *Come on, fatty, do it. We'll never talk to you again if you don't.*

Even then, Ruby knew it wasn't true. It didn't matter what she did—eating the worms, not eating the worms—nothing would make a difference in what the cool kids thought of her. She'd still be excluded for being fat. For living with her grandparents. For wearing hand-me-down clothes. For not following some unwritten set of rules she didn't understand. But she'd shoved the worms in her mouth, even knowing this, mashing them between her teeth viciously, feeling them squirm and fighting not to cry.

She'd swallowed, and almost immediately gagged, thrown up, and the school nurse had sent her home, humiliated, unable to look her grandfather in the eye as he drove her home in a battered Cadillac nearly as old as her.

But this isn't like that. Sapphire isn't one of those kids. So what is Ruby doing? Maybe, just maybe, a part of her thrills to the idea of stealing from Forsythe, starting a new life—one where no one would recognize her as a grease-stained waitress with a dead-end job and no prospects in a tiny little town in the middle of nowhere.

Bunching up her skirt, Ruby hurries after Sapphire. At any moment, Ruby expects the whoop of sirens, the cutting beams of flashlights picking her out. But there's only the hush of their feet over the lawn. Up close, Ruby can see how huge the house actually is. About halfway back the windows are covered with iron bars.

"What are those for?"

"The building was used as a sanitarium for a while. The nuns didn't need all the rooms, so they converted it into a hospital."

"We're breaking into an abandoned madhouse?" Ruby's voice catches. Her skin feels clammy. "I think I'm going to be sick."

Sapphire ignores her, pointing to one of the windows. "Do you think you could pull the bars off?"

Ruby considers the bolts. They're rusted and one is missing. It even looks as though someone tried to break in before them and gave up.

"I think so."

Her pulse thumps in her palms, and she takes a deep breath, setting her feet. She thinks of Harv Salmetti and Toad Face, her taunting classmates in the school yard and the worms. She yanks hard, twisting. The metal groans, resisting, then with a sudden puff of brick dust, the whole thing comes away in Ruby's hands.

She staggers back and Sapphire catches her. For a moment, neither of them says anything, then Sapphire grasps Ruby's shoulders, kneading them and leans close with a hot, fierce whisper. "You did it."

Ruby drops the bars, her arms trembling, more in exhilaration than fear. A grin plants itself on her lips, and without waiting for Sapphire's say-so, she steps forward and forces the window open.

The zing of adrenaline in her blood is even better than the alcohol. Lacing her fingers, she holds them out, a step for Sapphire's foot.

"Ladies first."

The impressed look on Sapphire's face heats Ruby with pride. Ruby boosts her through the window, and once she's inside, Sapphire calls down to her.

"Go around to the back. I'll unlock the door."

"We make quite the team," Sapphire says, meeting Ruby at the back door with a grin.

Inside, Ruby follows Sapphire down a long hallway, rooms opening to either side, some with abandoned bed frames, others with sagging mattresses, and all with paint peeling like shedding skin. At the end of the hall, there's a pair of pocket doors. Ruby shoves at them, ignoring the unoiled track shrieking its complaint.

Beyond the door, the house is sane, with glass-shaded lights burning, a threadbare woven carpet, and a grand staircase leading to the second floor.

"Up here." The steps creak under Ruby's weight, but Sapphire makes no sound, moving on the balls of her feet.

"This is where Forsythe keeps his collection." Sapphire pushes open a door.

"Oh. Wow." Ruby breathes out.

There are carved idols, insects cased in glass, canopic jars, hammered gold bracelets, and a massive, illuminated manuscript in a gold case embossed with jewels. Sapphire moves through the room, examining each object, but Ruby can only stand in the doorway, stunned.

"This. It has to be this." Sapphire holds up a necklace, and Ruby's mouth drops open.

Golden beads chime softly; they make Ruby think of feathers and spread wings. In the center of the necklace sits a scarab as long as her finger, carved from lapis lazuli and chased in gold.

"Try it on," Sapphire says.

Without realizing it, Ruby has stepped into the room. She blinks, shaking her head, but she's already reaching for the necklace. She wants to feel it against her skin, but at the same time, the idea of putting it on is revolting.

Sapphire steps behind her, draping the necklace around Ruby's throat. The gold is warm and heavier than it has any right to be. It chases the breath from her lungs. She's dizzy, wanting to claw the necklace away, but when Sapphire asks if it's too tight and moves to adjust it, Ruby bats her hands away.

Sapphire's lips move, but the words are lost in a rush of dark wind. Torchlight flickers at the edge of Ruby's vision. She's somewhere else; the walls are stone. Then Sapphire is shaking her, eyes wide with fear.

"Come on. We have to get out of here." She grasps Ruby's arm, dragging her.

Ruby stumbles in Sapphire's wake, her body numb and distant. It registers finally that Sapphire is saying "What's wrong?" over and over again.

"The necklace," Ruby gasps.

Her voice is scraped raw. She can barely breathe. Together, fumbling, they get the necklace off and it drops heavily to the grass. Chill air hits Ruby like a slap, and her teeth chatter.

"What happened?" Sapphire says.

At the same time, Ruby says, "We have to take it back."

"We can't. Didn't you hear the front door open? Either Forsythe is back or the guard saw us."

The inside of Ruby's skull is filled with the steady hum of wings; it's impossible to concentrate. "I need to lie down."

"This was a mistake." Sapphire reaches for Ruby's hand, but Ruby's legs won't cooperate.

Sapphire's eyes widen. She slips her shirt over her head, revealing the camisole underneath. Using the folded cloth, Sapphire scoops up the necklace. With the gold sheen hidden, Ruby's legs unlock, but they still tremble.

"What are we going to do?"

"I have money, credit cards," Sapphire says. "We could get on a train."

"A train? To where?"

"I don't know. I don't know." Panic edges Sapphire's voice.

It's all starting to unravel. Ruby takes a deep breath, forces her voice to remain even. "We'll take the necklace to the bridge. We'll throw it in the river and forget the whole thing."

Looking stunned, Sapphire nods. Ruby concentrates on putting one foot in front of the other and not thinking about anything else. Her skin itches. She twists her fingers into the slithery fabric of the skirt, fighting their desire to pluck the necklace from Sapphire's hands. Just one more look couldn't hurt, could it?

Wind tugs a curl of hair free to brush against her cheek, making her jump. Ruby stops, and Sapphire nearly collides with her. They're already at the mid-point of the bridge, water glittering darkly below them. Ruby reaches for the shirt-wrapped bundle, but stops.

"You do. I can't."

"I can't either." Sapphire looks stricken.

"We'll do it together."

Ruby places her hands atop Sapphire's meeting her eyes. Even through the cloth, the necklace feels warm. There's a faint buzz, an insect trapped beneath the combined weight of their palms. They step closer to the rail, and Ruby peers over the edge. She's struck by the impression of falling, not down, but up into the sky—the lights on the black water a scatter of stars.

"I still can't do it," Sapphire says.

"Neither can I." Ruby's voice husks.

A streak of light in her peripheral vision draws her attention. Ruby turns her head just in time to track a shooting star, blazing toward the horizon. And there, where it disappears, a blaze of light upon the water—a massive ship making its slow way from the harbor out toward the open water. The harbor itself is visible, other ships docked and glowing welcomingly. A slow grin stretches across Ruby's face, pulling up until her cheeks until they ache.

"I have an idea," Ruby says, pointing at the ship. It's ridiculous and impractical, and Ruby has no idea how much Sapphire has on the credit cards she mentioned, or whether she's even willing to share it. But for one moment, everything feels possible. "We're not going to take a train, we're going to take a cruise."

RUBY WAKES WITH HER HEART POUNDING, SWEAT STICKING HER nightgown to the small of her back. It takes a moment to orient herself, to recognize the thrum of the ship as more than the rush of blood in her ears.

As they stood on the pier watching the cruise ship pull in, everything still seemed like a grand adventure. But once they were on board, watching the shore dwindle, doubt had settled in.

"I can't afford this." Panic needled her with a silent tally of necklaces she's have to steal to pay Sapphire back.

But Sapphire had only waved Ruby's concerns away. "Call it a present from my aunt."

The breezy way Sapphire had said it, someone who'd never needed to worry about money, made Ruby's stomach twist. It was still a lark for Sapphire; she didn't need to steal.

And now, in the dark, the doubt is even worse, edging on panic. The shore is miles away. Only water surrounds them. Ruby's never been this far from home before, and it's so big out here.

It's all unraveling; the walls of the tiny cabin are closing in. She tries to breathe, calm herself and ignore the unfamiliar shadows on the wall. Something rustles in the corner of the room.

"Sapphire."

In the narrow bunk beside hers, Sapphire groans and rolls over, putting her back to Ruby.

"Sapphire!" Ruby bunches the sheets in her fists, listening for the rustling noise to come again.

Sapphire pulls her pillow over her head. Ruby untangles herself from the sheets and stands, shaking Sapphire's arm.

"What's happening?" Sapphire's words are slurred; she fumbles the sleep mask from her eyes.

"I heard something."

"Ships make noise."

"It wasn't the ship. I think we should…"

The rustle is unmistakable this time. Ruby instinctively lifts her feet, nearly falling onto Sapphire's bed.

"Ow, you're hurting me." Sapphire pulls away even as a shadow skitters across the room and disappears under the door.

"There!"

Sapphire's eyes widen. "I saw it, too."

"What was it?"

Something tickles at the back of Ruby's mind—the sensation of wings against palm. The memory of feeling weightless and dizzy and of torches flickering at the edge of her vision creeps back under her skin. She kneels dragging Sapphire's hastily-packed suitcase from under the bed and flips it open.

"What are you doing?"

Ruby ignores her, pawing aside Sapphire's clothing to reveal the necklace nestled at the bottom of the suitcase.

"Did you touch it?"

"No. What's going on?"

With trembling hands, Ruby lifts the necklace so Sapphire can see. The metal is no longer warm. It no longer buzzes in her hands. The scarab is gone, the bezel's tines bent as though the jewel forced its way out.

"We have to follow it." Ruby's voice is flat. "Get dressed."

She grabs a handful of clothes from Sapphire's suitcase and tosses them on the bed before gathering her own clothes—new ones, bought for her by Sapphire, because there wasn't time to go back home. If she gives herself even one moment to think about how ridiculous this is, she'll break into hysterical laughter and never stop.

Carved scarabs don't run lose on cruise ships. But as she dresses, Ruby listens for the rustle and tick of tiny legs. There's no such thing as living jewelry but then she isn't a thief either. She doesn't do things like this. But she did. And now she has to face the consequences.

"Come on." Ruby's pulse thumps as she steps into the corridor, Sapphire close on her heels.

"I guess it's good luck we picked a ship full of octogenarians after all," Sapphire murmurs, tension clear in her voice, despite her best effort to hide it. "They're all asleep or in the casino. It's like a ghost ship."

Ruby freezes at the click-click of jointed legs.

"That way."

They follow the sound through the silent dining rooms, past the empty cigar lounge, making their way to the theater at the aft of the ship. Plaster columns painted with hieroglyphs guard the door. Of course, Ruby thinks, they couldn't have ended up on a ship with a Greek theme, or a tropical theme, or anything other than Egyptian. Inside the theater, tiered seats lead down to the darkened stage.

"What do we do if we catch it?" Sapphire asks.

"Shove it back in the necklace and throw the whole thing overboard. Like we should have done on the bridge." Ruby surprises herself with the vehemence in her tone.

Halfway to the stage, Ruby freezes. Sapphire bumps into her with a sharp intake of breath. The curtains rise, drawn by an invisible hand and lights snap on, pooling overlapping colors—amber, emerald, sapphire, and ruby. The stage is flanked by two impossibly tall figures, mirror images of the goddess Isis, each one with a wing raised to stretch across the top of the stage, meeting in the middle.

The shadow skitters across the stage, larger now, six legs moving in a blur as it scales the figure of Isis on the left.

"What..." Sapphire starts to say, and the words die in her throat.

The scarab, grown to the size of Ruby's fist, settles at Isis' throat. With a grinding noise, the statue turns her head, fixing Sapphire and Ruby with baleful eyes the color of blood. Isis rips her wing away from the wall in a shower of plaster dust. More dust plumes into the air as the goddess steps from the stage.

Ruby scrambles back, her heel catching on the step behind her. She goes down, knocking into Sapphire's legs, sending them both tumbling.

"Throw the necklace at her," Sapphire yells.

"What?"

"It's the kind of thing that would work in a movie."

"Just run!" Ruby pushes Sapphire ahead of her.

She glances over her shoulder at the statue. At least it's slow. The thought isn't much comfort as Isis rips a seat from the nearest row and hurls it toward them. Ruby ducks.

"Run a zigzag pattern," Sapphire yells.

"That's crocodiles." Ruby pants, but does as Sapphire suggests, cutting back toward the stage. Maybe there's another way out.

From behind, Isis is hollow. The edges of plaster where she pulled her body away from the wall are ragged. Her feet grind as she pivots back toward the stage and takes a heavy step. Too heavy. A tiny fissure runs up the goddess' leg.

Another chair hurtles toward them. Ruby catches it awkwardly, staggering. She does her best to heave it back toward the goddess, but her strength, not being supernatural like the statue's only gets her so far. The chair falls short and as she's trying to catch her breath, another chair comes their way. This one misses, striking the second Isis statue, shattering its leg.

"We have to get out of here. There's got to be another exit." Ruby pulls Sapphire toward the stage. "Isn't Isis supposed to be the protector of children?"

"She's also the goddess of marrying her brother and raising him from the dead, so she's not all sweetness and light."

A chair hits the painted screen at the back of the stage and the catwalk it hangs from trembles.

"There's the door."

"Shit. It's locked!" Sapphire smacks the door with the side of her fist. "Emergency exit my ass."

"Try the other side."

Ruby turns just as a golden arm smashes down between them,

knocking her off her feet. A crack races up the goddess' arm and part of it crumbles she draws back for another blow. Ruby scrambles toward stage left. She can't see Sapphire anymore, and panic squeezes her tight. If anything happens to Sapphire and it's her fault…

Tears blur her vision and Ruby blinks them back, furious. She shoves to her feet, ready to throw herself at the plaster goddess and tear her apart with her bare hands if she has to.

"Get down," someone yells and Ruby is yanked, hard.

She lands on her knees. There's a crash and plaster dust fills the air. Ruby coughs, her eyes stinging. Isis' left arm, broken off at the elbow, lies on the stage. Ruby whips her head around, looking to see who pushed her and her mouth drops open.

The woman is almost as tall as Sapphire. What she lacks in height, she makes up for with silver platform heels, and a frosted-blonde bouffant with a pair of rabbit ears perched on top like a crown. She's flanked by a woman in a green dress and a woman in a copper dress and they both look angry. Ruby's mind whirls, grasping after some piece of information that feels so irrelevant she can't help speaking it aloud.

"You're the singers from the lounge show on the Lido Deck."

The blonde takes her eyes off the goddess for an instant and looks at Ruby.

"Shh, you'll blow our cover. We're actually here to save the world." She winks, and as the gold-and-plaster goddess lunges toward them, the three women spring into action.

The one in the rabbit ears drops to a crouch and comes up with what looks like a spear in her hand. She hurls it, and the tip punches through

Isis' leg. The goddess' plaster feathers sweep the space where the three women were standing an instant before. More dust rains down and Ruby throws her arms over her head.

The woman in green takes a sash from around her waist, whipping it over her head like a lasso. The ends are weighted with jangling coins, lending the cloth momentum. With a flick of the woman's wrist, the cloth catches the goddess around her left ankle. The woman in green pulls back and the goddess stumbles.

Isis raises her wing to swat, but the woman in copper is there, planting her feet in a wide-legged stance and firing a gun. Ruby claps her hands over her ears. The goddess reels back, a smoking hole where her left eye used to be. Hairline cracks craze her cheeks and Isis lets out a hollow, impossible roar.

"Now you've done it," the blonde says, grim.

"Got a better plan?" the woman in copper snaps back.

"Aim for the scarab." Ruby doesn't know where her voice comes from, but it's there, ragged and choked with plaster dust.

The three performers who aren't performers exchange a look and the blonde shrugs. "You heard the lady."

The woman in copper takes aim, but as she does, Isis reaches above her head, snagging the lighting array with her blade-like wing. Sparks explode. Ruby covers her head again. A can light hits the stage, narrowly missing her. On the far side of the stage, there's a shout of pain. Sapphire.

Ruby ignores the chaos, crawling toward the sound. There's smoke in the air now, and Ruby gropes blindly until her hand finds warm flesh, sticky with blood. Her heart lurches into her throat, but slender, calloused fingers find hers and grip hard.

"Ruby?"

"I'm here. I can't see."

"Something is pinning my leg." Sapphire's voice is raw.

By feel, Ruby finds part of the lighting array. She grips it, palms slicked with sweat and heaves upward. Sapphire hisses in pain.

"Don't move," Ruby says.

She stands, still holding the twisted section of metal. There's a shout. Isis howls, and a golden leg narrowly misses crushing Ruby as the goddess staggers backward.

Putting all her rage and fear into the motion, Ruby swings the lighting rig as hard as she can. The resulting crack reverberates through the theater; in its wake, there's a moment of ringing silence. Then Isis' entire left leg crumbles. The goddess pitches to the side. Chunks of plaster hit the stage. A blur of shadow breaks free, skittering across the stage, running for the second plaster goddess.

The woman in the bunny ears snatches her spear. "Oh, no you don't!"

In a graceful leap, she clears the rubble and drives the point down, pinning the scarab to the stage. There's a crack like thunder, a flash like lightning, and Ruby is on her back, blinking. A hand reaches to help her to her feet.

"Still with us?" the woman in green asks.

Ruby nods, but her shaking legs betray her and she folds back into a sitting position.

"Sapphire," she croaks, pointing, and the woman in green nods.

The blonde smoothes a hand over her bouffant as the woman in copper retrieves the broken pieces of lapis lazuli from around the point of the spear, which Ruby sees now is actually a harpoon. The woman in copper hands the broken pieces to the blonde, who frowns.

"Cursed," she says.

"You don't say." The woman in copper rolls her eyes.

"It's her ankle," the woman in green calls from the edge of the stage. "Penny, will you give me a hand?"

Penny holsters her gun. Between them, the two women get Sapphire upright, her weight on only one leg.

"Do you know anything about this?" the woman with the bunny ears holds out the broken pieces of the scarab.

Ruby swallows, her throat raw. The woman arches a perfectly-shaped eyebrow, waiting.

"We stole it." Ruby's voice is so small in the large space of the ruined theater. "From a man named Forsythe."

"Mmhmmm." The woman nods, as though none of this comes as a surprise, but she wanted to see how Ruby would answer, testing her. "A lot of people could have gotten hurt, or even killed."

"I know." Ruby grinds the heels of her hand into her eyes, glad for once she isn't wearing make-up. "It was stupid. We were stupid. We thought..."

Ruby stops. She can't even say it out loud. A hollow laugh bubbles up through her. She looks around at the shattered remains of the goddess and the twisted lighting rig. In the tiered rows of seats, there are gaps where the plush covered chairs have been torn free like rotten teeth. And here she is with clothes pulled over her nightgown, covered in plaster dust, and she just stopped a living statue from destroying a cruise ship.

"Are you going to arrest us?" Ruby asks.

The woman reaches out a perfectly manicured hand. "We're not that kind of heroes."

Ruby blinks, staring at it for a moment before lifting her gaze to the woman's violet eyes. After a moment, she takes the woman's hand and uses it to steady herself as she gets to her feet.

"How did you know to be here?" Ruby asks.

"My bunny-sense was tingling."

Ruby's mouth forms an "o," and it's a moment before the woman's deadpan expression cracks.

"I'm kidding," she says. "We've been keeping an eye on Forsythe ever since the necklace disappeared from a shipment of artifacts bound for the St. Everild University Museum."

"Why didn't the scarab attack him?"

"Maybe it needed a woman's touch?" Her tone is light, but Ruby can't help shivering, the adrenaline wearing off and leaving exhaustion and fear in its place. She starts when the woman puts a hand on her shoulder.

"That was quite the move with the lighting rig. You're awfully strong."

"So I've been told." Ruby tries to smile, but it doesn't quite work. The hollow laugh threatens her again.

"Will she be okay?" Ruby asks as Penny and the woman in green help Sapphire off the stage.

"She looks strong, too. I'm sure she'll be fine." One corner of the woman's mouth lifts in a wry smile, her eyebrow arching again. "So, Ms. Jewel-Thief, what exactly was your plan?"

"I don't know. I was going to run away and join the circus, and then everything went wrong." It sounds ridiculous out loud, but Ruby no longer feels like laughing. She's tired, empty, and she wants to go home. But there's nothing to go home to. She has the house, the physical structure, but without a job she can't pay the electricity bill and keep the water running. She could go back to Mr. Salmetti, beg, but the very thought puts bile in her throat. Everything her grandparents tried to give her, all ruined. Ruby shakes her head, wiping at her nose and mouth with the back of her hand.

"I don't have a job anymore, and because of me, Sapphire's lost hers and…"

"Shh." The woman squeezes Ruby's shoulder. "I think we can help you out in that department, if you're interested. My name's Bunny. What's yours?"

"Ruby."

"Ruby." Bunny smiles, and the same warmth surges through Ruby as when Sapphire first called them twin gems, tingling all the way through her body.

The way Bunny looks at her, a hint of mischief in her eyes, sets Ruby's pulse racing. She's seen what these women can do; she can only imagine what kind of job offer they have in mind. No more Mr. Salmetti, no more having to deal with anyone like him ever again. The way Bunny looks at her tells Ruby something else, too—for the first time since her grandparents, she's found someone, several someones, who look at her and see more than her body.

"Perfect," says Bunny, her smile deepening. "You'll fit right in."

Passion Between The Sheets

1 oz white rum

1 oz apricot brandy

1 oz Cointreau

1 oz apricot nectar

Passionfruit, muddled

Separate the flesh of the passionfruit from the seeds and muddle in the bottom of a highball glass. Combine remaining ingredients in a cocktail shaker with ice. Shake well and strain over muddled passionfruit.

The Ruby Crush was a false start. This drink is much more Ruby, even though the name may sound like a joke. My Ruby is almost as innocent as Starlight when it comes to sex. No, wait, I take that back. Starlight is innocent and shy. Ruby isn't innocent, or shy. It's love that she's missing out on, and until you've been touched by someone you truly love, well, you might as well never have been touched at all.

I wonder where that leaves me? If you reach for someone, to touch them, and they don't reach back?

But I'm getting off track. The truth is, I think Ruby intimidates people. No one expects her be as strong as she is, and I'm not just talking about the way she can lift things. The other thing is, people can be fucking shallow. Bodies are just bodies. They need to get the fuck over it.

Anyway, passion—that's what Ruby is all about. She can be every bit as fierce as Bunny when she wants to, and she barely even realizes it. One day she'll find someone as passionate as she is and together, they'll set the world on fire. But god help them if they ever hurt her. They'll have to answer to me.

PENNY IN THE AIR

PENNY CROSSES HER ARMS AND GLARES AT THE YOUNG AIDE BLOCKING the steps to the plane. He shifts his weight, glancing at the tablet in his hand as if the key to dealing with her might be written there.

"Ma'am, I really don't think..." His voice breaks, as Penny steps closer. In her chunky copper heels, she's a good inch taller than him.

"Just how the hell do you think I'm going to protect the president without my gun?" She pats the M9 Beretta, Stella, holstered at her side.

"The only weapons allowed on Air Force One are carried by the Secret Service. Ma'am."

Penny has to hand it to the kid—he isn't backing down. Even if he looks like an overwhelmed toddler, about to cry. She's tempted to show him just what she can do without Stella, but forces herself to take a deep breath. She mashes peach-flavored gum between her molars extra hard, counting to ten before leaning back to give the poor aide some space.

"Look." She racks her memory for his name. "Jonathan. I know you're just doing your job, but Mindy… *President Kelly* requested me specially, and if this gun doesn't get on the plane, neither do I."

"I'm sorry, but…"

"Oh, give her a break, Jonathan."

"Yes, Ma'am." As the president breezes between them, Jonathan snaps to attention so fast Penny is amazed his spine doesn't crack.

"It's his first month on the job." Mindy, impeccable in her perfectly tailored navy blue suit, turns to Penny with a wry smile, taking in the knee-high boots and copper minidress. "And you've gotten taller since I last saw you."

Penny resists the urge to tug down her hem. Mindy's seen her drink a room full of Sigma Phi boys under the table without flinching, and was there to hold her hair back the next morning; she's seen Penny covered in mud after beating out seven other cadets during the Exhibition Challenge on the obstacle course at Ft. Bragg, and she didn't hesitate a moment before throwing her arms around her in a huge hug. But her oldest friend has never seen Penny looking like this before. And her oldest friend just happens to be the leader of the free world now.

Penny squares her shoulders, daring Mindy to comment further. President or not, she can't help doing it with a smirk. Mindy returns the expression a moment later.

"It suits you," she says, before turning and climbing the stairs to Air Force One.

As silly as she might feel, the dress brought Penny luck when the Glitter Squadron fought the Lizard Men, and she's worn it ever since. The same goes for her hair, teased high enough that she feels the need to duck as she follows the president onto Air Force One.

"Posh," Penny says, taking in the surroundings.

"Sit anywhere you like. Can I get you a drink?"

Penny almost says yes, then shakes her head. "Not while I'm on the job. Speaking of—the kid's got a point. Wouldn't the Secret Service be better off handling this? Not that I'm not flattered."

"I trust you. The Department of Homeland Security pays them. There's a difference." The president gestures at the men in black suits standing unobtrusively at either end of the cabin. "Even senators on the other side of the aisle have heard of your team's reputation. There's no one I'd rather have watching my back."

"What exactly am I watching your back against?"

It's almost imperceptible, but Mindy flinches. If Penny didn't know her so well, she wouldn't have seen it at all.

"Mindy." Penny puts warning into her voice. "Tell me."

The president opens her mouth, but before she can speak, Jonathan interrupts. "We're almost ready to leave, Madame President."

The moment is gone. Mindy smiles, and Penny recognizes the poker face that made her bane of the campus back in their college days.

"I'll leave you two to get settled. I have some work to do."

Mindy moves toward the front of the plane and her private office. The two Secret Service goons take their seats. Another man enters and introduces himself as the pilot, and then comes the service crew. Only Penny is left standing until Jonathan stops short of touching her arm and points instead.

"How about over there?"

To her annoyance, Jonathan takes the seat across from her. She swaps the current wad of peach gum for a fresh stick, and stares deliberately out the window. After a moment, the engine thrums to life. Penny's stomach does a little flip. It isn't fear, but she clamps down on the armrests just the same.

The plane's lift thrusts her back in her seat. There's a sensation of weightlessness, the thrill of leaving the ground.

Aching blue surrounds them, and it opens up a space in Penny's heart. She should be the one in the cockpit, flying Mindy's plane. She should also be a retired Air Force veteran. A decorated one, with a combat readiness medal and a gallant unit citation. But for that, the Air Force would have had to let her fly.

Penny resists the urge to put a hand to her sternum and press at the emptiness behind it. Instead of all those *shoulds*, Penny has a fucking *denied* stamped in red across her pilot license application. Good enough for the grunts, but not the elites. Good enough to get shot at, but not shot down, tumbling like Icarus from the sky.

Clouds skim over the wings as the plane rises. It shouldn't still hurt, all these years later, but it does. It leaves Penny breathless. This is where she belongs. The quality of light up here is different; it tastes of peaches and honey, and…

"I know we got off on the wrong foot." Jonathan's voice is soft, but Penny whips around to glare at him as he breaks into her thoughts.

Her expression cows him, so he has to swallow and find the words he just lost. "I actually admire the Glitter Squadron. I'm kind of a fan."

Penny manages to keep from rolling her eyes; he's young.

"May I ask…. What's Bunny like?"

"Seriously?" The word explodes from Penny.

Jonathan flinches, and she regrets her tone. At the same time, there's the itch at the back of her mind, the voice she can't quite shut up, no matter how much she wants to: Bunny, always Bunny.

Jonathan rises, cheeks flushed, and moves to another seat.

Penny looks at her hands. They're shaking. *Remember to breathe.* She does, and forces herself to examine her anger despite the fact that she thinks Dr. Popov's "techniques" are nothing more than pop-psychology bullshit. She tries the visualization exercise, picturing her anger as a diamond-hard core, buried under her breast bone. It pulses occasionally, setting off flashes that contribute to the trembling of her hands.

And just like that, the world turns night-vision green. Gunfire rattles in the darkness, accompanied by bursts of light. Penny's body wants to rock back and forth. It wants to scream. It wants to curl up tight. It wants to set everything on fire.

She stands, not bothering to check whether they've reached safe cruising altitude. No one stops her. Before she realizes it, she's crossed the length of the plane, mounted the steps, and is simultaneously knocking and sliding open the president's private door.

Mindy is halfway to rising, reaching for her desk drawer, but she stops, seeing Penny. Still, tension remains, even when Mindy resumes her seat. Penny glances at the desk drawer. Is Mindy keeping a weapon in there?

"Sorry." Penny closes the door behind her and tries a smile. "Can I get that drink after all?"

Mindy rolls her shoulders, a forcible attempt to relax, and pours

Penny a healthy measure of Glenmorangie. A matching glass, ice melting, sits at the president's elbow.

"You okay?" Mindy asks.

No. Penny nods. Mindy knows her well enough not believe her, but she knows enough not to push either. She pats the chair next to hers, and Penny sits.

"You asked what was going on." Mindy refills her own glass, not meeting Penny's eyes. "I may have told a tiny white lie about the mission being to protect me."

Penny tenses, but says nothing as Mindy open the middle drawer of her desk and pulls out something that looks like a blade. It gleams in the light. Penny looks closer. Not a blade, a feather.

"Careful," Mindy says, even as Penny touches the razor edge. Blood wells on her finger and she sucks in a breath before putting her finger in her mouth.

"What the hell?" The next sip of her drink tastes like earth and smoke and iron.

Mindy leans back, tired lines etched around her eyes. "Do you remember the attack on the Pentagon last year? The explosion that sent half the building up in flames? Killed over a hundred people."

"No."

Mindy twirls her glass, watching legs of amber liquid run down its side. "*That's* because it never happened. A group calling themselves the True American Nation—we used phone taps, surveillance, all the usual tricks. We knew about them, but we couldn't root them out. Might as well have been goddamned ghosts."

Mindy picks up the feather, turning it to catch the light. There are shadows in her eyes that weren't there even a year ago.

"Has Bunny ever told you about the Area 51 Project?"

Penny starts, and amusement tugs briefly at the corner of Mindy's mouth at the reaction before weight settles around her shoulders again. She rolls her neck, and the bones pop.

"The short version is, there are numerous supernatural beings on the government payroll."

Mindy pulls a laminated ID card from the pocket of her blazer. Tilting it into the light reveals a ghosted hologram of a classic, cartoonish alien head—bulbous skull, pointy chin, over-sized eyes.

"You're shitting me," Penny says.

"I wish I was." Mindy's voice almost cracks, surprising Penny.

Her friend's hand trembles, and it takes two tries for Mindy to slip the card back into her pocket.

"I fucked up, Penny." Her voice is barely audible. "Big time."

"Mindy, what—"

But Mindy shakes her head. After a moment, she takes a shuddering breath, and her voice is clearer, steadier, when she speaks again.

"We managed to capture an individual suspected of being in the True American Nation's inner circle. We didn't have any hard proof. It was a gamble.

"This is a harpy feather." Mindy's fingers hover over the coppery surface without touching it. When she looks up, the rawness of her expression startles Penny, but this time the president holds eye contact. Mindy downs the rest of her glass, and shakes herself as if to physically shed the weight of her words. When she sets her glass down, her face is impassive, and she sits straighter.

"The harpies got the information we needed. We sent in a strike team, clean and quick."

Penny reaches for her friend, but before she can touch her, Mindy draws her hand back.

"Don't. Whatever you're going to say, don't." Mindy's voice is hard, but there's sorrow in her eyes. "I haven't gotten to the worst of it yet.

"To say the harpies work for the government is to put it in generous terms. We keep them locked away in a secure facility in Area 51. They do not get to see daylight. They never see the sky. They're winged creatures and we daren't let them fly."

Penny understands that fire, white and hot, in Mindy's throat.

"Why?"

The single word sounds so cruel.

Mindy offers Penny a cracked, humorless smile. "They don't exactly blend in. If the public knew the government kept trained…mythological torturers at its beck and call, and was willing to use them against its own people…"

There's something else, something in Mindy's expression that makes Penny feel as if the floor of the plane is about to drop out beneath them.

Mindy slides a photograph from under the papers scattered on her desk and turns it so Penny can see. The image is blurred, the resolution poor. She can just make out a young boy, arms bound behind his back, mouth gaped in fear.

"This arrived yesterday." Mindy places a second photograph beside the first, a school portrait. The boy's mop of brown hair, his freckled face, his gap-toothed grin, are hauntingly familiar. "They have my nephew. Joshua. He just started kindergarten."

She's never met the boy, but Penny still has the baby pictures Mindy sent when Joshua was born saved on her computer. Weariness replaces the rage in Mindy's features, soaking all the way through her bones.

"There was another enclave of harpies. I don't know where they came from, or why they waited until now, but they want their sisters back. If I don't give them what they want, they'll kill Joshua."

Mindy takes a final object from an open desk drawer—a second feather—and sets it beside the first. This one is battered, torn. Or chipped might be a better word. Penny still can't tell whether the feathers are organic or metal. Either way, this one is tipped with dried blood.

The president's expression is stark, her voice flat. "I know where they're holding him."

Penny stares at the president, Mindy, her friend. But there's nothing to say. The weariness in Mindy's eyes is a thin veneer over the horror buried deep at their core. Penny glances at the battered harpy feather again. Mindy authorized torture, and possibly used it herself. Who tortures the torturers? Penny doesn't ask the question aloud. She doesn't want, or need the answer.

Whether Mindy held the knife or gave the order, the result is the same. A fault line runs through her now, and only force of will holds her together. Penny recognizes it; the same rough edges run under her skin, matching wounds that will never heal.

Penny takes a deep breath. Part of her wants to capture this moment,

Mindy's expression—the hardness, and the pain, owning every decision she's made, every ounce of what she's done.

She wants to broadcast that image to the world as a fuck-you to the pundits who will call Mindy emotional and irrational, accuse her of leading with her heart instead of her head. Because she knows Mindy will be judged differently from other presidents. Her actions will be scrutinized and dissected under a different lens.

And the other part of Penny—here and now, thousands of feet in the air—doesn't give a fuck about any of that. Mindy isn't the leader of the free world. She's Penny's friend, blood sister, twin of scrapes and bruises and a thousand childhood adventures; brave defenders of their neighborhood, treehouse architects, junkyard warriors, and wild shining knights on sixteen-speed horses.

Mindy is family, and where family is concerned, the free world can go fuck itself. Penny straightens and looks Mindy in the eye. "I've got your back."

PENNY TUCKS HER LEGS BENEATH HER, BOOTS ABANDONED UNDER her seat, and massages the back of her neck. The battered paperback in her hand is folded near in half along the well-worn lines cracked into its spine.

On the seat beside her there's a sheaf of papers she's already leafed through a dozen times. Satellite images, maps, photographs showing multiple hidden entrances to the Toquima Cave system.

"I had no idea these existed." Penny had said when Mindy handed her the pictures.

"Of course you didn't." A quirked, broken grin crossed Mindy's face as she tapped the logo on the folder holding all the pages together. The alien head, smug in its serenity, looking guilelessly back at Penny.

Fuck Bunny and her security clearances. But Penny had studied the maps, the images, everything Mindy had given her. She was as prepared as she was going to be.

"I thought you could use this."

Penny starts, looking up to find Jonathan holding out a steaming cup of coffee.

"I didn't know how you take it, so I brought cream and milk and sweetener and sugar." Jonathan empties his pocket onto the tray table.

"Just black actually, but thank you."

"I just wanted to say I'm sorry. I really am honored to be working with you."

"Thanks." She wishes he would go away, but he doesn't move. "Good coffee."

It's the closest she can bring herself to an apology. Jonathan glances at the paperback splayed face down now on top of the papers.

"What are you reading?"

A smile touches Penny's lips. "A Zippy Terwilliger book."

Jonathan returns a blank stare, but takes the seat across from her. Penny turns the luridly painted cover so he can see. It shows the titular hero in her bomber jacket and leather flying helmet against a jungle backdrop. A silver airship looms above Zippy, and zombies in various states of decay peer menacingly from the trees.

"They're kind of kids' books, I guess. The author churned out four or five a year. They're terrible, really. I mean the geography and ecology are all messed up, and people are constantly saying things like gee whiz and practically every second line of dialog ends in an exclamation point." Penny shrugs, setting the book aside. "I used to read them all the time as a kid. They're relaxing."

"I used to like the Honor Dodge books." Jonathan's voice is hesitant, as if he's afraid Penny will slap him if he says the wrong thing.

"I read one or two of those. Honor's like Zippy, but in space."

Penny thinks about the endless summer days she and Mindy spent reading Zippy Terwilliger adventures in Mindy's treehouse. The same treehouse they'd retreated to years later to get shit-faced drunk after Penny was denied her pilot's license.

"Zippy was kind of my hero growing up." Penny shrugs. "I wanted to be a pilot, but…"

She stops, frowning. She has no intention of spilling her guts to this kid, and she changes tack. "What about you? What do you want to be when you go grow up?"

"I…" Jonathan blushes, looking flustered.

"Sorry." Penny lifts the corner of her mouth, softening words. "I couldn't resist. You barely look old enough for college, let alone a job."

"I am twenty-three." Jonathan's defensive tone and the way he puffs himself up only widens Penny's smile.

"We'll be landing in fifteen minutes," a member of the flight crew says, collecting their cups.

Penny slips her boots back on and fastens her seatbelt. Jonathan bounces one leg up and down, burning off nervous energy. Penny watches him, sidelong. He doesn't look like he'd even play a violent video game, let alone be involved in a real-world combat situation. If Bunny were in this situation, she'd say something comforting like everything's going to be okay. Penny prefers silence to lying.

"Follow my lead. Move when I say, and keep quiet."

The two Secret Service goons nod. They might be twins—broad-shouldered giants with identical haircuts, carved from slabs of stone. Either because, or despite, the fact they're both ex-military, Penny finds herself wishing for Bunny and the rest of the Glitter Squadron at her back instead. But Mindy insisted it would be Penny and Penny alone carrying out this mission. She won't even be able to tell the Squadron about this if she survives.

Dust coats Penny's legs from the climb. Feeling foolish, she waves the alien-head ID card in the empty air in front of her. But it works. There's a faint click, and seemingly solid rock folds back to the reveal a narrow entrance to the caves. There's just enough light to show the petroglyphs marking the walls. Even though Mindy assured her the harpies don't know about this entrance, Penny is glad the goons have their weapons drawn.

When shrieking harpies fail to burst forth and attack them, Penny lets out a breath. She slips Stella into her hand, and steps into the mouth of the cave. The weight of the gun in her hand reassures her, and there are knives sheathed in both of her boots, just in case. She gives the signal, and the goons follow her as she snaps night-vision goggles in place.

Deeper in the cave, jagged teeth of stone in sharp, radioactive green hang from the ceiling and rise from the floor. In between them are bundles of sticks and mud, vaguely nest-like shapes. Something snaps beneath Penny's boot. A bone. She doesn't look a second time to verify her first impression—it's human.

She gestures the goons forward. She should feel vulnerable in a copper minidress and knee high boots, but the sheen—even in the darkness—is polished armor. Bunny is either having a good influence on her, or a bad one.

A few more steps and in, Penny sees them. Hanging upside down like bats, a dozen or more women with razor-sharp wings folded around their bodies sleep with their talons buried in the stone.

A sound catches her attention, a small, fragile sound. Human. Penny creeps around a jutting stalagmite. Mindy's nephew crouches in a cage woven of the same sticks used to make the nests. Penny eases the night-vision goggles from her eyes, plunging herself into total darkness.

Her vision adjusts. Tears run from Joshua's wide-open eyes, making tracks on his dirt-smeared cheeks. His whole body shudders, the occasional hitching of his breath the only sound in all the silence.

Penny gestures to the goons to hold their positions and creeps forward. The boy catches sight of her, his eyes widening further. He almost yells, but Penny closes the distance, and holds her finger to her lips.

"Your aunt Mindy sent me. I'm here to take you home." She says this as quietly as possible, but her voice still sounds overloud.

Penny glances behind her, but without the night-vision goggles she can't see the goons or the creatures nestled overhead. But she needs the boy to see her eyes.

"I need you to stay very still, Joshua, and be very quiet. Can you do that?"

The boy nods. Once Penny is certain of him, she lowers the goggles, reducing the boy to a terrified smear of green light with too-big eyes. She still can't believe Mindy's brother found someone to marry him, let alone have his baby. Her memories of Bobby mostly consist of him and his smelly friends playing terrible music in Mindy's garage, thinking they would all grow up to be rock stars. She gave Bobby a bloody nose once, though she can't remember why; her mother grounded her for a week.

Penny smiles in the darkness. But the woven branches forming the cage are stronger than they look. Her hand slips, drawing blood, and she swallows a curse. She pulls one of the knives from her boot, sawing at the branches. Her palm is slick with blood, and she's acutely aware of the minutes ticking by. How long before the harpies wake? How long until she's out of time?

The rest of the branches are easier to untangle. She reaches through the new gap in the bars and pulls the boy free. He smells like sweat and urine, but Penny hoists him over her shoulder. She signals the goons to retrace their steps.

They're almost clear when one of the goons trips, crashing to one knee. The sound echoes through the cave, answered by the thud of Penny's pulse. She holds her breath. Then there is a sound like a hundred umbrellas being unfurled at once, like a thousand knives being drawn, and a chorus of shrieks full of hunger and rage.

"Go!" Penny breaks into a run, heedlessly shattering bones under her chunky heels.

Joshua clings to her, whimpering softly. Outside, Penny rips the goggles off. Earth slides under her feet, but she keeps her balance despite the weight of the boy slung over her shoulder. A shadow passes overhead and Penny skids to a halt, dropping to a crouch and pushing the boy behind her.

She fires Stella. Joshua wails. The shots go wide; the harpy folds her wings, diving.

"Shit." Penny snatches the boy's hand, dragging him in her wake.

One of the Secret Service goons reaches the car at the same moment she does and launches himself into the driver's seat. The other goon is nowhere in sight. Penny shoves the boy into the backseat and dives in after him.

"Drive!"

Talons scrape the roof. Metallic wings sweep forward, shattering the rear window. Penny throws herself over the boy as broken glass rains onto the seat. The car surges forward. A shriek of frustration sounds behind them, louder than the roar of the engine.

Penny straightens, shaking glass from her hair. "Are you okay?"

There's a scratch on one cheek, but as far as she can tell, the boy is unharmed. He nods, but there's a glazed quality to his expression. She wouldn't blame the kid for going into shock.

"You better like gum." She hands him a peach-flavored stick.

Joshua accepts and chews mechanically. Penny wills the car to go faster. Her heart lurches in relief as the plane comes into sight. She twists around. No wings blot the sky, but that doesn't mean the harpies aren't following them.

Mindy waits at the bottom of the steps, her face breaking into an expression of relief as Penny helps Joshua from the car. The boy runs, flinging himself at his aunt's legs.

Even when they're aboard, and the plane door closes, Penny can't settle. They left a man behind, and they're about to lift into the air where the harpies await with razor sharp wings.

THEY'VE BEEN FLYING FOR ALMOST AN HOUR, BUT PENNY IS NO calmer. The remaining security goon—Penny still doesn't know his name—touches her arm. She starts, realizing she's gripping her armrests hard enough to press her knucklebones out against her skin.

"Relax. This thing is proofed against nukes." He smiles, but there's a shadow to it, evidence of pain.

They left a man behind, and Penny doesn't even know this one's name. Bunny would know his name.

So she doesn't say: *Proofed against nukes, but not mythological creatures.* And she tries to return his smile, but the muscles twitch in her cheek instead.

The goon's eyes widen. He points, and Penny turns to the window behind her. A winged shape hurtles toward the plane, talons outstretched.

She's already on her feet as Mindy enters the main cabin, eyes red with exhaustion.

"They're here," Penny says.

Mindy presses her lips into a thin line, but doesn't respond. Rubbing sleep from his eyes, Joshua emerges behind her. There's a sound like nails on a chalk board, but much worse. The harpies are trying to get in.

The pilot noses the plane down, as if he can hide them in the clouds. Joshua makes a low, whimpering noise, clinging to his aunt's leg.

"Get him into your suite. Take Jonathan and any non-essential crew members. Lock the door. You stay in there, too."

Penny makes a shooing motion. Mindy looks like she's about to protest, but after a moment she gathers her nephew in her arms and obeys.

Penny glances out the window just in time to see a harpy land on the wing. This is the first chance she's had to get a good look at one of the creatures. Her wings are cream and blue and bronze, the tips of her feathers wickedly sharp. There's a blueish cast to her skin; her lips and nipples dark enough they might be black. There are bones and feathers woven into her hair, or maybe the feathers *are* her hair.

There's a thump from the other side of the plane. Through the small, oval window in the door, she sees a harpy baring her teeth. The creature hammers the window with her fist. The security glass holds, but trembles with each blow. After a moment, the face disappears, and then the whole door shakes as one of the harpies strikes it full force.

Penny gives the security goon's smile back full force now, trying to be reassuring, but it feels more like a grimace. "There's no way they can get in."

The goon licks pale lips and doesn't respond. For all his size, Penny realizes he might be as young as Jonathan, maybe younger. He's not wearing his tinted glasses anymore; his eyes are bloodshot. The goon they left behind—maybe they were twins after all.

Shit.

"Hey." Penny grabs the goon's wrist with just enough force to get his attention. *What would Bunny do?*

"What's your name?"

"R-Ruston, ma'am."

"Okay, Ruston. We're going to get through this, you and me. And we're going to make sure all the others get through this, too. You got that?" It takes all Penny's effort to keep her voice even, to keep it from being too hard.

How the hell does Bunny do it? She lets go of Ruston's wrist, moving to the other side of the plane. There are at least a dozen harpies darting in and out of the clouds. Some are armored in bronze, complicated and lovely. Most are unarmed, but Penny catches sight of one with a spear.

"Shit!" Instinct sends Penny reeling backward.

The harpy dives, striking the plane. There's a terrible sound as the spear punches through layers of metal—more than it should be able to. Fine. Penny smoothes her hands over her dress, gathering her thoughts. Calm, cool, and collected. Just like Bunny would be.

But she isn't Bunny, and she doesn't have the Glitter Squadron to back her up. It's just her. She's been to fucking war. She's saved the fucking world countless times. But never like this, never alone.

Another strike. The inner wall of the cabin shudders, but the spear's point doesn't emerge. There's a scraping sound as the weapon is withdrawn. No damage. Then Penny notices a tiny, pinhole wound.

It isn't like in the movies; the plane doesn't explode. But if she doesn't do something, they'll lose cabin pressure.

What would Zippy Terwilliger do?

Penny squeezes her hands into fists, and lets go. She isn't Bunny. She isn't Zippy. She is only herself. Penny takes the wad of peach-flavored chewing gum from her mouth and presses it against the hole. That simple act is enough to snap the world back into focus.

"We need to open the door," she says.

"What?" Ruston looks at her like she's lost her mind.

"We can't do anything from inside the plane, and if we don't do something they'll rip us apart. Get the pilot to tell us when we're at an altitude where it's safe."

Ruston's mouth works for a moment, but he trots off. Blows continue to rain against the outside of the plane. After a moment, Ruston returns with a shell-shocked member of the crew.

"Be ready," Penny says.

The crew member stations herself beside the door, hands trembling. Penny plants her feet, weapon drawn. Ruston takes a position beside her.

"As soon as you open the door, get out of the way," Penny says to the crewwoman.

The woman nods. Her lips move, silently counting. Penny sees the moment come, and at first it seems like the woman is going to freeze, lose her nerve, then she wrenches the door open and scrambles aside, wedging herself between two seats, arms over her head, making herself as small as she can.

Penny fires. It's pure instinct. A harpy fills the open doorway for one moment, then Penny's shot hits home, and the bird woman falls. Two more harpies crowd in to take her place.

All they want is their sisters' freedom.

"Take the one on the left!" Penny shouts over the rush of air.

They're low enough now that the open door doesn't want to suck them outside, but the plane feels unsteady. The space is too close to fire again. Penny lashes out with a kick instead, catching one of the bird women square in the face. There's a satisfying crunch; a gout of blood—blue-black—soaks the woman's lips and chin. She tumbles back, her wings snapping wide, beating the air to regain her balance and keeping her from tumbling out of the plane. Penny ducks under the sweep of blade-like feathers, and comes out of her crouch with one of the knives from her boot. She drives it into the bird woman's hand where she braces it against the wall.

This time, the harpy's shriek is human. As she struggles to pull the blade out, Penny kicks her hard in the stomach. The woman falls out the door, leaving the blade embedded in the wall. Penny yanks it free, wiping harpy blood onto the copper of her dress.

If this were a Zippy Terwilliger story, in the end the bad guys would be tied up and handed over to the proper authorities, wearing hangdog expressions. Or, if like the Pirate King they did happen to "die," they'd pop up again in the next adventure with some over-complicated story about how they escaped death once again. There'd be no smears of blood, no harpies screaming as they plunged through the clouds. Mindy wouldn't have shadows under her eyes, and the knowledge of torture weighting her mind. And at the end of the day they'd celebrate with a pot of tea and a plate of warm scones.

Penny turns, whipping her blade through the air. Perfectly balanced, the knife buries itself in a harpy's chest. Before Penny can reach for the knife in her other boot, another harpy takes the fallen one's place. Ruston aims, but the harpy lashes out, swiping talons across his face. He screams, dropping his weapon. His knees fold, hands clutched to his cheek and blood seeping between his fingers.

The harpy's wings snap wide, buffeting the space with air. Penny staggers, and the moment she does, the harpy is on her. She knocks Penny onto her back, driving the air from her lungs. Starbursts cloud Penny's vision. There's a horrible wheezing sound she recognizes as her own, not helped by the harpy's weight on top of her.

Talons slash. Penny jerks her head to the side, rocking her body so the harpy lifts just enough to allow Penny to get her leg up and draw her other blade. The harpy snaps her wings wide again, using them for balance. Penny strikes; the blade skitters off patterned armor.

The knife is knocked from Penny's hand. Pain shoots from Penny's wrist to her elbow. Even if she could reach the blade, she doubts she could get her fingers to close. As she tries to shake off the tingling sensation, the harpy catches Penny's arm, slamming it back against the floor. Before the shock even registers, the harpy rears back, burying her talons in Penny's shoulder.

Penny howls.

The harpy squeezes, making the blood flow faster, grinning. She leans in and lets out an avian shriek, a sound of triumph, disconcerting from human lips. There's nothing human about the bird woman's eyes; they're golden, like a hawk's, dilated so wide the black reaches almost to the edges.

Penny wants to fall into those eyes, hypnotized prey. Her thoughts skitter, slipping like the blade off the harpy's armor. No knife. No gun. The world threatens to go black, rocking with the sound of explosions, the smell of charred flesh, the sound of a child wailing over a twisted body, burned beyond recognition. The scent is in Penny's mouth, in her nose, clogging her throat.

She needs to get up, get away, get air. Her fingers scrabble, talons of their own, ready to claw the memory of scent out of her skin. Instead, they catch on one of the pins from her teased-up hair. They close. They strike. She jams the pin into the endless gold-rimmed blackness. And she can breathe.

The harpy's scream is a horrifying mix of human and avian. She paws, blind, trying to pull the pin free, smearing blood on her face and hands. Penny bucks and the harpy slides off her, trying to crawl away from the pain. The feathers of her folded wings tear gouges in the carpet. The bird woman sobs, a deep, sick noise in her chest and her throat. An animal sound.

And the animal in Penny answers. The human in her answers, too. It is equal parts mercy and cold, calculated opportunity as she retrieves her fallen blade and plunges it into the space between two of the harpy's vertebrae, just at the base of her skull.

Cradling her numb and bloodied arm, Penny uses the toe of one chunky, copper boot to roll the harpy's limp body over. The creature's eyes are more blood now than black and gold. Shaking with adrenaline, laced with exhaustion, Penny kicks the harpy's body through the open door and watches it fall, leaving shed feathers and smears of blood behind.

Life isn't a Zippy Terwilliger story.

"How's Joshua doing?" Penny asks.

Penny and Mindy sit across from each other at a trestle table tucked beneath the shade of a tree in the White House rose garden. The scent of a dozen varieties of roses makes a gentle perfume, attracting the hum of bees.

"A few scrapes and bruises. None the worse for wear. My sister-in-law is a wreck, terrified to let him out of her sight. I think I may be off the Christmas card list this year." Mindy offers a wry, tight smile.

One of the White House staff arrives with a tea tray and sets it down between them.

"Tea and scones." Penny smiles. "You remembered."

"Of course." Mindy lifts a scone, picking at it, but Penny never sees her take a bite.

Her own stomach feels too tight for food. She looks away. At a discreet distance, two security goons stand at the ready. With a start, Penny recognizes Ruston, angry gashes marring his face. Penny's shoulder twinges in sympathy. Her puncture wounds, Ruston's soon-to-be-scars— the marks the harpies left on them will never fully heal.

"I'm shutting down the Area 51 project," Mindy says, drawing Penny's attention back. "I'll hold a press conference. The voters deserve to know what kind of president they elected."

"You're risking the office."

"Probably." Mindy shrugs.

Penny doesn't know what to say. Everything Mindy worked for... But it's not her place to try to convince her friend otherwise when she's made up her mind. Instead, she reaches for the bag at her feet and hands it to Mindy.

"What this?"

"Just open it."

Mindy pulls out a hardcover book, looking at it for a moment before smiling.

"It's the anniversary edition," Penny says. "The first five volumes, bound together, including the one with Zippy in the haunted maze. I know that one was always your favorite."

Penny watches Mindy admire the luridly painted cover showing Zippy in her plane soaring through an achingly blue sky while below her swamp creatures and werewolves reach after her and howl their frustration.

"I thought maybe you could read them to Joshua sometime. Well, when he's a bit older."

"Thank you," Mindy says, still looking at the cover, her expression wistful. "I think he'd like that."

The shadow beneath Mindy's skin is closer to the surface now. The decisions she's made are like a bruise, one that will never fade. Penny can't imagine being in her friend's shoes. She can barely imagine being in her own shoes some days, the things she's done in the name of freedom and saving the world. All she can do is take it one day at a time.

After a moment, Mindy rises and tucks the book under her arm. "The free world doesn't run itself, no matter how hard I wish."

Mindy's smile is lopsided. Penny stands, and for a moment, they're awkward, president and citizen. Then Mindy pulls her into a hug, and just for a moment Penny feels some of the tension melt away. Some, but not all.

"Feel free to stick around and finish your tea. No one will kick you out, I promise."

After a moment, Penny resumes her seat. She isn't in the mood for tea and scones, but she's not ready to leave either. Just for now, she wants to pretend this is all there is to the world—no wars to fight, no terrible decisions to make.

A figure crosses the lawn, and Penny tenses. The tension doesn't go away completely when she recognizes Jonathan. The young aide's expression is sheepish, nervous even, and Penny forces her own features to soften, gesturing to the chair across from her.

"I don't want to bother you," Jonathan says. He meets her eyes, but it doesn't last long. "I just wanted to say again what an honor it was to meet you."

Despite herself, Penny grins. She rises and holds out her hand. Jonathan stares for a moment, stunned, before accepting it. She can't quite resist squeezing hard enough to feel the shifting of his bones, but to his credit, Jonathan doesn't grimace.

"Not so bad, working together." Penny studies him for a moment before letting go. "Ask your boss for my contact information. I'll give you a tour of our headquarters sometime, and introduce you to Bunny."

The blush coloring Jonathan from his throat to the tips of his ears makes it all worthwhile. He stammers gratitude. After the third "thank you," Penny leaves him, smiling to herself as she crosses the lawn. She's reluctant to leave the peace of the rose garden, but ready to head back to the Glitter Squadron and home. The free world won't save itself, after all, no matter how much she wishes.

The Copper Top

1 oz Stoli Orange

1 oz Peach Schnapps

1 oz peach nectar

1 oz Grand Marnier

Crushed ice

Combine first three ingredients in a cocktail shaker and blend well. Pour over crushed ice in a high ball glass. Using a spoon, gently pour the Grand Marnier to create a layered look. Garnish with orange peel if desired.

Well, that was a bust. I spend all this time designing Penny the perfect drink, and she won't even try it. She's constantly chewing on that peach gum like a wad of cud, but God forbid she give this a try. She said it's "too girly" and I said, "Honey, exactly what is it you think you've got between your legs? Just because you pack a big gun doesn't mean you have the hardware to match." Honestly, she and CeCe both need to lighten up when it comes to their booze—Little Miss I-don't-touch-anything-mixed and Little Miss-Mister bourbon-straight-up and Jack-no-ice. Boring! It's like they both think they've got something to prove to the world, you know? News flash, honeys, the equipment you're born with has nothing to do with how strong or weak you are. It hasn't nothing to do with anything about you. You don't have to prove anything to anyone. Besides, some people would kill for what you've got.

THE DEVIL COMES TO THE MIDNIGHT CAFE

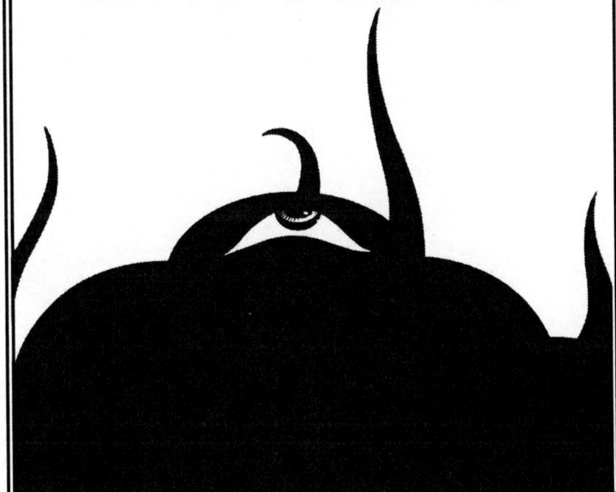

Jazz, whiskey, and cigarettes, each smoother than the last; this is CeCe's kind of night, and the Midnight Café is her kind of club.

Tonight her velvet suit matches the smoke in the room, her grey coattails as sharp as soft fabric can be. Her shoes and walking stick gleam sleek black in what little light is offered. Everything here is dim except the conversation, sparkling even at a hush. Bottles line the mirror behind the bar and as long as you're flush, you never need to see the bottom of a glass.

On stage, a set ends in a murmur of horns. Without turning, CeCe slides another bill across the bar to keep the amber flowing. Tonight, she's celebrating—the Glitter Squadron saved the world again. Though she'd never admit it where Bunny or Sapphire could hear her, it feels good to be a part of something valuable.

Her tobacco is imported. Turkish. Each cigarette black with a filter that would glow underneath UV lighting. CeCe exhales rings of smoke toward the ceiling, and then the lights dim further, leaving a single spot pinning the stage.

There's a sharp whistle followed by a low patter of stomping and applause. CeCe straightens. The last element of a perfect evening steps onto the polished floorboards of the stage.

Madeline. She doesn't stride but rather slinks to the microphone. She grips it with both gloved hands and appraises the audience with a knowing smile. A brush mutters across the snare, joined a moment later by the mourn of a saxophone. The drums step in full, heartbeat strong, a white-hot shock of noise bringing the crowd alive with wolf whistles and catcalls as Madeline parts her gorgeous crimson lips and rasps in a breath as effective as dragging her nails lightly up each and every spine in the room.

As much as CeCe wants to live in the moment, there's a match striking a small flare of regret that stinks of sulfur. *She* should be up there on stage with Madeline. Except nobody wants her crooning anymore; they want Madeline's bluesy, sultry heat. And deep down CeCe knows she was never half the singer Madeline is, even in her heyday as the Velvet Devil of the Midnight Café.

Besides, CeCe has the Glitter Squadron now. She has saving the world. She comes and goes as she pleases. The team needs her more than she needs them, and that's the way she likes it.

CeCe gives over all her attention to the performance. She watches Madeline's throat, the way it works beneath the pool of shadows untouched by the spotlight. Lips next, then the glitter of her eyes, brighter than diamonds, and last the spill of auburn hair over shoulders smooth as marble.

All eyes in the room are on Madeline, attention magnetically pulled toward the stage. But of all the gazes drinking her in, the one Madeline meets in return is CeCe's.

CeCe raises her glass—a heavy-bottomed rocks glass minus the ice, poured with two smooth fingers of Bushmills Sixteen-Year-Old Single Malt—a salute, and Madeline smiles at her before turning back to the others, the audience captive as her voice opens wide. CeCe holds onto her smile, watching Madeline sing, and watching the crowd watch her. Do they think they know her? Madeline is more than a perfect face. She's wit and laughter, speaks at least three languages, and climbs sheer rock walls on vacation just for fun. The last time Madeline dragged her along, one of the only times, CeCe watched in amazement from below as Madeline reached the top, taking only a moment to catch her breath before singing first in French, then Italian.

CeCe can say she's met some very unique souls, but none claim her like Madeline. CeCe had a family once, but domesticity didn't work for her. She found the Glitter Squadron, and it fit, but there was still some raggedness to the edges of her life. But then she discovered Madeline.... Her past, her present, her future—it all aligned. If anyone asks, CeCe will say she's still working it out, but in truth, she has it figured. She's the satellite orbiting the Glitter Squadron, the velvet antidote to all their lamé. She's the lone wolf to their pack. She owes all that understanding, finding her place in the world, to Madeline.

The song ends. Lights glint from the beads covering Madeline's dress as she takes her bow, before making her way to the back of the room. CeCe is waiting, and catches Madeline's waist, stealing a kiss before releasing her to the chilled glass of Chardonnay waiting on the bar.

"Great set tonight, doll." CeCe opens her monogrammed cigarette case, offering one to Madeline. She keeps the case evenly stocked—her own Turkish cigarettes on one side, and the Virginia Slims Madeline prefers on the other.

"You really think so?" Madeline's cheeks are flushed.

CeCe lights Madeline's cigarette with a silver lighter that matches the case, before lighting her own.

"You killed it. You always do."

There's a hint of rosewater—which CeCe thinks of as Madeline's scent—as Madeline leans back. There's something else though, wood-smoke and, oddly, cinnamon. A rim of crimson stains Madeline's cigarette filter as she blows a thin stream of blue toward the ceiling. She leaves another perfect imprint on the glass. The color makes CeCe hungry.

"I was thinking maybe you could come with me this weekend." Madeline speaks without looking at CeCe. "Stolen Chimney. Utah. They say Moroni fashioned the rocks as a warning."

There's a strange rigidity to Madeline's posture, one CeCe finds herself echoing. It's irrational, but she's searching Madeline's words for a trap. Is she hoping to be taken up on her offer or turned down?

The moment she had it all figured out, while Madeline was singing, slips through her fingers. CeCe is lost again. There are days where Madeline feels like a puzzle CeCe's meant to solve, but doesn't have all the pieces. The best she can do is flash a smile, play it cool.

"No can do, doll. Top-secret business afoot." Even casual mentions of the Glitter Squadron bother Madeline.

This time is no exception. She flinches, then picks a fleck of ash from her lip, distracted. "Okay."

CeCe thinks she hears relief in Madeline's tone, even though her shoulders remain tight. Madeline starts as CeCe brushes fingers over her arm, but immediately softens the reaction with an apologetic smile. Madeline swirls her wine glass—restless and uneasy.

"Is everything okay?" CeCe is afraid of the answer.

Madeline gives her a brief, frightened glance. "Just tired."

It's pure lie, another trap, another hole in the puzzle. CeCe sips her drink, swallowing the amber smoke of her whiskey to chase away the doubt. She touches her lips briefly to the curve of Madeline's neck, simple and uncomplicated. Madeline gratifies her with a delicious shiver.

"What do you say we get out of here?" CeCe keeps her hand on the small of Madeline's back, expecting her to lean into the touch.

Madeline surprises her by pulling away. There's a hard edge to the brightness in her eyes, not quite anger, but closer to fear. "Is that all I am to you? Someone to warm your bed?"

The words, unexpected, rock CeCe back in her seat. "Doll, slow down. Where is this coming from?"

A minute ago, everything was tense, but cool, and now the world is falling out from under her. CeCe struggles to catch up while not letting any of it show. She's the Velvet Underground Drag King, after all. She has a reputation to maintain. Clark Gable telling Scarlett he doesn't give a damn, that's her.

Except she does give a damn. Even though she's never said it aloud, CeCe is ninety-nine percent certain she's in love with Madeline. And she's never been in love before. Women were creatures that came and went before Madeline; they were there or they weren't and it didn't matter. Confusion, touched with fear, makes CeCe's pulse jump. Her first instinct is to withdraw. Deep down she knows that this is what caring gets you, relying on other people instead of doing your own thing. It gets your heart broke.

Madeline reaches for another cigarette. Instead of waiting for CeCe to light it, she plucks the lighter from CeCe's fingers. It takes her three tries to get the flint to spark. "At New Year's, we talked about Paris," Madeline says. "It's April now."

"You want to go to Paris? We'll go to Paris. We'll go tonight." There's an edge to CeCe's voice, rising to match Madeline's tone.

"Paris isn't the point." Madeline drops her just-lit cigarette into CeCe's glass. "I've never even met your friends. You're ashamed of me."

"Come on now." CeCe tries for lightness, struggling to keep her voice even. "Any woman would be proud to have you on her arm."

"I don't want *any* woman. I want you, and I want to know you're with me, and not just because of this." Madeline gestures to her body.

"Babe…" CeCe reaches for Madeline's hand, but it's jerked away.

"No. Everyone looks at me, but they don't see me. Maybe…" She hesitates, standing, gathering her purse and rummaging inside. Her voice drops, so low it's now a confessional whisper. "Maybe there isn't anything else to me."

"Maddy, that isn't—"

The clatter of Madeline's keys hitting the floor interrupt CeCe's words. Flustered, Madeline stoops to retrieve them. Her cheeks are flushed, eyes too bright. "I can't do this anymore," Madeline says.

CeCe reaches frantically for the right words but Madeline has already whirled precariously on needle-thin heels, heading for the door.

CeCe brings the épée up to her mask, saluting the end of the match. Butch sketches a quick bow across from her before removing his mask. Even though he doesn't run with the Glitter Squadron anymore— he's a small-business owner but, as he's quick to tell anyone who asks, not the respectable kind—they still meet up to practice every now and then, keep their skills sharp.

"I've got to run, but same time next month?" Butch asks.

CeCe nods, pulling off her mask and gloves, and running fingers through her sweat-damp hair. "Same time next month."

She tries to hide the note of disappointment in her voice. She was hoping Butch would suggest a drink, or even another match. Despite the burn in her muscles, CeCe could go again. She considers looking for another partner, but even another round of parry, riposte, lunge, and feint would only be a delaying tactic. Eventually she will have to go back to her apartment, where she will inevitably think about Madeline and their fight.

To hell with it, CeCe thinks. She's not going to spend her nights slinking around; she's going to face the music. At home, she showers and dresses in her finest. Wine-red velvet tonight, sharp as blood. When every line of her pocket square is precise and crisp and her shoes are buffed to a high shine, CeCe heads back to the Midnight Café. She's no whipped dog to run scared with her tail tucked between her legs after one little fight.

She slides into her usual seat at the bar, cool as ever, consciously keeping her leg from jiggling or her fingers from drumming on the bar. She doesn't smoke her cigarettes any faster than usual, or gulp her drink, and she definitely does not look at the vintage art-deco pocket watch with its glittering silver fob chain.

The Elysian Quartet's set ends, and CeCe straightens, convincing herself the sudden speed in her pulse is only her imagination. Madeline always follows the Elysian Quartet, but CeCe doesn't recognize the blonde who takes the stage.

CeCe catches the bartender's eye. "What's with the new girl?"

The bartender shrugs, but CeCe notes the way his gaze moves toward the door beside the stage. CeCe leaves a twenty on the bar and the rest of her drink untouched.

Her suit picks up bloody highlights from the exit light as she ignores the *Employees Only* sign and pushes through the stage door. A narrow corridor leads to the dressing rooms. CeCe knocks on Madeline's door, presses her ear to the wood, but only silence answers.

What if Madeline's gone for good? What if CeCe has fucked up irrevocably by failing to follow some arcane rule she doesn't understand? Maybe Madeline wants to settle down, start a family. CeCe's never considered herself a family man; it's not her scene, but she could convince herself to be domesticated. For Madeline. But what if it's something worse? The thought nags at the back of her mind—the distraction, the tension, the sudden anger. It's not like Madeline. So what if this isn't about her, or them at all?

CeCe shoulders the door, and to her surprise, it gives. The dressing room smells like rosewater and cinnamon. The scent is an imprint, as if Madeline was just here, but the room is decidedly empty. The new scent, the one that doesn't belong to Madeline, but which CeCe smelled on her the night she stormed out, is there too, increasing her unease.

The lights circling the mirror over Madeline's vanity are on, but the rest of the room is dark. Tubes of lipstick, compacts, and jars of cold cream — nothing seems out of place. A photograph tucked into the mirror's frame catches her eye.

CeCe swallows around a lump in her throat. Her and Maddy, cheek to cheek, smiling for the camera on New Year's Eve. CeCe tucks the photograph into her wine-red pocket. Madeline is her girl. Come hell or high water, CeCe will figure out where she lost her and how to win her back.

Something else catches her eye, crammed into the trash can under Madeline's vanity. A long-stemmed rose, the stem snapped, petals bruised as though Madeline tried to grind it out like a cigarette. Another suitor? An unwelcome one?

CeCe's thoughts whirl. She's so distracted, she nearly collides with a woman who appears out of nowhere as CeCe steps back into the hall. CeCe blinks. For a moment, she's looking into a mirror. Except the colors are flipped, everything just slightly askew.

Where CeCe is all velvet, the other woman's suit is midnight silk. Her creases are knife-crisp, the blackness interrupted only by the bloody slash of her tie. CeCe's hair is blonde-ash; the woman's slicked-back do is as black as her suit, one lock worked into a jagged, lightning-strike curl over her right eye.

"Excuse me." The woman smirks, shouldering past CeCe. "I've got a show to do."

The woman walks with a faint limp, as though compensating with reality for the affectation of CeCe's crystal-topped cane. The shape of her from behind is wrong, her shoulders too bulky. Or maybe it's just a trick of the light.

The red exit sign casts the woman's shadow behind her. Wrong. The door slams; CeCe jumps, pulse echoing with the slam. The scent of cinnamon lingers in the air. Wrong. She needs to find Madeline.

CeCe recognizes she's in a dream, but she can't wake up. The dream doesn't behave the way a dream should, either. Everything is too sharp, too linear. It's a sliver forced into her mind, and she can't dig it out.

She follows the hall behind the stage at the Midnight Cafe, and pushes open Madeline's dressing-room door. The geography of the dream-room is all wrong. It's bigger than CeCe's apartment; the racks of costumes frame a heart-shaped bed. Madeline pours from the bed, boneless in ecstasy, hair spilling like russet ink, eyes closed and lips parted. The woman with the lightning-strike curl and sharp-angled black suit raises her head from between Madeline's legs. "Mine," she says. "Mine."

CeCe jerks awake, her heart pounding. There's a weight on her chest, crushing her. She isn't alone.

Thrashing and scrambling at the covers, she stands and nearly falls. It's a moment before she can convince herself the shadows aren't leaking toward her, the world isn't about to end.

"Shit." She runs a hand through her hair; goosebumps rise on her skin.

She forces herself to breathe, to examine the dream, the strange angles of it. It doesn't fade the way dreams usually do. If anything it sharpens, and that in itself kicks something loose in CeCe's mind. Fragments of half-remembered mythology, related by an ex-girlfriend who fancied herself a medieval scholar. Incubus. Succubus. She can't remember which is which, but aren't they both demons that prey on people in dreams?

Ridiculous. CeCe shakes her head. It *was* just a dream, her subconscious trying to tell her to man up or she'll lose Madeline for good. She glances at the clock, decides fuck it, and calls Madeline anyway.

CeCe loses count of the rings before hanging up. It's two a.m. Where would Madeline be if not at home? CeCe pours herself a drink before crawling back into bed, pulling the blanket around her shoulders. The room is cold, even though the windows are closed.

Her heart wants to crack in two, the image from the dream re-asserting itself, overwriting what she knows to be reality. She loves Madeline, and Madeline loves her. Except… Except.

CeCe slams the glass down hard. This isn't her. It's like the dream, a sliver beneath her skin. But she's stronger than this.

She sucks in a breath, snapping the world back into focus. The chill retreats from the room. Think rationally. When everything else is eliminated whatever remains, however impossible, must be the truth.

This is what CeCe knows: She loves Madeline. And because she's never been this certain about anything else in her life, she refuses to believe Madeline would simply give up on her and walk away. There's something else afoot—a demon, worming its way into her dreams, cocky, announcing her presence and intent. The question is, now that CeCe knows it's out there, gunning for her, gunning for her girl, what is she going to do about it?

CeCe returns to the Midnight Café.

The blare of horns assaults her the minute she steps through the door. The music is blood hot, the place jumping, bodies packed shoulder to shoulder. The spotlights normally trained on the stage swing over the crowd in a pulsing, strobing panic. Everything is too bright and sharp and loud.

CeCe stands in the door gripping her cane, dazed. Like a magician's reveal, the lights swing back to the stage, illuminating the singer. Of course.

The demon wears dark red today, her suit the color of drying blood, her tie a slash of ink. She dips the microphone low, like a dance partner, and the crowd goes wild. Her voice steps up CeCe's spine, but not the way Madeline's does. This is an assault; voltage-dipped nails, driven with the power of a nail gun—Bam! Bam! Bam!—between each vertebra.

It brings back last night's panic; loneliness in the midst of a crowd, as though the demon sings for CeCe alone. Punctuating the point, the woman raises her head, echoing her motion from CeCe's dream. She grins and the lyrics are lost in a rush of blood pounding in CeCe's ears. The demon's lips shape a word meant for CeCe alone: *Mine.*

The demon throws a dark wink, tipping her hand. Even though she knows what will come next, it still tears CeCe's heart out. As the song ends, a single spot sweeps to the side of the stage, illuminating Madeline. Her beads are black and crimson tonight. The light hugs her as it always does, but instead of CeCe, it's the demon waiting to circle her waist, pull her close.

Wrong.

The demon whispers something in Madeline's ear. Madeline laughs, head back, too-bright teeth flashing in the spotlight. The music kicks up again, a physical wave pushing CeCe away. She's not wanted here. Madeline has made her choice. She wants nothing to do with CeCe. She wants to be left alone.

CeCe slams through the door, not waiting to hear the music Madeline and the demon will make together. She's outside, in the rain. Of course it's raining. Alone. The word echoes, nipping her heels, chasing her all the way home.

It's a Tuesday, or a Wednesday. CeCe doesn't remember and doesn't care. Just like she doesn't remember falling asleep fully clothed. She has a vague sense that the phone has been ringing off and on. The Glitter Squadron is used to her going AWOL. Eventually they'll give up, but just to be safe, she yanks the cord out of the wall, and crawls back into bed, piling the covers over her head.

The world has gone away; she's the only one left. Alone.

But knocking insists otherwise. CeCe staggers to the door, opening it only to make the pounding stop, not because she wants to talk to whoever is on the other side. It's a moment before her eyes focus, and a moment more before her brain catches up.

"Sapphire?"

"Honey, you look like shit." Sapphire's nose wrinkles. She purses her lips, then sighs. "I'm not going to stand in your doorway all day, so you'd better invite me in."

When CeCe doesn't move, Sapphire pokes her in the chest with a long, gem-studded fingernail, forcing her back a step. Sapphire's floor-length fishtail skirt hisses behind her. Her nose wrinkles again, taking in the disarray; she nudges an empty bottle aside with one glittering platform sandal and raises an eyebrow.

"Taking good care of yourself, I see."

"What do you want?" CeCe hasn't moved from the door, and in fact is gripping it in order to stay upright. None of this makes sense. Bunny she could understand, or Esmeralda. Sapphire doesn't even like her.

"Charming. You weren't answering your phone. I thought someone should check to make sure you weren't dead. Good to know you're at least face-up in the gutter."

CeCe opens her mouth to snap a retort, but what comes out is, "Madeline left me."

"Oh, honey." Sapphire's expression flickers through a complicated range of emotions—animosity and sympathy and the urge for a smart-assed remark.

CeCe almost smirks, but it isn't in her. God help her, she almost wants to hug the other woman when Sapphire says, "You want me to make you some tea?"

Defeated, CeCe nods. She isn't Clark Gable, keeping her cool. She's just CeCe, falling apart. She needs to sober up, wake up, figure out how to put her life back together. She needs to get the image of Madeline with the demon's arm around her waist out of her head.

"Wanna talk about it?" Sapphire asks when she returns from the kitchen with two steaming mugs of tea.

CeCe finally moves away from the door. She almost asks if Sapphire has a flask on her, surveying the dismaying ruin of her liquor cabinet littering the floor.

"All right, let's try this, then," Sapphire says. "Do you love her?"

"I… Yes." CeCe runs a hand through her hair, a futile attempt to slick the fallen strands back into place.

"Okay. Good start. Now, go after her."

"It's not that simple." There's a hollow space inside CeCe's skull. "She was laughing. There's another…woman."

CeCe can't bring herself to say demon. Because it sounds ridiculous in the light of day, with all the alcohol gone. It would be easier, gentler to believe something supernatural stole Madeline away from her, but the cold hard truth of it is she wasn't stolen. CeCe lost her.

"She looked happy," CeCe says.

"Looks are deceiving. Do you *know* she's happy? Did you ask her?"

CeCe opens her mouth, but no words come out. She closes it again, frowning.

Sapphire taps a nail on the table for emphasis, drawing CeCe's attention. "If this was just about you making excuses to be miserable, then I would let it go, but Madeline's happiness is wrapped up in this, too. Stop being such a candy-ass coward and let her into your life already."

CeCe looks up, stunned. Sapphire might as well have slapped her, but perversely CeCe finds herself chuckling.

"The traditional response is 'thank you,'" Sapphire's tone is sour.

"It's just, I always got the sense you didn't like me. But here you are, trying to put my love life back together."

"Honey, most of the time I think you're an arrogant, self-centered little prick. But—" the corner of Sapphire's mouth lifts in the faintest of smiles—"that doesn't mean you're not family."

CeCe feels something unknot inside her; maybe having a family isn't such a terrible thing after all. "Thanks. You're a swell gal."

Sapphire snaps her fingers, pointing a warning finger at CeCe's chest. "Don't you *gal* me. I'm all lady. And don't you forget it. Now, go get your girl back."

CeCe is stone-cold sober for the first time in what feels like forever. She rests her hand on the dresser for a moment before opening the top drawer. Bu
ried under a ball of socks there's a velvet box.

The ring inside is an art-deco dream. She bought it at a pawn shop, the same one where she got her pocket watch, the week after she met Madeline. It's been hidden in her drawer ever since. Holding the ring crystallizes her, drives away the rest of her fear, or at least holds it at bay. She should have given the ring to Madeline long ago. She can only hope Sapphire was right and it isn't too late.

Music beats a pulse through the Midnight Café's skin, even from outside. It thrums in CeCe's bones as she reaches for the door. Hot jazz. The hottest.

It's like a wave from a blast furnace when she steps inside. Sweat-slicked bodies writhe in a space cleared by pushing the tables up against the walls. It's only dancing, but it might as well be sex. The air reeks of it, and the demon is eating it up. On stage, she howls, sweat beading her skin, but rather than looking like exertion, she glows as if lit by flames.

Once again the demon's suit is the flip-side mirror image of CeCe's— blacker than black, with the flourish of a purple pocket square and tie. A single flower, its petals the same velvet nap as CeCe's suit, decorates her lapel.

As the demon dips the microphone low, leaning toward the crowd, a trick of the light paints the shadow of horns on her brow. The song comes to an end, and the demon sweeps a bow. Her jacket strains at the shoulders, as if against folded wings. Or maybe it's just a bandage; maybe CeCe and the all-too-human-woman can exchange binding tips when all is said and done.

Two conflicting truths exist in CeCe's mind: She's lost Madeline to another woman, and a succubus stole her girl away. Her head buzzes, struggling to keep the thoughts straight as she pushes through the crowd.

"And now, fools and follies, ladies and gentlemen, sinners each and every one of you—I'd like to invite my special lady to join me on the stage."

A sickening sense of déjà vu makes CeCe's stomach lurch, and she freezes halfway to the stage. Madeline's dress glitters like moonlight as she takes her place at the demon's side. She scans the crowd, looking lost for a moment, and CeCe's pulse skips on hope. She's the one who should be up there beside Madeline—the Velvet Devil and the Silken Angel. But Madeline's gaze passes over her, snagging on a blank space as though CeCe doesn't exist.

"Before we start our next set." The demon winks. "I have a happy announcement. Not one hour ago, this little lady here agreed to be my wife."

CeCe's ears ring, drowning out the thunder of applause, the whistles, whoops, and hollers. Madeline smiles as though the corners of her mouth are lifted with strings, a doll, moved by the demon beside her. Her eyes are glassy.

"I object!" CeCe pushes toward the stage.

"Well now, I don't believe anyone asked you." The demon's voice is honey and tar, the edges of her smile cutting sharp.

"She's already spoken for." CeCe hates the way her voice quavers.

The demon smirks. The shadow of a tail twitches behind her. "Funny." The demon lifts Madeline's hand, showing a band of black metal. It looks heavy, and it absorbs the light. "The only ring I see on her finger is mine."

"Madeline? Doll?" CeCe reaches for Madeline's other hand. Her fingers are cold. Up close, the blush on Madeline's cheeks no longer hides the pallor.

Madeline starts, jerking back. Her eyes focus on CeCe, but she shakes her head.

"I can't…" Madeline's voice is strained. Her gaze losing focus again.

"Fight it," CeCe says. "It's a trick."

"I think you'd best leave the lady alone." The demon's face is inches from CeCe's. "She's with me."

CeCe ignores her, keeping her gaze on Madeline.

"Maddy, I know you can hear me." She begins to croon, low and sweet, one of the old songs from her Velvet Devil days.

Her voice cracks, losing the thread of the melody. Sweat gathers at the small of her back. Madeline's expression grows pained, like she wants to turn her head and look at CeCe, but she can't.

"You're too late," the demon says.

"I'm not going anywhere."

The demon cocks an eyebrow. "Will you fight for her then?"

CeCe finally tears her gaze away from Madeline, gaping at the demon.

"What do you think, ladies and gentlemen?" The demon addresses the crowd, arms spread wide. "Shall we duel for the lady's favor?"

"She isn't a prize," CeCe says, but her words drown in wave of applause.

"Last chance." The demon drops her voice low again, turning back to CeCe. "Time to tuck your tail between your legs and run."

"Like hell I will!" CeCe draws the handle of her cane from the base, revealing a thin sword.

Running with the Glitter Squadron has taught her a thing or two about always being prepared.

She leaps onto the stage. A brief electric shiver makes its way from CeCe's polished wingtips to the crown of her slick-coiffed head. She flourishes her sword, vamping as she prepares to lunge.

"Tsk. Tsk." The demon wags a finger. "I can fight dirty, too."

A thunder-crack fills the air accompanied by a flash and the scent of black powder and cinnamon. The demon's jacket shreds as two powerful bat wings snap free, beating the air and lifting her off the ground. The horns aren't just a shadow on her forehead anymore, and instead of shiny black shoes, cloven hooves peek out from her trouser cuffs.

Cries of surprise fill the air, and panicked footsteps rush for the door, leaving CeCe, Madeline, and the demon alone.

"Surprise." The demon bares fangs and dives at CeCe.

CeCe dodges, rolling, and springs up with her sword-cane brandished. She can't help thinking of Errol Flynn as Robin Hood, battling for his ladylove against Basil Rathbone as Sir Guy of Gisbourne. Adrenaline-high and emboldened by the image, she slashes at the demon's face, drawing a line of red on her cheek. This is nothing like sparring with Butch, this is the real deal, and she has no intention of holding back.

The demon snarls, landing with a force that shakes the stage. She grasps Madeline's shoulders, shoving her toward CeCe. Madeline stumbles, letting out a choked noise of surprise. CeCe drops her sword, catching Madeline.

"Are you okay?"

Madeline's face is tear-wet; a tremor runs the length of her body, physically trying to shake free of the spell holding her. But it still has its claws in her, and panic skitters across her features. She fights CeCe, eyes wide, trying to escape.

"What have you done to her?" CeCe whips around to face the grinning demon.

The terror in Madeline's eyes breaks CeCe's heart, but she lets Madeline scramble away. CeCe reaches for her sword, ready to smash the smile from the demon's face. But the demon is too quick. She kicks the blade away and catches CeCe by the throat, lifting her and slamming her into the wall backing the stage.

CeCe's vision blurs, her eyes stinging as she pries at the hand gripping her throat. The demon relaxes her hold just enough to allow the tips of CeCe's polished shoes to scrape the stage. She leans in close, her lips brushing CeCe's ear, breath hot.

"I can give her things you can't."

Stars burst behind CeCe's eyes.

"Pleasure. Fortune. Fame. I can make her a star," the demon purrs.

"She doesn't want…"

"You don't know what she wants." The demon squeezes, cutting off CeCe's words.

CeCe kicks, shoes scuffing the stage, but she can't get purchase. The tiny hairs on CeCe's ear bend under the weight of the demon's breath.

"How about this, then? Two for the price of one, the three of us, all cozy together?" The demon snickers, pushing images into CeCe's mind—the demon's lips on her throat, Madeline naked and crawling toward both of them.

CeCe reaches for another image—Madeline on New Year's Eve,

eyes bright, talking about Paris; Madeline, sweaty from rock-climbing, trying to cajole CeCe into coming along this time; Madeline speaking to her sister on the telephone, discussing their mother's cancer diagnosis and fighting back tears. This is Madeline—not CeCe's gal, and not the demon's. Her own goddamn person, the person CeCe wants to share her life with.

"I don't deal with devils." CeCe hears the rasp in her voice. She wants to accompany the words with a dramatic gesture, but her hands play traitor, hanging limp at her sides.

"I'm sorry, Madeline." CeCe wheezes, struggling to draw in enough breath. "I love you."

If she could reach the velvet box in her pocket… But she can't remember why the box is important. It's hard to focus.

A wordless yell and the sound of splintering wood breaks the spell. CeCe drops as the demon releases her, hitting the stage on her knees, gasping for breath. Behind the demon, Madeline holds the remains of a splintered chair.

"Get the hell away from my woman." Madeline's arms tremble, but she shifts her gaze to CeCe, eyes bright and wholly focused now. "You okay?"

CeCe's swallows against the bruise left by the demon's grip. "Yeah."

"Good. Then let's kill this bitch."

Madeline gets the tip of her shoe under CeCe's sword and flips it into the air. CeCe manages to catch it and pushes to her feet, ignoring the pain. She steps to Madeline's side, slips her arm around her waist, and together, they face the demon.

"Madeline, honey, babydoll…" The demon's voice is all liquid sweetness again, plucking at them, a faint prickle at the base of CeCe's spine.

"No one calls me *doll* except for her." Madeline jerks her head to indicate CeCe, driving toward the demon with the chair.

The demon jumps back, wings snapping wide. The microphone stand goes over with an electric whine. A table crashes to the ground and one of the lights overhead pops, raining shattered glass on the stage.

CeCe leans into the wind of the demon's wings. The succubus howls, lifting higher before tucking her wings and diving at them.

"Get down!" Madeline grabs CeCe and they fall, a tangle of bodies trying to shelter each other.

Pure instinct makes CeCe bring her sword up at the last minute. Too late, the demon's eyes widen. Momentum impales her on the sword, and there's a sound like the demon's suit ripping, only worse. A flash of negative light, a dark so painful CeCe lets go of the sword to shield her eyes. Black powder and sulfur and cinnamon scorch the air. The demon is gone, leaving only a curling wisp of smoke in her wake.

Madeline lets out a cry. The black ring on her finger sparks like ignited gunpowder. There's a second flash, and it vanishes, leaving an angry, red scar.

"Maddy..."

"I'm okay." Madeline curls one hand protectively around the other, looking dazed. "You?"

"I've had worse days." CeCe surveys the now-empty bar, the overturned tables and chairs, the cracked mirror behind the bar. "Better ones, too."

Broken glass crunches under Madeline's shoes. She stoops, picking up scrap of purple. It takes CeCe a moment to recognize the flower from the demon's lapel, its petals bruised almost to translucence.

"Did we kill it? Her." Madeline trembles, shock setting in as the adrenaline wears off.

Her gaze is miles away. Haunted. What did the demon make Madeline see? What did it make her do? Is it possible, despite everything, Madeline actually loved her? CeCe pushes the questions away. "I don't know," she says, voice soft.

Madeline lets the flower fall, turning to look at CeCe. "When the demon had you by the throat, you said you loved me. Did you mean it?"

Old habits and old fear almost put a smart remark on her tongue, but CeCe pushes it down. "Sure." CeCe looks at her shoes. "Of course I did."

"You've never said that to me before."

"Yeah, well, I meant to." The velvet box in her pocket digs into her and CeCe fumbles it free. "I mean, I know I should have."

She still can't bear to look at Madeline. What if she sees the echo of fear in her eyes, the ghost of whatever spell the demon laid upon her? Worse, what if there isn't a spell but CeCe still doesn't see love? What if she's blown her chance? CeCe holds the box out.

"Anyway, this is for you," she says.

Daring a peek from the corner of her eye, she watches Madeline open the box and trace the ring with the tip of one finger.

"How long have you had this?" Madeline asks.

CeCe's cheeks flush hot. She feels like a kid caught with her hand in the cookie jar. "Since the week I met you."

"Idiot." The smile in Madeline's voice makes CeCe look up.

More glass crunches under Madeline's heels. She puts her forehead against CeCe's. Warmth comes from her skin and over the lingering scent of sulfur CeCe catches a hint of rosewater. And cinnamon. The demon's smell.

Madeline touches CeCe's chin, anticipating her move, and keeping her from looking down again. There's sorrow in Madeline's eyes, but hope, too.

"I went looking for the succubus. Not her specifically, but someone like her. And I did it long before we had our last fight. I was lonely and scared of the way I felt about you. And at the same time I wanted to make you see me, see that I could be part of your life. All of it."

CeCe flinches, but Madeline holds her in place.

"Just hear me out," she says. "I know you say you're not a joiner, but you have this whole other life with the Glitter Squadron. You claim you're not part of the team, just occasional back-up when they need you, but I know that's not true. They're your family."

Madeline sighs, and a sad smile touches the edges of her lips for a moment. "I love singing, but it's not saving the world." Madeline puts her fingers over CeCe's mouth to silence her. "I'm not some fragile thing to be left behind while you go out and face danger. I'm not the girl you come home to at the end of the day either. If we're in this, we're in it together. Okay?"

Madeline takes her fingers from CeCe's lips, stepping back a pace.

"You saved my life tonight. I don't think anyone could accuse you of being fragile." CeCe offers a crooked smile, but doubt remains in Madeline's eyes, her expression searching.

CeCe doesn't think of Madeline as an accessory, or a treasure to be protected. Maybe she needs to say as much. If Madeline is a puzzle to be solved, then so is CeCe. Neither of them are mind-readers, and she has to remember that.

"You could put that on, if you wanted to." CeCe gestures at the ring.

After what seems like an eternity of CeCe listening to the blood pound in her ears, Madeline returns the smile. Her expression is sly, amusement brightens her eyes, meeting CeCe halfway. Together, they'll muddle through somehow.

"If I didn't know better, I might think you were proposing to me."

The tension drops from CeCe's shoulders and she straightens, looking Madeline straight in the eye. "What do you say?" She lifts Madeline's chin. "Be my best gal for good?"

"I say yes." Madeline leans in and touches her lips to CeCe. "But I want a costume to go with this ring. From now on, you and me are a duo."

CeCe catches Madeline around the waist. "Doll, you've got yourself a deal," she says and spins Madeline around once before setting her down and leaning in for a longer kiss.

When she comes up for air, CeCe grins. "You and me, we make a pretty good team."

After the fiasco with Penny I didn't even bother trying to come up with a drink for CeCe. But you know what? Today, I can't even be mad at her; her wedding was *glorious*. I've never seen her look so handsome—dark blue velvet tails, midnight silk cummerbund and top hat, and this darling little peacock feather boutonniere that matched Madeline's bouquet. Lilies and feathers and white roses—and guess who caught it? Now I just need a prince charming to match.

The entire Glitter Squadron stood as CeCe's groomsmaids of honor. You should have seen the dresses Es made us. Madeline's back-up band stood as her bridesmen in matching jewel-tone suits. We were a whole rainbow spread out on either side of the happy couple. Except for M, of course. M doesn't do weddings. Just as well. It would have given me nightmares for weeks. Ugh. But in happier news, rumor has it the Glitter Squadron might just be getting a new member. Es is working on a costume for Madeline as we speak, a sort of belated wedding present. It should be ready by the time they get back from Paris. The Silk Songstress. It has kind of a nice ring to it, don't you think?

THE STORY OF M

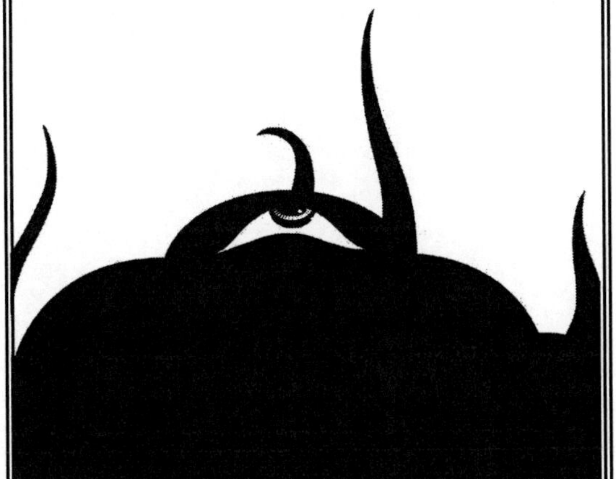

THE STORY OF M IS NOT A STORY YOU WANT TO HEAR. WITHOUT A beginning or an ending, starring one so thoroughly versed in the language of pain it may well be a native tongue. The story of M has eyes framed by leather. The story of M has lips that never part. There is nothing here, not for you. Just leave it be and move on.

★

Penny asked me the other day what kind of drink I would make for M. I told her, "Honey, fuck if I know." Who knows what M drinks. It might be ouzo, it could be a lake of petrol on fire.

It's funny, not in the ha-ha kind of way—I wouldn't even recognize M if we met on the street. Assuming M ever does anything as normal as walking down the street. Bunny must know something about M, even if the rest of us don't; she recruited M at some point. Or maybe M just appeared. I try not to think about it too much. It gives me the creeps. *M* gives me the creeps. I know, I know—it isn't kind and it isn't fair, but it's true.

I can't explain it exactly. All I know is M is pain. I wonder sometimes what it would be like... No. I don't wonder. Shit. I don't know what I'm trying to say. Thinking about M gets my head all messed up. Now *I* need a drink. Look, as far as I know, M is a breathing, animate slab of leather, through and through. I am *not* making M a drink, and I am *not* going to think about it anymore.

So why can't I stop? And why am I still afraid? Why are there some things I can't tell the Glitter Squadron about who I am? Who I want to be? Even Ruby. My Ruby.

Because what if I'm wrong? Then it will all be for nothing. My mother will never have grandchildren. Nobody will carry on my daddy's name. I could, now, I guess freeze some before it's too late and find someone to carry my child one day down the line, but it wouldn't be...right. Because this isn't me. This isn't my body. Not yet.

I suppose there's my answer. It's not all for nothing. I'll tell the rest of the Glitter Squadron soon. I'm just not quite ready.

THE OPENING BARS OF "SOMEWHERE OVER THE RAINBOW" CHIME through the Glitter Mansion's front parlor. Esmeralda smiles, as she does every time their headquarters' doorbell rings, thinking of the heated battle and the resignation that finally led to the custom tone. Sapphire had rolled her eyes and called "Over the Rainbow" too cliché. Penny had argued for the 1960s *Batman* theme song, which Bunny pointed out would sound terrible with chimes. Starlight had pushed for the *Twilight Zone* theme, which led to Sapphire rightly asking, "How would that even work?" In the end, they'd drawn straws and Bunny had won. With a satisfied smirk, she'd had "Somewhere Over the Rainbow" installed.

Setting her magazine aside, Esmeralda unfolds herself from the couch, but Bunny is there ahead of her, waving her away.

"I've got it."

Esmeralda retrieves the magazine, but reading is pretense now. It's been a while since they had a case. She turns a page for show, listening to the low murmurs from the front door, while trying to surreptitiously keep an eye on the hall.

"We can talk in my office," Bunny says.

Esmeralda glances up as Bunny and the woman pass, and her stomach does a flip. The magazine slips from her hands. Her mother can't be here. It's impossible. She doesn't know about the Glitter Squadron. Can't know.

Neither Bunny nor the woman—who isn't Esmeralda's mother, of course she isn't—glance her way. Esmeralda lets them pass before letting out a breath, pulse still skittering. Biting her lip, she counts to ten, then creeps down the hall.

Bunny's office door is open just a sliver. Esmeralda peeks through, trying to get a better look. It isn't her mother, but the woman looks so similar she could almost be her mother's twin. The idea nags at the back of her mind, but Esmeralda can't make the pieces fit.

It isn't just the woman's looks. The woman's outfit reminds Esmeralda of the ones her grandmother brought back from Villahermosa for Esmeralda and her sister when they were little. The embroidery on the white cotton blouse and wide skirt is exquisite, and the woman's hair is woven around her head in tight braids like a crown, studded with bright red flowers.

Esmeralda stares at the woman, heavyset, who even looks to be about her own mother's age. The main difference is her brow, carefully cultivated to grow over the bridge of her nose, like a Frida Kahlo portrait come to life, and a faint shadow darkening her upper lip.

The truth hits Esmeralda all at once like a shock of cold water. The silver framed photograph from on top of her grandmother's piano;

the sound of glass shattering and hushed, angry words; the feel of the banister against her palms as Esmeralda and her sister peered down from the second floor, straining to hear.

"Oh." Esmeralda releases a breath; her hand isn't fast enough to stifle the sound.

Heels click as Bunny crosses the floor. Guilt freezes Esmeralda in place, so she's still standing there, gaping, when Bunny opens her office door all the way. The woman behind Bunny looks up, startled. Before Bunny can toss an accusation, before the woman can get a good look at her, Esmeralda flees.

When she's safe in her own room, Esmeralda sinks onto her bed. She should have apologized, but the dual shock of thinking her mother had found out about her life with the Glitter Squadron, and realizing who the woman in Bunny's office must really be...

Esmeralda opens one of the drawers under her bed, pushing scarves and belts aside until she finds the photograph tucked away at the bottom. She brushes her fingers across its surface. She snuck downstairs after her mother, grandmother, and sister had gone to bed, and retrieved the photograph from the trash under the sink. She'd never seen her grandmother and mother argue quite like that before, and she had to know. Touching the photograph now, she almost expects to find coffee grounds and the remnants of broken glass dusting her fingertips, but they come away clean.

The photograph is black and white, taken when her mother was only sixteen. The house in the background is Esmeralda's grandparents', the rear fin of her grandfather's Cadillac, his pride and joy, just visible at the left of the frame. A young man stands with his arm around her mother's shoulders. They're both wearing uniforms from their high school tennis team, her mother holding her racquet. They are both smiling, her mother's smile shy, awkward, like she isn't certain of her growing body yet, where the young man's smile is easy. Yet there's the faintest shadow, tucked into the corner of that smile, barely noticeable, except Esmeralda knows to look. The young man in the photograph—now the woman in Bunny's office—Mamá's brother.

Trying to reconcile the impossibility of the situation makes Esmeralda's pulse race all over again. Her mother's brother, the uncle she's never met—never even knew existed for the first several years of her life beyond cryptic whispers of "shameful behavior" quickly silenced whenever Esmeralda or her sister walked in the room—is right down the hall. Should she say something? Introduce herself?

The thought makes her palms sweat. What would she even say?

"Mind telling me what that was all about?"

Startled, Esmeralda drops the photograph. Bunny stands in the doorway, one hand on the knob, the other on her hip, brow arched, waiting. Sheepish, Esmeralda retrieves the brittle square, with her mother and uncle's faces staring up at her. She clutches the photograph hard.

"I think the woman you were talking to is my uncle. I mean, I'm not sure. I've never met him. Her."

"Whoa." Bunny's expression changes in a blink; she steps into the room.

Esmeralda makes space for her on the bed, handing over the photograph. "That's him with my mother when they were young."

Esmeralda studies Bunny's nails; it's easier than meeting her eyes. Today they're metallic violet, picking up the subtle hints of purple shimmering in Bunny's dress. Esmeralda can't help thinking of storm clouds.

"That's not what I was expecting. You wanna talk about it?"

"It's complicated," Esmeralda says.

"I have time." Bunny gives her the edge of a smile.

Esmeralda's known Bunny the longest of any member of the Glitter Squadron. In fact, she's known Bunny longer than almost anyone else in her life, besides family. After her parents' divorce, her mother moved them around so much there was never time to settle down, make friends. Putting down roots was dangerous; it was only a matter of time before they were ripped up again. But things are different, the Glitter Squadron, their mansion, this is home. She can trust Bunny with this tale.

"I didn't even know I had an uncle until I was ten," Esmeralda says.

Bunny pats her hand and gives her an encouraging smile. Esmeralda releases a breath that's shakier than she would like.

"When my parents got divorced, we stayed with my grandmother for a little while. It was supposed to make things easier on my mother while she took care of court stuff and finding us a new place to live. I think it made things worse though. They were both tense nearly the entire time we stayed there."

Looking back now, Esmeralda understands. She can't imagine living with her mother again at her age, going back home after having spent so many years building her own life. After a week, they'd be at each other's throats, and back then they'd lived with her grandmother for at least three months. The incident with the broken picture had taken place one of the first nights they'd been there.

"One night, my mother and grandmother got into a big fight. My sister and I hid upstairs, trying to listen in, and I saw my mother take one of my grandmother's photographs and deliberately smash it."

Esmeralda picks up the photograph lying on the bed between them. This time, she focuses not on her uncle, but the girl beside him, her mother. Both siblings squint in the sunlight, her mother all knobby knees and elbows with none of the soft roundness she has now, still growing into her body. It's her eyes that strike Esmeralda, unshadowed, unlined, so free of the cares that have filled them all of Esmeralda's life.

"I couldn't ask my mother or grandmother about it of course. But I got the whole story later from family friends."

Esmeralda sets the photograph down again, remembering the almost gleeful expression of her grandmother's two oldest friends, taking turns to relate the story after a few glasses of sherry. They'd told it as if they were discussing characters in a telenovela, and not real people's heartbreak and pain.

"Eduardo was…is…barely a year older than my mother. My grandfather wanted him to take over the family tailoring business, but he wasn't interested. He dropped out of school and traveled, picking up odd jobs, making just enough to get to his next destination. There were postcards, occasional visits home, just enough contact that everyone assumed he would settle down eventually. Then one day he turned up out of the blue and announced he was moving back to Mexico, to Juchitán in Oaxaca to live as a muxe."

Esmeralda pauses, taking a deep breath, looking at Bunny without fully raising her head. "In Zapotec culture it isn't..." She falters, then tries again. "Muxes are a third gender, fluid—not male or female. They simply are."

Bunny keeps her hand on Esmeralda's.

"There are some parts of Mexico City that are as accepting as Juchitán, at least now, but not when my grandfather grew up. He was very traditional. His idea of Mexican life was very different from the traditions and culture in Juchitán. When my uncle chose to leave, my grandfather saw it as more than just a man choosing an unnatural lifestyle, going against God, he saw it as Eduardo renouncing his family and his culture.

"He took Eduardo's choice personally, told him he was no longer part of the family, and if he ever tried to come home, he would be treated as an intruder. My grandfather would call the police and have him thrown in jail."

Bunny's fingers tighten, an involuntary motion. Esmeralda shrugs, apologizing for a man she's never met, but whose blood flows in her veins.

"My grandmother's friends, the ones who told me the story, said he would never admit it, but Eduardo leaving broke my grandfather's heart. I never knew him but they said he was a proud man, stubborn, but family meant everything to him. At the time Eduardo left my grandfather was very sick. He'd been hiding it from the family, and he died less than a year after Eduardo left. I think my mother blamed Eduardo for their father's death. She never forgave him."

"That's some heavy stuff," Bunny says, gaze distant for a moment, frown tugging at the corners of her mouth.

Esmeralda knows that Bunny hasn't spoken to her own family in years. For all she knows Bunny could have a niece or a nephew out there somewhere. She can imagine that person seeing Bunny walking down the street one day and feeling the way Esmeralda feels now.

Even though she knows it isn't the same, Esmeralda understands how Bunny must feel, how her uncle must feel. Esmeralda talks to her mother, but she's never said one word about the Glitter Squadron. Her mother thinks Esmeralda is just an accountant, that her day job is her life, not the identity she pulls on like a sweater to hide her true self. If it *had* been her mother in Bunny's office, and not her uncle, what would she have done?

"So what did Eduardo want?"

"Well." Bunny stands, taking up what Esmeralda has come to think of as her battle pose, legs braced akimbo, chin up, body tense and ready for motion. Maybe it's all the talk of family, but Bunny seems more agitated than the situation requires. There is a quiver beneath her skin; all she needs is an excuse to take something down with her harpoon.

"There's a situation with a church in your…your uncle's community. Some construction work woke something. Now the church is haunted. Haunted galore: statues weeping blood; flickering lights; unearthly wailing. The whole shebang."

"Perhaps it's a miracle?" The response leaps to Esmeralda's lips before she can stop it, tasting of bile the minute it hits her tongue. "Sorry." Esmeralda looks down, abashed. She can almost feel rosary beads passing through her fingers—penance for backtalk, for anything Mamá or the sisters at an interminable succession of Catholic schools considered unladylike. For blasphemy like this, Esmeralda might have had her backside striped by a ruler.

"So a ghost." She sighs. "Why did she come to us? We fight the corporeal, if not exactly the normal."

"We *do* have a reputation." Bunny grins. "Not just for saving the world, but…I mean, look at us." With a smooth gesture, she shows off her glorious curves, the light glinting off her dress, the frosted coif of her hair.

"Point taken." Esmeralda returns the smile, but there's a painful edge in it. It feels like holding a piece of broken glass in her mouth, trying not to get cut. There's so much more she wants to ask Bunny about Eduardo, jealous of even their brief interaction. With all the moving they did, family is the only thing Esmeralda has ever had to root her, but at the same time she has so little in common with hers. Eduardo might actually understand her.

Has he ever even see a picture of her, or her sister? Did he try to come to her grandmother's funeral?

Bunny touches her shoulder, startling her. "You were a million miles away there."

"Family."

"I understand." Pain flickers in Bunny's eyes so briefly Esmeralda almost misses it—a ghost beneath Bunny's skin darting close to the surface before disappearing again.

"I told Eduardo to come back tomorrow. At ten." Bunny leaves the words there, pointed, before gently closing Esmeralda's door behind her.

★

Esmeralda knocks before entering the parlor.

"Hi. Um. Hello."

Eduardo turns from studying the glamour shots, publicity photos, and framed press clippings from the Glitter Squadron's many exploits that decorate the wall. She clutches a beaded handbag close as her eyes light on Esmeralda, wary. Her outfit today is every bit as beautiful as the one she wore yesterday. Esmeralda admires the intricate stitching, the crisp way her skirt falls—evidence it's been freshly pressed.

"Bunny will be along in a moment. But I wanted to talk with you."

Esmeralda hesitates. She can't shake the feeling that it *is* her mother standing in front of her, and her heart pounds. She's tried so many times to tell her mother about the Glitter Squadron. It's been on the tip of her tongue, but she chickens out every time, and every time she does, it hurts. She can imagine Mamá's judgment, the way she would look at Esmeralda if she knew where her daughter was—who she was talking to—right now. Esmeralda's stomach clenches, but she forces herself to smile.

"Please, sit. Can I get you anything? Tea? Water?"

"I'm fine, thank you." Eduardo sits. The wariness hasn't left his eyes; faint lines surround them, a map, tracing his life's pain.

Esmeralda tries to reconcile the woman in front of her with the smiling youth in the picture.

"My name is Esmeralda." She holds her breath, waiting for a flicker of recognition. But, of course, if Eduardo knows of her at all, it would be by the name on her birth certificate. "Here." She thrusts the photograph toward him, only considering a moment too late that it might be cruel.

Eduardo stares at the picture in her hand, but doesn't touch it, knuckles white where she grips her handbag. "Where did you get that?" Eduardo's eyes narrow.

The impulse to flee is strong but she forces herself to stay put. Eduardo's expression changes from suspicion to alarm, then she relaxes just a fraction, looking at Esmeralda more closely. Does she see traces of her sister, her mother, even her father in Esmeralda's eyes, the tilt of her chin? "Silvia is my mother," Esmeralda says. "My grandmother is Sofia."

"You're…?" Eduardo doesn't finish the sentence.

"I'm your niece."

Esmeralda's throat tightens. Her eyes prickle, and all she can think is how Bunny will chide her for ruining her make-up if she cries. Esmeralda puts her hand to her mouth, blinking until the tears retreat. "I'm sorry. I made a mess of that. I meant to…" She shakes her head.

"You look like her." Eduardo's voice breaks, dropping a tone, heavy with emotion.

Eduardo stands. It startles her to realize she's taller than her uncle.

"Let me look at you."

Esmeralda can't help laughing, a broken sound that is almost a sob. She half expects Eduardo to pinch her cheeks, but she only touches the air around Esmeralda's shoulders, her arms, taking the shape of her without contact. There's admiration in her eyes, but they're crowded with ghosts, too. There's so much Esmeralda wants to ask, but she barely knows where to start.

"Do I have cousins?" The moment she says it, Esmeralda is afraid it's the wrong thing to say. The look of regret in Eduardo's eyes in unmistakable.

"No." But the softness in her tone forgives the question, and a bittersweet smile touches her lips. "I was married for a little while. Her name was Isabel. But it didn't work out."

"You have a great-nephew," Esmeralda says. "My sister's son. I brought a picture." She holds it out, shy—her sister and her nephew on the very same beach where, a day later, she would meet Bunny.

This picture, Eduardo does take, studying it a moment before handing it back. The sorrow-touched smile returns, but there's something like fondness in her eyes. Esmeralda wishes she was better at this, wishes she knew what to say. She falls back on business.

"Bunny told me about the church—."

"You'll help?" The hope in Eduardo's eyes is heartbreaking.

Esmeralda takes a risk and squeezes her uncle's hand. "It's what family does."

BUNNY KNOCKS SOFTLY, AND ESMERALDA LOOKS UP. SHE'S BEEN sitting on her bed with her knees tucked up, her e-reader propped against them. She's read the same paragraph at least five times.

"Want some company?" Bunny holds a large bottle of Pinot grigio and two glasses etched with shooting stars.

"Thanks." Esmeralda smoothes the blankets and pushes pillows out of the way.

Bunny pours for both of them and hands Esmeralda a glass. "How are you doing?"

"Okay. I guess. It's a lot." Esmeralda swirls her glass before taking a sip.

"Have you spoken to your mother yet?"

"No. And I don't plan to. Not unless Eduardo asks me to, that is." Esmeralda presses her lips together. They're silent for a moment, then Esmeralda shakes her head.

"It's funny. I was thinking about the mission, and I can't even remember the last time I was in a church."

"Raised Catholic?"

"Communion, confirmation, the whole thing. My mother and I had a big fight about it when I was fifteen. I told her I didn't want to go to church anymore, and she said as long as I lived under her roof I would go and that was the end of it."

Esmeralda feels the familiar surge of guilt at talking to Bunny about her family. Esmeralda talks to her sister almost every day, but even she doesn't know about the Glitter Squadron for fear it will get back to their mother. More and more, Esmeralda feels the gap; only part of her is with her family when she's with them. The rest is with the Glitter Squadron. It feels dishonest and worse, it makes her feel fractured. If she continues to pull in opposite directions, something will break.

"I envy Starlight sometimes." Esmeralda takes another sip of her wine. "I know it sounds like a horrible thing to say, what with her mama being so sick, but they're so close. They share everything, you know?"

Bunny nods, refilling both of their glasses without a word. She twists the bottle to ensure not a single lost drop.

"Sometimes I think the only reason I stopped going to church when I left for college was to spite my mother, and I don't even know why. Maybe it was a belated teenage rebellion thing. I remember thinking how stupid my mother must be to believe in God. It seemed so clearly like a myth to me, and I actually pitied her."

Esmeralda shakes her head. Bunny offers a small smile.

"Teenagers," Bunny says. "We always think we know everything at that age."

"It's embarrassing. I mean how arrogant do you have be to think you have everything figured out? But it's weird." Esmeralda pauses. "I mean, we've fought aliens and werewolves. I've seen how big and strange the universe is, but I still can't help thinking my mother's beliefs are wrong. Does that make me a horrible person?"

Bunny reaches out, covering Esmeralda's hand briefly. "Just because her beliefs are fine for her doesn't mean they're right for you. Have you ever told her you've fought wolfweres?"

Esmeralda snorts. "I thought they were were*wolves*."

Bunny's smile widens. "Oh, honey, they were pure Tex Avery wolves who thought they were man enough to take on the Squadron. Poor things."

Bunny pats Esmeralda's hand again. "There, see, all you needed was a little wine to cheer you up. One more glass, and you'll be right as rain and ready for the mission."

"Sure." Esmeralda makes herself smile, wishing the confidence she tries to convey with the expression was real. Bunny always knows the right thing to say, but Esmeralda still can't quite shake the doubt gnawing at the back of her mind.

★

THIS IS ESMERALDA, AND SHE HAS NEVER FELT STRONGER OR MORE foolish in her entire life. The sweat and metaphorical dust of the road—a plane journey in reality—sluiced off in the shower, her skin shed and applied anew, she is a warrior.

Five foot six standing flat, she is nearly five nine in platform boots patterned subtly with scales but almost entirely hidden under the gleam of her green, flared, body-hugging jumpsuit. She is a seventies wet dream—low slung gold belt circling her hips, neckline cut practically to meet it, arms bared, dark hair teased into a soft cloud framing her face, and peacock feathers trailing away from the corners of her eyes, which are lined in shimmering beetle-green and gold.

As strong as she is right now, as ready as she is for battle, she can't shake her nerves. She has the sudden feeling that her whole life has been about playing dress-up—adopting the trappings of her mother's religion, then slipping into the clothing of rebellion and atheism. In her mother's neighborhoods, she was too white. In her father's, too Latina. A whole lifetime of trying to blend, trying to fit in. What if that's still what she's doing now?

The other members of the Glitter Squadron are goddesses. Esmeralda is a woman who took a walk on the beach one day and found herself face-to-face with a sea monster, handing an Amazon a high-heeled shoe as a weapon.

Bunny squeezes Esmeralda's arm, bringing her back. "This is your show. We'll follow your lead."

Esmeralda breathes out. Bunny believes in her, and aside from Bunny, she has the most experience on this team. She can do this.

Esmeralda forces herself to put one chunky, glittering heel in front of one chunky glittering toe and keep going until she reaches the church door. She isn't a girl playing dress-up; she is a member of the best, most bad-ass team in the world. She's faced eels from outer-space, beach-blanket vampires in bikinis, and wolves in tuxedos. Ghosts should be a piece of carrot cake.

Cold radiates from the wrought-iron handles set in the church's wooden doors despite the heat of day. There are watchful eyes from some of the buildings surrounding the church, but otherwise the Glitter Squadron is alone.

Esmeralda half expects frost to spread across her palm as she touches the handle. It's not just the cold, the whole building feels wrong. It doesn't match the architecture of the streets around it. It looks like it was picked up and dropped here from another place, which in a way, it was. On the plane Eduardo told them about the British lord who built the church, mashing up styles, and filling it with stolen treasures from all around the world.

The illusion of out-of-placeness is only deepened by the construction equipment huddled nearby, even though they're only tearing up the neighboring lot, not the church itself.

Esmeralda takes a deep breath and yanks open the door. Despite the chill in the handle, the inside of the church is almost warm, humid. It's also green, like being underwater, and ripples of light play across the walls and the ceiling reflected from some non-existent pool. *Drowned*; the word drags damp fingers up Esmeralda's spine.

Her heels echo on the floor; Bunny, Penny, and Starlight follow behind her. She can almost hear the breaths they aren't taking, the reverent hush. Inside the lack of sound, there's an eerie sense of a fifth source of held breath.

Esmeralda walks the aisle toward the altar. Statues in niches line the sanctuary, Catholic saints whose names she cannot remember. Where they've wept, rust-colored stains mar their cheeks and their robes.

In contrast to the saints, tiles that look like they were uprooted from a mosque are embedded in the floor between the pews. There's Hebrew writing carved into the walls, and bits of bas-relief sculpture that look like they could be Sumerian.

The effect of all the belief embedded in the objects jumbled into the church makes Esmeralda's head buzz. Her knees threaten to buckle. Ingrained memory tells her to kneel, to pray.

Esmeralda's breath catches. The hush, the stone eyes of the saints on her, the painted crucifix—they stir something deep inside her. Her mother's faith isn't her own, but there's still a wanting inside her. Esmeralda wants to believe in something larger than herself. She wants the Glitter Squadron, her chosen family, to fit together with her blood family.

Esmeralda sinks to her knees in front of the communion rail, the wood worn smooth. It stops the trembling in her legs, even though the padding in front of the rail has long since rotted away.

"Are you okay?" Penny is at her side.

Esmeralda nods, neck stiff. It's a moment before she can get her voice to work, and even so the church tries to swallow it. Cold-damp seeps up through the tiles into her knees. The weight of the space presses down on her.

"I have to do this."

Doubt flickers in Penny's eyes, but she steps back. To Esmeralda's surprise, Starlight kneels beside her, licking her lips, looking frightened as a doe. She gives Esmeralda a tentative smile, and Esmeralda manages one in return. Penny and Bunny hang back.

Esmeralda bows her head, and closes her eyes. She almost wishes for her mother's rosary, the smooth beads to pass through her hands and calm her. The words of a prayer come to her lips with surprising ease. She shuts out everything—the watery light, the damp chill rising through her, the sense of held breath, waiting.

It's not as much a prayer as an apology. As the words flow through her, she focuses on memories of sitting next to her mother in an uncomfortable church pew, trying not to fidget in her stiff, itchy Sunday clothes, listening to the priest drone, and wishing to be anywhere else in the world. She tries to remember exactly how her mamá looked—tense walking into the church, but relaxing over the course of the sermon. Her mother's faith helped her when she had nothing else, starting over again, building a new life for herself and her daughters.

Is it really that different than Esmeralda and the Glitter Squadron hanging out after-hours on Exclusively Lime Green's roof deck, testing out Sapphire's latest alcoholic concoctions? Her family, chosen and blood—Esmeralda imagines fitting them together like pieces of a puzzle. The knot of fear inside her loosens. She is big enough to hold both truths inside her and the knowledge calms her, letting her focus on the task at hand.

Esmeralda opens her eyes, rising. Starlight glances at her uncertainly, standing as well. She's about to speak when the calm is shattered by an unearthly shriek filling the air, followed by a terrible grinding as one of the statues turns on its base. A fresh line of blood runs from between its clasped palms.

Starlight ducks, clapping her hands over her ears at the noise. Penny's hand goes to her gun, but Esmeralda gestures her back.

"My name is..." She hesitates, taking a deep breath. "I was born Christina Joanne Garcia Layton. My *name* is Esmeralda. These are my friends. We're here to help you. We only want to talk."

The shriek drops to a growl, a terrifying sound Esmeralda feels in her bones. One of the statues falls over with a crash, and Esmeralda jumps. The whole church shudders, stained glass shivering in the windows.

The temperature drops. Water-stained Bibles and hymn books on the edge of decay fly from the back of the pews, pages flapping like torn wings. Esmeralda's mind races, grasping for anything about demons, exorcism, but all she comes up with is Linda Blair's head spinning and pea soup.

"Stop it," Esmeralda shouts. "You can't scare us off. We're not going anywhere until you talk to us."

The wailing stops abruptly. The light shifts, blue-green, warm and cold. A figure appears behind the altar.

Esmeralda bites back a scream. The word *drowned* pushes into her thoughts again, but the thing looks dried, like a mummy—leathery flesh tied around stick-like bones. Cords of wet hair hang down to its feet, pooling water on the tile floor.

Penny's 9 mm is out, aimed. "Shit!"

Esmeralda steps forward instead of back, eyes on the thing behind the altar. "No!"

The thing shrieks, fury and pain. The glass in the windows trembles, on the point of shattering. The Bibles and hymn books thump to the ground all at once.

Esmeralda acts on blind instinct, reaching for the creature's stick-thin wrist. She expects her hands to sink through the horrid flesh, to have it crumble like dust. But her fingers close. The creature yanks backward, but Esmeralda doesn't let go. All the statues turn to face her now, eyes weeping sticky, red tears. A sob builds in Esmeralda's chest, but she tightens her grip.

Images wash over her—not quite words or pictures—but fragments of both. Limbs bound, dark brackish water, and the stumps of trees. A body marked with ritual scarring, and clothed in fine linens and beads, the holy and profane.

Esmeralda steps back, nearly falling. Bunny is there to catch her. The creature sways, wails—not rage this time, but a soft, keening sound.

"She's just a child," Esmeralda says. "They hurt her. There was some kind of ritual, a binding to keep her body and her soul trapped together as they sacrificed her to make her into a little god."

She takes a deep shuddering breath and risks another glance at the creature. It regards her with eyeless eyes, pain and fear rolling off it in waves. Esmeralda sorts through the jumble of images and emotions, trying to put them into words.

"They drowned her, and they buried her, and she felt everything. It was like sleeping, only she couldn't wake up. Her dreams were meant to protect her people, but sometimes she had nightmares.

"People used to leave offerings where she was buried. But they died off or drifted away. They forgot, and she was alone for a very long time until a man dug up her bones, stole her and took her a long way from home. She was afraid. She tried to talk to him, but he thought she was a demon, so he buried her under a church. She slept for such a long time, hiding from the pain, but then there was noise digging into her dreams, waking her up."

"The bulldozers tearing up the yard," Starlight says.

Cheeks wet with tears, Esmeralda takes a wobbly step toward the creature. No, the child. She feels hollow and wrung out, frightened, but she goes to the girl and folds the child in her arms. At first the girl recoils, but Esmeralda tightens her grip.

She strokes the damp hair, fighting revulsion and the feeling of bones scarce-wrapped in skin.

She thinks of her nephew, and does the only thing that makes sense to her in this moment—low and sweet, she sings a lullaby. The memory of her mother's hand brushes her forehead, soothing her fever as a child; the memory of her grandmother, humming the same tune as she cooked, a faraway look in her eyes.

Esmeralda presses her face into the dead stringy hair, ignoring the scent of water and earth and rot, and weeps. "No one is going to hurt you anymore," she whispers. "You're safe here. You're with…family."

She doesn't know how much time has passed, but when Esmeralda opens her eyes again, the light in the church has shifted to a pale gold. It no longer looks drowned. Bunny and Starlight have their arms around her, and she's shaking.

"I'm okay," she manages, but her throat feels raw.

"You really scared us for a second there," Bunny says; a hint of moisture dews her perfect lashes, and she blinks it away. Esmeralda smiles.

Her arms are empty, and she feels a brief ache for the space where the bones of the terrible drowned thing nestled against her.

"What happened to—"

"It vanished," Starlight says.

"She. She has...had a name." Esmeralda says. "Once."

The others exchange a glance, but say nothing.

Esmeralda draws herself up. "We need to talk to my uncle and her community and convince them to accept the child as part of their family."

Esmeralda squints against the sunlight; with her eyes half-closed, the church looks almost lovely, peaceful, despite its decay. "What did the members of the historic society say?"

"Most of them were surprisingly open to the idea of adopting a ghost child." Half of Eduardo's mouth rises in a smile. "They've been caring for the church for years, trying to raise enough money to restore it and turn it into a proper museum. If the ghost is part of the church, they'll care for her too."

They stand in silence for a moment, looking at the church, and the shadow of construction equipment falling across it. Eduardo will do the best she can for the dead girl, Esmeralda knows that. She only hopes it will be enough.

"When I first moved to Juchitán," Eduardo says. "I didn't know anyone. My father didn't want anything to do with me and I'd resigned myself to the idea that I would never go home again. I starting thinking of myself as a ghost, and thinking of my new home as the City of the Dead."

Eduardo turns away from the church, and Esmeralda has to hurry to keep up, despite Eduardo's shorter legs and her longer skirts.

"It's what I wanted, I was living *my* life, but it was still lonely. Then I started to get to know people—muxe who had been living here their whole lives, their families, their neighbors and friends. I reached out to people I'd met while traveling, people who felt like they didn't fit in their communities, weren't accepted for who they were for whatever reason. I told them this was a place they could call home."

Eduardo casts a glance at her, and Esmeralda's heart turns over, thinking of Bunny and the Glitter Squadron. Her uncle built a community, not just one house, but a whole neighborhood of like-minded people finding each other. She wonders about the other people living here, divided between the home of their birth, and the home of their hearts. She wonders if it ever stops hurting.

"A lot of people living here felt the same way I did when I first moved. We couldn't go back. Like your ghost."

"Except she didn't have a choice," Esmeralda says.

Eduardo turns, her expression heavy, weighted with memory, but transitioning to a sorrow-touched smile. "We'll make your ghost feel welcome as best as we can. She can find a new family here the way we all found ours."

Eduardo reaches out a hand to Esmeralda; her fingers are thick and blunt, her skin rough, but her grip is warm and strong. Esmeralda squeezes back.

"New lives seemed like a good excuse to begin our own new traditions. We started celebrating our deaths and rebirths by holding our own Day of the Dead celebrations whenever someone new joined our community. I think it would be appropriate to hold one tonight, for *her*, don't you think?"

Eduardo pauses, her expression a blend of reticence, hope, regret. "If you want to…I mean, I know you're all very busy and…"

"No, no." Esmeralda squeezes her uncle's hand, trying to calm the erratic beat of her heart. "Of course we'll stay."

Esmeralda does her best to ignore the echoes of her mother in her uncle's face.

She looks down, afraid to mention her mother's name and reopen Eduardo's old wounds. Eduardo returns the pressure of fingers against her hand, as if reading her thoughts, and Esmeralda feels a rush of gratitude.

"We would love to celebrate with you," she says, and for the first time since meeting her uncle, Esmeralda allows herself a genuine smile.

THE NIGHT IS WARM BUT NOT HUMID. OF COURSE, THE GLITTER Squadron is dressed to the nines. Bunny wears white, one shoulder bare, her skirt falling in gossamer layers so she looks like a delicate flower turned upside down. She is radiant and the absolute center of attention of the small knot of admirers gathered around her. Esmeralda would expect no less, and the sight makes her smile.

Starlight wears a pink dress with a knee-length skirt and an empire waist sewn with tiny rosebuds. She wears a pink bow, holding her hair in a high ponytail, but from the way she fidgets with the ends, twirling them around and around her fingers, it looks like she wants to pull the strands over her face and hide.

"You look beautiful." Esmeralda gives Starlight's arm a reassuring pat. "Go make some new friends. I promise they won't bite."

Starlight blushes.

Esmeralda's smile widens. "I'll rescue you if you look like you're in trouble. Now go." She gives Starlight a nudge, and reluctantly, Starlight obeys.

Penny is the one that surprises Esmeralda the most, having allowed Eduardo to give her a makeover. She wears an elaborate Chiapas-style dress, thickly embroidered with flowers in silken thread, her copper hair braided into a blossom-studded crown. Esmeralda wonders if the outfit appeals to Penny because the wide skirt provides so many places to hide her weapons.

Music spills over the gathering, and the air is heavy with the scent of food. Candy sugar skulls and marigolds decorate the long table, between plates heaped with tamales and turkey and elaborate braided loaves of egg bread. Everything is lit with colored paper lanterns and candles, giving the whole gathering a soft, surreal glow.

A muxe roughly Eduardo's age is dressed as Catarina, the queen of the celebration, holding court at one end of the long table. Men and women and muxe fill the rest of the seats, Zapotec and American, people from here and from around the world, gathered by Eduardo on her travels. Children dart around the outskirts of the party. A brief flicker, and Esmeralda thinks she catches sight of her ghost girl running with them, but when she turns her head the glimmer is gone.

After everyone has eaten their fill, the tables are abandoned in favor of an impromptu dance floor, and the musicians step up their playing a notch. Esmeralda watches Bunny whirled onto the dance floor by a succession of partners. Starlight shyly follows a beautiful young man, allowing him to lead her through the steps of a dance. Penny stands on the periphery, arms crossed, watchful, but even she wears the edge of a smile.

Esmeralda joins in a few of the dances, trying to remember the steps her grandmother taught her, getting it hopelessly wrong, and laughing. She dances once with her uncle, and once with Bunny, but always she returns to the edges of the celebration. She's warm and full of good food, and she can't remember the last time she felt this comfortable with people she barely knows. Yet her heart still hurts. Surrounded by friends, new and old, she is lonely.

"Homesick?" Eduardo slips up beside her.

"That's the word." Guilt needles her, she should be happy, blessed with all this love, but she can't quite shake the restlessness.

"I know the feeling."

"Is there a phone I could use somewhere? I'll pay for the long-distance charges."

The way Eduardo looks at her reminds Esmeralda so much of her mother. They have the same eyes, and Eduardo's are so full of kindness that Esmeralda can't help being hopeful. Family is family after all. Eduardo gestures to a nearby house owned by one of the people at the party, and Esmeralda slips inside.

The strains of music follow her, fading away to be replaced by the thump of her heart. Esmeralda finds the phone, but still hesitates before lifting the old-fashioned plastic receiver. She dials before she can change her mind, pressing the phone to her ear and closing her eyes. On the third ring, her mother answers. Esmeralda has to swallow hard before she get out even the simplest words.

"Hi, Mamá. It's…Christina." She grips the phone harder, wiping away a silent tear before answering her mother's question. "Mamá, everything is fine. I just wanted to talk." Really talk, this time, Esmeralda thinks. "I missed you, and I wanted to talk, that's all."

Persephone's Kiss

1 oz vodka

1 oz PAMA liqueur

1 oz pomegranate juice

1 tbsp honey (heated to soften)

Pinch of chili powder

Combine all ingredients in a cocktail shaker filled with ice. Shake well, and pour into a chilled martini glass.

Despite her name and the color of her outfits, I've always associated Esmeralda with red, even more than Ruby. It's a secret red, deep and hidden, like a jewel at her heart. Besides, after that spooky shit with the church in Mexico—Starlight told me all about it—it seems fitting. Esmeralda went into the land of the dead and brought her uncle back home. Okay, I know that isn't quite Persephone's story, but it seems apt—death and family and all. Esmeralda didn't lose her uncle like Orpheus lost Eurydice. She found her. She's even trying to organize a reunion between her mother and her uncle. What I wouldn't give to be a fly on that wall! Not that I'm hoping for disaster. I think it's sweet. I'm happy for Es. We're her family, but her family is her family too, you know? We all have to find our place in the world. I'm glad she found hers.

THE ULTRA FABULOUS GLITTER SQUADRON SAVES THE WORLD AGAIN

OR THE GREAT G-STRING MEN TEAM UP EXTRAVAGANZA

THE ABANDONED FACTORY LOOMS BEHIND BUNNY, FRAMING HER AS she takes up her battle pose and looks at each of them in turn, a leader sizing up her troops.

"Penny, you and Esmeralda go through the right entrance. Sapphire and Ruby, to the left. CeCe, you stick with Silk and keep an eye on the perimeter. Starlight and I will go in head-on. Everyone got it?"

Three pairs of heads nod at Bunny, standing in the center of the semicircle they've formed in front of her. Only M doesn't nod, arms crossed, standing outside the Glitter Squadron huddle. As the group breaks, M slips away, disappearing into the shadows of the ruined building.

Starlight presses against Bunny's side as they approach the abandoned factory's front door.

"Sweetie, you're tangling my spangles," Bunny says.

Starlight pulls the glittering ropes of her dress free, and gives Bunny more space. Es has been teaching her how to sew. She'd thought it would be fun, trying to recreate one of Bunny's outfits, but now she feels a little silly. They're twins in shimmering silver flapper dresses and laced up go-go boots, 'twenties glam and 'sixties swing mashed into one. Bunny's trademark ears and her harpoon set them apart, but still—it's no wonder the other members of the Glitter Squadron think of her as Bunny's little shadow.

After Mars and Machu Picchu and the thing with the gargoyles in Texas, she should be one of them, all sequins and poise. But sometimes she's afraid they still see her as the frightened girl who could barely do her own make-up, knock-kneed in her roller skates, and cowering in front of a trio of space eels. She's grown up so much since then; not just a roller girl anymore, but a glamorous roller woman.

Gathering herself, Starlight moves slightly ahead of Bunny, picking her way over the shattered bricks and debris littering the factory floor. Bunny glances at her askance but says nothing, and Starlight continues on, steps precise. She squares her shoulders, chin up, as if the smashed-out windows and the shadow-haunted corners don't bother her.

Starlight assesses their surroundings, then clicks on her flashlight, playing the beam over the abandoned machinery hulking around them—primordial bones, pulled up from the depths of tar pits and put on display. She turns her beam toward the far corner, illuminating a fall of debris spilled from a hole in the ceiling.

As her light touches the ragged hole in the floor above, something creaks, and despite herself, Starlight jumps. Her pulse punches against her skin, but she takes a deep breath, keeping the beam of her light steady. It's only one of the other members of the Glitter Squadron, it has to be.

Even though they know better than to make a sound. Something skitters over her foot, and she swallows a scream.

Her flashlight beam jerks, an involuntary reaction. The edge of the light catches a shadow slipping away, leaving an impression of something unnaturally large, with too many legs, and something like horns.

"What..."

Bunny elbows her for silence. "Lights off."

Starlight swallows, but obeys. As her eyes adjust to the fresh darkness, there's another sound. A chirr of wings. A flash, followed a split second later by the bark of Penny's gun. Instinctively, Starlight falls back as Bunny moves forward, harpoon loose and ready in her hand. Penny fires again and there's a crash, the sound caroming off the factory's empty spaces.

A shape darts past her, close enough to touch. Starlight whirls, trying to follow the motion and a sound like pebbles across the skin of a drum. As she tries to orient herself, someone crashes into her. Hard. Starlight goes over in a tangle of limbs, the flashlight knocked from her hand and landing with a faint crunch beyond her reach.

She flails, and hands flail back. Hands, skin, human flesh. A lot of it. Starlight twists, getting her feet under her. "Get off!"

Before she can deal with the person who landed on top of her, a beetle the size of its namesake car barrels toward her. Its carapace is crimson and spotted with Rorschach black splotches.

She scrambles to stand as panic flows through her veins. She braces for impact, bereft of even the flashlight to defend herself. Starlight doesn't like guns, but right now, she wishes she'd let Penny talk her into borrowing one of her weapons after all.

"Behind me!" Penny appears, yanking Starlight back and firing.

CeCe and Silk rush in from outside, drawn by the noise, just as Bunny vaults over a fall of debris. She drives the point of her harpoon into the giant bug, slowed but not stopped by Penny's bullets. The beetle's wings clatter, a warning sound. Bunny wrenches her harpoon free, readying it for another blow when something whistles through the air.

Bunny jerks as a stone cracks against the beetle's shell. The creature spins toward the new threat at the same moment as something else flies out of the dark. A boomerang.

"What?" Penny says.

A second stone whistles through the air, bouncing harmlessly off the beetle's carapace. This time Starlight tracks its source, and her mouth drops open. A man with a sling dangling from one hand drops with an athletic grace from atop one of the broken machines. He's barefoot. In fact he's naked except for a leopard print g-string.

Starlight finally turns to see the man who collided with her, undressed almost identically, except his g-string is a green that pure jade would envy. Dust coats his dark, oiled skin. A third man appears, retrieving the boomerang. His g-string is silver, the color of shark skin.

For a moment, everything stills, fabulous women and scantily clad men blinking at each other in confusion. Then the beetle rattles its wings, and time lurches forward again. Bunny stabs her harpoon into the point where the beetle's head meets its red, armored shell.

There's a sickening crunch and Starlight turns away. When she looks back, Bunny is pulling her harpoon free, standing atop the conquered beetle. Everything about her stance is a challenge; her grip on the harpoon no more relaxed now that the immediate threat has passed. She brushes a strand of frosted blonde hair out of her face, and fixes her gaze on the man in the leopard-print g-string. Only now his tiny undergarment is tiger striped. Starlight blinks. Did she only imagine the spots before?

"Just who the fuck are you supposed to be?"

"We could ask you the same thing." It's the man with the boomerang who answers, Australian accent and all.

"None of your fucking business, that's who." Penny moves closer to Bunny, pistol still drawn.

"Ladies." Sapphire approaches holding up her hands, then glances at the three near-naked men. "Gentlemen. Let's all be civil here. None of us are covered in chitin, so I'm going to go out on a limb and say that puts us on the same side."

Penny sets her jaw, keeping her stance hard, but Bunny steps down from atop the beetle's carapace.

"That's better." Sapphire flashes a charming smile. "Now, let's start again. We're the Ultra Fabulous Glitter Squadron. Enchanted to meet you, I'm sure."

"We're the G-String Men." A fourth man emerges, posture relaxed as though he's out for a mid-day stroll, not in an abandoned factory fighting a giant beetle. His hair is a sun-bleached surfer's tangle, his skin tanned to match. "Exotic dancers by day, world-saving heroes by night." He punctuates the words with a thrust of his bedazzled crotch. "Though sometimes it's the other way around."

A bottle spins away from his foot as he approaches Bunny. Without asking permission, he lifts Bunny's perfectly manicured hand, and touches his lips to her knuckles. Starlight flinches, ready for Bunny to tear him apart, but for the first time in Starlight's recollection, their unflappable leader is too stunned to react immediately. Not that Starlight blames her. The incongruity of the whole thing, and the idea of saving the world in nothing more than a glittering g-string. It's ridiculous.

"Name's Zack," the man says. "But no one calls me that. I'm the Big Kahuna."

He scans the other members of the Glitter Squadron, tossing a wink at Starlight. Heat rises to her cheeks, and she looks away.

"It would be my honor to give you ladies free tickets to our next show."

"We're not interested in that right now." Penny's voice cuts across the stunned silence. She kicks the beetle with the side of her boot before getting right in Big Kahuna's face. "What do you know about this thing?"

Kahuna's expression doesn't change, which only makes Penny's nostrils flare. Her fingers twitch, but Bunny steps in smoothly, drawing their attention.

"Any knowledge you can share would be helpful. We should pool our resources." Despite her disarming smile, it's clear she's still poised for a fight.

"Suits me." Kahuna shrugs.

"Lovely." Bunny's smile doesn't touch her eyes. "If you'd care to follow us, we can talk more comfortably at our headquarters."

Penny frowns, but keeps silent. Ruby and Sapphire exchange glances, like true twins, communicating volumes without speaking. When no one raises an objection, Bunny nods once, satisfied, and moves toward the door. A line of glittering women and scantily-clad men falls in behind her.

At the door, Starlight glances over her shoulder just in time to see M coalesce from the shadows. Moving cat-silent, M crouches by the fallen beetle. One leather-clad finger dips into the mess of the beetle's head before it is touched to M's lips. Starlight turns away but not fast enough to avoid seeing M shudder, not entirely in revulsion. Not fast enough to avoid the sickening mirrored response from her own body. She runs toward Bunny, hurrying to catch up.

Bunny reads the mood in the parlor. CeCe and Silk stand together in the far corner, CeCe ever so slightly in front of her new wife. Sapphire and Ruby occupy the opposite corner, Ruby worrying her lower lip with her teeth, Sapphire with her chin up and shoulders back, deliberately not looking at the G-String Men.

Three of the men share one of the parlor's long couches, Kahuna in the middle, legs splayed, leaning back. The other two sit forward, feet planted firmly on the ground. Boomer, the Australian, stands behind them with his arms crossed. Penny and Esmeralda occupy the couch across from them, Penny looking as though she's just waiting for an excuse, Esmeralda's smile tight. M is nowhere to be seen, which is not unexpected. Bunny isn't worried about M. She's worried about Starlight, standing in the doorway, sneaking glances at the G-String Man barely in green.

"Star, sweetie, why don't you grab us a pitcher of sangria." Bunny arranges her features carefully, smooth as her hair and the lines of her dress, keeping her voice light. "I'm sure we could all use a drink."

Starlight jumps, a guilty blush coloring her cheeks as she hurries from the room. Bunny shifts her attention to Kahuna, a different kind of tension crawling beneath her skin. Her jaw wants to clench, but she refuses to let it.

"Why don't we start with introductions?" Her smile is as sweet as she can make it, sickly so, she hopes.

She needs Kahuna to see what's behind her painted lips without her parting them; Boomer may be the one in sharkskin, but Kahuna is the one with teeth.

"Well, you know me and Boomerang already." Kahuna flashes his smile on cue; Bunny doesn't let her fingers close into a fist at her side.

"And this here is Bad Kitty." Kahuna points to the man in the animal print g-string, which turns from tiger stripe to a shade of tawny as Bunny watches. She doesn't let her surprise show, moving her attention to the man in green as Kahuna gestures to him. "And this is Flash Jr."

Bunny lets the Glitter Squadron introduce themselves, keeping an eye on Starlight as she reappears with the sangria. Bunny doesn't miss the way her blush returns as she hands Flash Jr. a glass.

"So what do you know about these killer ladybugs?" Penny asks, impatience winning out.

"Ladies first," Kahuna says.

"Not funny." Penny reaches for the gun that Bunny is now extra glad she insisted Penny leave in her room.

Bunny clears her throat. "I suspect we know about as much as you do. About a week ago, a homeless man was found dead outside the factory with strange marks on his body. Another corpse was found yesterday, same markings. Your turn."

The G-String men exchange glances; Bad Kitty is the one to speak up.

"We didn't know about the beetles, not specifically. We were at the factory to investigate odd seismic activity. Tremors. Nothing big enough to be called an earthquake." Bad Kitty looks away, mumbling like someone used to being disbelieved, if not outright ridiculed.

"We thought it might be Mole People." Bad Kitty shrugs. "We fought them in Switzerland a few months ago."

"I read about that in the *National Inquirer*. That was you?"

Bunny turns. Starlight's eyes widen, and she covers her mouth, murmuring, "Sorry."

"We'd been asking around," Bad Kitty says. "Some folks were willing to talk to us, but the stories were inconsistent, jumbled. No one was quite sure what they saw, just something strange. Most people just clammed up. I think they thought we were cops."

"We weren't even wearing our cop outfits." Bunny turns in time to see Boomerang wink, but he withers immediately at her attention, and she looks back to Bad Kitty.

"Is it any wonder?" Sapphire rolls her eyes. "If you *were* a cop, would you believe some raving lunatic claiming to have seen a giant beetle? Of course no one wanted to talk to you."

"Luckily, we're not cops."

A muscle in Bunny's jaw twitches despite her best efforts; she clenches her teeth to still it. Even though he hasn't spoken in five minutes, Kahuna's presence still sets her on edge. She takes a deep breath. There's an ache gathering at the back of her neck, threatening to creep upward.

She resists the urge to rub at the spot, too aware of how carefully she's holding herself.

"I suggest we divide into teams. Do some investigating."

"Whatever you say, boss lady." Kahuna tosses her a mock salute.

Bunny shifts. She's on the verge of thanking him oh-so-politely for his negligible contribution and kicking his all-but-bare ass out the door. But leadership is compromise, and making use of the resources at hand. And sometimes leadership is keeping unknown elements where you can see them. Her first priority is to keep her girls safe.

"Penny, CeCe, Silk. Tomorrow, I want you to go back to the factory with Flash Jr. and Bad Kitty. Investigate, but play it safe. If you see any sign of those creatures, get out. Esmeralda, you'll take Star, Ruby, and Kahuna. Try to track down those kids who found the first body, and talk to anyone you can who reported seeing something strange. Boomer, Sapphire, and I will do research."

Bunny lifts her chin, waiting for someone to contradict her. Some expressions are better shielded than others. Starlight's raw as a wound, and Bunny feels a moment of guilt. It's not that she doesn't trust her; she's a good kid. It's the world around Starlight she doesn't trust. Penny is uninterested in hiding her resentment. And Kahuna is openly amused.

Fine. Sometimes leadership is being unpopular, too. As the room disperses, Bunny catches Starlight's attention.

"Can I talk to you for a minute?"

Starlight glances toward the door; Bunny doesn't miss where her gaze lingers.

Starlight sits. And now that they're alone, Bunny is rattled. Space eels and killer deer she can handle; here, she's out of her depth. Ridiculously, a half-formed memory of a very-special episode of *Blossom* rises to Bunny's mind: Clair Huxtable inexplicably appearing in Mayim Bialik's kitchen to illustrate the female reproductive system in pink icing.

"Look, sweetie, I don't know if you've ever…"

Starlight's mouth twists downward and she isn't quick enough to hide the expression. Bunny can't help picturing her the way she looked when she first came to the Glitter Squadron. Her expression is transparent—the words building up to push back against Bunny even before she's finished her sentence oddly make her look more vulnerable now than she did before Bunny first did her make-up.

"I'm not that young." Starlight's words are hasty and the tips of her ears are red. "My mama gave me the talk ages ago. I know about…all that."

Starlight waves a hand dismissively, but she doesn't meet Bunny's eye. A fist squeezes Bunny's heart, once, and hard, before letting go. She breathes out. Then she breathes in, and Bunny lets her voice drop, her tone coming closer to its natural timbre than it has in years. She tries not to wince because it feels important to let Starlight see this side of her. This is Phillip's confession, not hers.

"I was going to ask if you'd ever been in a serious relationship. I know it's none of my business." Bunny goes on before Starlight can answer. "I just don't want to see you get hurt."

Starlight's blush fades to a glow, a frown turning the corners of her lips. The play of emotions, so close to the surface brings the fist back to Bunny's chest, and this time it doesn't let go so easily.

"Is this the part where you tell me to avoid making the same mistakes you did?" Starlight tries to sneer, but it doesn't work. The tone doesn't suit her. The underpinnings are still visible beneath her skin. It hurts. Because Bunny remembers what it feels like to be afraid and to lash out, thinking no one else in the world is afraid except for you.

"No, sweetie." Bunny shakes her head. "I *was* the mistake. I know men like Kahuna and Boomer and Bad Kitty and Flash Jr., because I've been the asshole leaving a trail of unreturned calls behind. I've slipped out of more windows and climbed down more fire escapes than you'd believe."

"But you don't know anything about Flash Jr." The minute the words are out, Starlight's eyes go wide.

"Neither do you, sweetie. That's all I'm saying. Just be careful."

Bunny sees the instinct to protest, the teenage rebellion, even though Starlight isn't a teenager anymore. For all her youth she's probably a hell of a lot smarter and more grown up than Bunny was at her age, or even ten years older. It took a tentacle rising out of the sea, killing a man and ripping a dog in half, to wake Bunny up and get her to finally stop acting like a spoiled, selfish child. Starlight's been a hero since she was seven years old.

It's not a new thought, but it strikes Bunny like a blow to the gut every time. No matter how fast she runs, no matter how hard she fights, she will never completely leave Phillip Howard Craft behind.

"I'll be careful. I promise," Starlight says. She hesitates a moment, then darts in quick to plant a kiss on Bunny's cheek.

For the second time today, she's stunned beyond words, and it's her turn to blush now. Dazed, Bunny watches Starlight leave the room, touching her cheek only once she's gone.

★

Dust-coated and bone-sore, Penny drops Stella on the table at Bunny's elbow. "Well that was fucking pointless." The safety is on, of course, but the sound of the gun hitting the wood has the desired effect. Bunny flinches and Penny smirks.

Some days are better than others. Today is not one of the good days.

Her fingers literally itch—something she thought was a figure of speech until now. She's sick of asking *how high* every time Bunny says *jump*, and if she doesn't shoot or punch something soon, it'll be a some*one* who gets the brunt of her rage.

"You sent us on a wild-goose chase."

"You didn't find anything?" Bunny resumes her infuriating calm, the shock of Penny's gun and the bluntness of her words already worn off.

Penny wants to shake her. Just once she wants to see their goddamned fearless leader rattled. Bunny's mild expression is flint, sparked against the kindling covering the hollow space inside.

Penny knows it isn't Bunny—it isn't *just* Bunny—under her skin, making it itch like it wants to crawl off her bones. It's everything. But if she keeps feeding the burning ball of rage she won't have to look at the white-hot point of light fueling it.

If she stokes the fire high enough, it will immolate everything—the nights she wakes, sweat-drenched, from dreams tinted emerald green. The nights starburst explosions of gunfire rake closer, even after she opens her eyes. The fire will burn away the shaking, covers pulled high, jaw clenched tight, and scorch to ash those dreams that don't even afford her the mercy of green-tinted night vision. The dreams where everything is clear and bright in the unforgiving light of day, and the only color is red.

It isn't Bunny, but Bunny is here.

"The factory was empty. Even the bug's body was gone."

"Gone?" Bunny rises; Penny straightens as if she can match Bunny's height, legs braced, hands on her hips.

Behind Bunny, the laptop shows an article about rhinoceros beetles. While she's been crawling through dust, Bunny's been sitting on her padded ass, surfing the web.

"Other beetles must have come back and collected it. That would indicate intelligence, an organized society. Maybe there are some kind of funeral rituals taking place." Bunny taps her nails against the table, pondering.

"Or maybe wild dogs ate it. Or some sick-fuck collector is working on the world's biggest shadow box display. We don't know what happened. We don't know anything." Penny is breathing harder than she should, her face hot.

"Do we have a problem here?" The change in Bunny's stance is almost imperceptible.

She's standing the way she stands just before a fight—not holding her harpoon, but she might as well be. Tense and ready. Maybe Bunny can be rattled after all.

Armed or not, she has height and weight on Penny. But she's untrained, and fuck it if Penny is going to back down from the hardness in Bunny's eyes, even though she's seen it make four star generals quail. Generals know fuck-all compared to the grunts on the front line.

"You're the problem," Penny says. "You throw orders around like you've got a fucking clue and you expect us all to fall in line."

"If you have a better idea…"

"Ha!" Penny can't hold back the barked laugh, even though it leaves her throat raw. "As if you'd listen."

"Are you saying you have a problem with my leadership?" Anger creeps into Bunny's tone, an edge behind the steel in her eyes.

It betrays her weariness, matched by a slant in the hard line of her shoulders—evidence of the effort it takes her to hold herself together, hold all of them together. Instead of backing off, Penny drives in hard.

"I'm saying I've fucking been to war. I'm saying I've fucking been a soldier and I'm the only one here with any real experience. You're just playing dress-up."

Bunny's face goes white, blood draining from the blow. Her mouth drops open, a painted circle, but no words emerge. It's just as well because Penny's ears ring, and everything is bright and hot and tangled up inside her. She is directionless rage crackling like lightning, striking everything, everyone, within reach.

"You put on a dress, and it's brave. You're a goddamned hero standing up to the status quo. When I put on a dress, I'm doing what's expected, I'm fulfilling my role. You know what happened when I put on a goddamn uniform and went to war? They still talked over me, looked past me, and when they weren't looking at me and thinking about fucking me, they were looking at me and waiting for me to fail. If you ever get sick of people ignoring your opinion, you can take off your dress and go back to being one of them. I don't have that luxury. I can't stop being who I am."

For a moment, Penny thinks Bunny will hit her, wishes she would. Blood, an ache in her jaw, would keep the words from coming. Because she doesn't hate Bunny. And deep down she doesn't believe a word she's saying.

There's a hollow place under the anger, a hole she needs to fill with Bunny's pain so nothing else can creep in. It isn't right; it isn't fair. But she watches herself keep doing it. She doesn't stop. Because if she stops…

Penny leans forward, daring Bunny to react, strike back. Instead, Bunny crumples. The smooth mask of her face collapses in on itself, and she breaks eye contact, something Penny has never seen her do.

"Neither can I." Bunny's voice is so soft it's barely audible.

The hollow space inside Penny fills with sickness so violently, she begins to gag.

"Penny, wait," Bunny calls, but Penny ignores her, stumbling in her chunky, grit-caked heels to her room and slamming the door.

A knock comes a few minutes later, soft enough that Penny can pretend she doesn't hear it. She holds her breath, jaw clenched tight and body trembling.

She waits until enough time ticks by that the Glitter Squadron settles for going to bed angry. Only then does Penny release something between a laugh and a sob.

Undressing is quick and efficient, like field-stripping a weapon—boots, dress, bra, panties, holsters, sheaths—everything in a neat pile on the floor. Without turning the light on, she examines herself in the full length mirror. The only visible scars are the ones left by the harpy, four perfect talon marks driven deep into her shoulder. She touches them experimentally, wishing for pain. But there is none, only the tight pucker of skin, smoother and shinier than the rest. And that isn't right. It isn't right at all.

★

M IS NOT SURPRISED BY THE KNOCK AT THE DOOR, OR EVEN THE HOUR. M is rarely surprised at anything. When the door is opened, Penny stands revealed in the hall light. She is naked and this doesn't surprise M either.

"I need you to hurt me." Penny's voice is husked, raw in place of tears.

M steps back, allows Penny inside, and closes the door.

There are no lights on in M's room. Illumination seeping in from the hall is just enough to show vague outlines—the handle of a whip here, the glint of a blade there.

M says nothing. M rarely does.

Penny squares her shoulders, back to M, waiting. There is a creak of leather as M reaches for a handle that fits perfectly into a gloved palm. Penny flinches only at the first blow. Whether it is the sound or the swiftness that startles her into motion is not M's concern. Only the handle, only the lash, only the precision of each blow timed to each breath and the stuttering beat of Penny's heart.

Every subsequent lash Penny takes in silence; she does not react again. Not until M stops. And then, it is merely a widening of her eyes as M steps in front of Penny so their gazes meet. Then tears frost Penny's lashes.

M touches a gloved finger to Penny's mouth, touches the same finger to the metal zipper glinting in place of lips. Wordless, M tells Penny what she already knows: No amount of pain will fill the hollow space inside; there's no number of scars she can take onto her skin to dull the rage. She will have to learn to live in her body and mind because her world has been irrevocably changed. She will not heal, not from this, but she will learn to endure, and she will survive.

It is only then that Penny breaks. She drops to her knees, body curling in on itself, an endless spiral of hurt without relief.

Silent, M leaves Penny shaking on the floor, closing the door on her pain-wracked body. M's job is done.

CeCe leaves Madeline sleeping and creeps downstairs. The Glitter Squadron house is too big; CeCe misses her apartment, *their* apartment, she reminds herself. Has to keep reminding herself. If it were up to her they'd be back at home, but Madeline insisted.

After the factory, CeCe emerged from the shower to find Madeline still in her white silk suit—the edges crisp, the cape framing her when she'd struck a heroic pose, white fedora tilted to shadow her face, but leaving a wicked smile visible.

She'd kept the domino mask on the entire time, even after letting CeCe strip her of everything else. After that, CeCe hadn't been in much of a position to refuse Madeline anything.

So she's here in the Glitter Squadron house, unable to sleep. And despite the shower she still feels half-moons of dirt pressed under her nails. Madeline's giddiness at her first real mission should be infectious, but all they did was patrol the grounds outside the factory the first time, missing all the action, then crawl around in the dust the second time with nothing to show for it.

CeCe doesn't let herself think *this was more fun when I worked alone.* Instead, without turning on the lights, she finds her way to the liquor cabinet, the one saving grace of the Glitter Mansion.

"Can't sleep either?"

CeCe starts at the voice, but keeps from spilling her drink. Sapphire lounges on one of the couches, elegant in a sheer, dark blue dressing gown over a satin slip nightdress. She raises a long-stemmed cocktail glass in a toast.

"Guess not." CeCe leans against the wall.

She still doesn't know what to make of Sapphire, hasn't ever since she showed up at CeCe's door and gave her the kick in the pants she needed to get Madeline back. Even at this hour Sapphire is immaculately made up, eyelashes thick, lids outlined and glittering, and not a hair out of place.

"Trouble in paradise?" Sapphire arches a sculpted eyebrow.

"No. Nothing like that." But the corners of CeCe's mouth turn down, betraying her. "It's just this place makes me itchy."

"Tell me about it." Sapphire pats the seat beside her. After a moment, CeCe perches on the far end of the couch.

"I don't bite, honey. Not until the second date."

Now it's CeCe's turn to raise her glass. "You're a swell gal, but I'm spoken for."

"But?" Sapphire prompts.

"Promise you won't laugh?" CeCe studies her drink, terrified of what she's about to say, and to who. But Sapphire helped her before, and like she said, they are family.

"Cross my heart and hope to die."

"Madeline and I are trying to have a baby." CeCe looks up, meeting Sapphire's eyes, waiting for judgment, for a smart-ass remark. But Sapphire's expression is grave, touched with just a hint of pain.

"Why would I laugh at that?"

"We… I mean she… Ah, hell." CeCe drains the rest of her drink, running a hand through her hair.

She looks at the wall, because it's easier than looking at Sapphire.

"We went to the clinic together and chose a donor. We don't even know yet if it worked, but what if it does, and it doesn't feel like my baby? What if I don't love it enough and I'm a crappy dad?"

"Honey, listen to me carefully—genetic material isn't what makes you a parent. If you want this, and it happens for you, you'll make a wonderful father."

CeCe wills the blood in her cheeks back down. The Velvet Underground Drag King does *not* blush.

"Madeline's adopted, right? Does that mean her parents aren't her parents? And Ruby was basically raised by her grandma and grandpa. Did an egg and a sperm make either of them who they are? No. It's the people who loved them."

"Yeah," CeCe refills her glass, and after a sip, she tries on a shaky smile. "Listen to me, moping and moaning again. You always catch me at my best, don't you?"

Sapphire takes a delicate sip. In the dark, her expression is hard to read. A flicker of movement catches CeCe's eye as she gazes out the parlor window—a shadow crossing the lawn. It's there and gone so quickly she shrugs it off.

"You won't tell anyone?" CeCe says. "I have a reputation to maintain after all." She lets her smile turn self-deprecating.

"As an emotionless hard-ass? Yeah, I know." Sapphire drains her drink, but makes no move to rise from the couch. Belatedly, it occurs to CeCe to wonder why Sapphire is drinking alone in the dark.

After a moment of awkward silence, the softness of Sapphire's voice makes her jump.

"I started hormone therapy."

Light from the window highlights Sapphire in profile—her nose, her lips, the sharp line of her cheekbones. She doesn't look at CeCe, making it impossible to tell if the brightness in her eyes is the light or something else.

"A secret for a secret, right? I haven't told anyone else yet."

"Oh." CeCe breathes out. Sapphire finally turns, smiles, but it's a fragile thing.

"I've got a reputation to maintain, too."

"Of course." CeCe says.

She feels she should say something, but doesn't know what. Her pulse thumps. Sapphire's smile softens, the edge of sorrow tucked away again.

"Goodnight, CeCe. Sleep well."

Feeling simultaneously dismissed and relieved, CeCe swallows. "Goodnight," she whispers, before slipping back upstairs.

★

Ruby glances back at the darkened house. The lawn is damp; she should be cold but her pulse trips, leaving her flushed and her breath uneven. At a flash of movement through the parlor window, she hurries away, expecting the door to open at any moment and pin her in a square of light.

Bunny would kill her if she knew she was out here on her own. And Sapphire would kill her twice.

Sheknows she's being reckless and stupid, but at the same time she can't shake the feeling the giant beetle in the factory is connected to her. The memory of tiny legs ticking across her skin lingers. The shiver-hum, the buzzing warmth, as though she never took off the cursed necklace. She saw Bunny destroy the scarab, but that doesn't mean anything.

Ruby won't be able to live with herself if anyone gets hurt on her account.

If this is her fault somehow, because of the necklace, then tonight is her chance to set things right, and she'll do it without putting anyone else in danger this time.

Sapphire and Bunny will never know, and Ruby will sleep sound knowing she did everything she could to protect them.

Dense woods untouched by developers occupy the lot across the street from the Glitter Squadron property. Moonlight touches only the slender trunks closest to the road, penetrating no further. Anything could be lurking there, but Ruby convinces herself it's not.

She steps toward the trees. There's a hissing squeak, and she lets out a squeak of her own, reeling backward. Her heel catches on the lip of asphalt, dropping her hard. The sound rises from a hiss to a rattle, and a beetle bursts forth from the trees, shaking its wings. It feints, trying to scare her off, coming close enough that its legs snag strands of her hair.

"Hsst!" A hand grabs her arm. Ruby whips around, lashing out and scrambling to her feet.

In her panic it's a moment before the hand registers as human. Flash Jr. stares at her wide-eyed. Before Ruby can ask what he's doing here, the beetle turns, ready to charge again. Ruby grabs Flash Jr., dragging him between the trees.

"We have to get back to the house," Ruby says.

More movement catches Ruby's eye, and she pushes Flash Jr. behind her. The absence of Sapphire at her back is suddenly palpable. But there's no hiss or chitter; Ruby stops just short of delivering a blow as Starlight draws up in alarm.

"Star?"

"Ruby?"

"What are you doing here?"

Starlight glances over Ruby's shoulder. The warning rattle of wings comes again before she can answer. The beetle lunges, and this time, Ruby lunges back, her body shaking with adrenaline.

The beetle veers away. Ruby grabs its leg, twisting, ignoring the spines digging into her flesh. There's a sickening crunch as the leg rips free. Ruby staggers back, still holding the limb as the creature disappears into the woods.

At Starlight's hand on her shoulder, Ruby jumps. She whirls, holding the severed leg like a club.

"I didn't see any more when…" Flash Jr. stops, guilty as Ruby turns on him.

"You were spying on us." Ruby's fingers tighten reflexively until a sharp spike of pain makes her suck in a breath.

"You're bleeding," Starlight says.

Ruby looks at the thing in her hand, ignoring the blood slicking her palm. Thick fluid oozes from the torn end of the leg — barbed, jointed, and if she straightened it out, it might be longer than her arm. She shakes her head. One thing at a time.

"You." Ruby grasps Flash Jr.'s biceps with her free hand, squeezing harder than she has to. "You're coming with us. No more skulking."

"What were you doing outside?" Starlight pitches her voice low as she falls in beside Ruby.

Ruby falters, then yanks Flash Jr.'s arm speeding her pace. She hopes the darkness is enough to hide the shamed blush trying to climb her cheeks. What was she thinking? *Oh, I have special beetle-sensing powers thanks to a cursed necklace I stole, so I thought I would track down the bugs myself and save everyone the trouble, la-di-dah.*

The self-mocking tone in her head makes her response come out sharper than she intends.

"I could ask you the same thing."

The darkness doesn't hide Starlight's blush at all. "I thought I saw something." The words are barely a murmur; Starlight keeps her gaze fixed on her toes.

Ruby doesn't miss the way Starlight avoids looking at Flash Jr. Guilt trips her, but they need to focus on the task at hand. With a jerk of her head, she motions Starlight to open the Glitter Mansion door.

"Go wake Bunny."

Starlight, desperate to escape, hurries to obey. Ruby guides Flash Jr. into the parlor.

"Sit." She pushes him roughly toward the couch.

There's a squawk of surprise, and Flash Jr. trips, knocking over a lamp.

"Sapphire?" Ruby blinks as her eyes adjust. "Why are you sitting alone in the dark?"

"I was trying to enjoy a little peace and quiet. Are we having a party?" Sapphire looks at Flash Jr., then the severed leg in Ruby's hand. "If so, count me out. That looks more like M's kind of thing."

The light snaps on. Bunny, perfectly coiffed as ever, missing only her signature ears, stands in the parlor doorway. One perfectly manicured hand holds her feather-trimmed white babydoll robe closed. Starlight hovers behind her.

"Would someone mind telling me what the hell is going on?"

When no one answers, Bunny steps fully into the room, drawing herself up. Because it's Bunny, even the fuzzy rabbit slippers on her feet are intimidating. Ruby speaks in a rush.

"I caught him snooping around outside." She points at Flash Jr. "And there was a beetle. I pulled its leg off."

Bunny frowns; Ruby feels the silent reprimand before Bunny turns her attention to Flash Jr.

"Did Kahuna put you up to this?"

Flash Jr. opens his mouth, then shuts it again, looking sheepish.

Bunny's gaze hardens; Flash Jr.'s shoulders slump.

"He's outside in a van with the others."

"Call him." Bunny snaps her fingers and points at the old-fashioned phone in cream and gold sitting on one of the parlor's many end tables.

Bunny turns her attention back to Ruby and the severed leg. "Let's have a look at that thing."

Ruby hands the leg over. Bunny's nose wrinkles.

"Go take care of your hand."

Ruby's heart sinks. Even trying to help, she's gotten it all wrong. It's the theater on the ship all over again. Ruby can almost taste the plaster dust at the back of her throat. Sapphire nudges her gently, breaking the spell.

"Let's get you cleaned up."

Sapphire guides Ruby toward the door, but they pause in synch, reluctant to miss the show. Bunny's frown deepens as she studies the leg. Esmeralda appears, taking in the scene with a glance.

"Is that from one of the beetles?"

Bunny nods. Esmeralda stops just short of touching the thing.

"Well." A slight smile touches Esmeralda's lips. "Good thing we know someone who can help."

Bunny looks up in confusion, then her expression clears. The answer comes to Ruby at the same moment.

"Doctor B?"

Bunny and Esmeralda both turn to stare at her. Ruby blushes again, this time without the benefit of the darkness to hide her.

"I'll go with you." Penny's voice is soft.

Ruby starts; she didn't hear her enter the room. Penny glances at Bunny, then her gaze skates away. Something passes between them that Ruby doesn't understand, but the tension is palpable—electricity before a storm.

The doorbell rings and Ruby jumps, nerves shattered. Penny opens the door to Kahuna, Bad Kitty, and Boomer. Kahuna offers a grin; the other two G-String Men have the grace to slink in behind their leader. At the fire in Bunny's expression, Ruby braces herself, expecting a tirade. But Bunny surprises her.

"I think you'd all better stay here for the night. If we're in this together, we're in it together. No more spying and second guessing. We have to trust each other."

Bunny waits a beat, as if waiting for a challenge. Ruby's heart goes out to Bunny. She can't even imagine trying to hold them all together. Ruby lets Sapphire lead her away to clean and bandage her hand to the sounds of Bunny playing the perfect hostess. Taking care of them. Like always.

"So, what do you think, Doc?" Esmeralda looks over Doctor Blood's shoulder, even though the information feeding from the electronic microscope to his computer means nothing to her.

She fights the urge to pace. The lab equipment makes her nervous. He's reformed; Esmeralda is a firm believer in second chances, but she can't quite shake the memory of gorilla men and rotting zombies.

"Call me Hector." Doctor Blood waves a distracted hand, peering through the microscope.

Penny snorts. Esmeralda shoots her a look, but Penny simply rolls her eyes, leaning in the doorway with her arms crossed. When they first met him he went by the name Richard, but who are they—of all people—to judge him for reinventing himself?

Hector leans back rubbing the bridge of his nose. "Oh."

"What is it?" Esmeralda asks.

Doctor Blood looks so much older than he did on Mars. His scars are no longer shiny pink; they're tired and white. Even though it was his choice, Esmeralda wonders whether working for the government under close surveillance is really better for him than jail. With the guards posted outside his door and the cameras perched in every corner of the room, he might as well be in prison. Except this way the government gets to reap the benefits of his brilliant mind under the guise of rehab, without ever paying him a dime.

Hector points at the screen. "*Lotis tyrannus regis.*" He shakes his head. His gaze wanders from the screen to the papers scattered across his desk. For a moment, Doctor Blood looks utterly lost, adrift amidst a sea of data and research that doesn't even belong to him anymore. Esmeralda makes a mental note to ask Bunny whether she'd mind her visiting Hector more often—not just when they need something, but because Hector himself needs a friend.

Penny unfolds herself from the doorway. "Spill it, Doc."

Esmeralda didn't see Penny arm herself before they left, but it doesn't mean she isn't packing.

"Hector, please." Esmeralda keeps her voice soft, despite her anxiety.

"It's something we were working on."

"Who's we?" Even as Esmeralda asks, pain flickers through Hector's eyes.

"My wife." He pauses, squaring his shoulders. "My *ex*-wife, Helena, and our lab assistant, Victor. We were studying aggression in insects, making them bigger and meaner and looking for ways to control their behavior."

"Why?" Penny says.

"Oh, you know, the usual." Doctor Blood offers a wry smile. "We were building better super soldiers. Or rehabilitating prisoners. Or curing cancer."

"Or taking over the world?" Esmeralda raises an eyebrow, trying to break the tension. She's grateful when Doctor Blood seem to take it as the joke she intended, even though he doesn't smile.

"Did you ever find a way to harness the aggression?" Penny asks.

"*I didn't.*"

"Could Helena and Victor have continued your work?"

The expression on Hector's face makes her regret asking it, but they don't have time to put kid gloves on to handle a former supervillain's battered heart.

"Who knows?" Something like a broken laugh escapes him. "Maybe they did, or maybe someone stole the formula. It doesn't matter."

"It matters to us." Penny moves closer, forcing Doctor Blood to look at her. "And we need to know how to stop them."

"I suppose I could…" Another vague gesture, taking in the lab.

"Don't suppose. Just get to work." Penny's voice is sharp and even

Esmeralda flinches. Before she can say anything to gentle the situation, Penny strides to the door and bangs it with the flat of her hand to let the guards know they're ready to leave. Esmeralda tosses an apologetic glance over her shoulder, then hurries to catch up.

"Well, we know what they are, but not where they are or how to stop them," Bunny says.

Even though Bunny is as perfectly put-together as ever, Sapphire sees the minute cracks in her armor—the strain of holding them all together, not to mention the added complication of the G-String Men. Penny will barely make eye contact with anyone; CeCe and Silk are secretive, whispering to each other; M has vanished, as usual; and Starlight can't stop staring at Flash Jr.

Meanwhile, the looks Boomer keeps giving her set Sapphire on edge. It's like he's trying to figure her out, and it frightens her in a whole different way than Kahuna frightens her. Kahuna with his undirected hunger, like he wants to devour the world. No wonder Bunny doesn't like him. And Bunny likes everyone.

"I say we search the factory again," CeCe speaks up and all eyes turn toward her. "There must be something we missed."

Penny frowns, but says nothing.

"Go with the flow, man." Kahuna kicks his feet up onto the coffee table.

From the tangle of his sun-and-surf gnarled white-boy dreads, he pulls out a joint. As Sapphire watches in horror, he sparks the cheap plastic lighter tucked into the waistband of his g-string.

"What the hell do you think you're doing?" Bunny's voice cracks with shock and she slaps the lighter—printed with a bare-breasted hula dancer—out of his hand. It clatters to the floor.

"Hey, man. I'm just trying to relax. This is how I get into the zone before a mission." Kahuna seems unfazed, but he leans forward, planting his feet on the floor and Sapphire catches the gleam in his eye.

How much is an act? He's still holding the joint, but he makes no move for the lighter.

"There's no smoking in this house," Bunny says.

"She does it." Kahuna indicates CeCe. Bunny and Silk both shoot CeCe a look, but the Velvet Underground Drag King merely shrugs.

"You have your vices, I have mine." Kahuna indicates the bar before retrieving the lighter, turning it in his hand.

Bunny clenches her jaw, but even though Sapphire sees the fight in her eye, she turns deliberately away from Kahuna and addresses the room at large.

"Since no one has any better ideas, we'll check the factory again. But we go as a group this time, no more splitting up. Make whatever preparations you need. We'll reconvene in half an hour."

Murmuring fills the room. Sapphire moves to Bunny's side.

"Are you okay, honey?"

"Fine," Bunny says, but the word is too tight.

Before Sapphire can push the issue, Bunny moves away. Always smiling, always taking the time to comfort others when they're hurting, but who does Bunny turn to when she's in pain? Sapphire watches her walk away, the cracks in her armor already spackled over. Compared to Bunny, CeCe was easy.

Turning, Sapphire finds Starlight lingering in the doorway. And Boomer hasn't moved from his place beside the unlit fire.

"He really isn't that bad, you know." Boomer gestures toward the window.

Kahuna has moved outside to the lawn. Smoke curls around him, and his ass, barely covered by the thin line of his g-string, is pointed defiantly at the parlor's picture window. Boomer frowns.

"I know he comes off as an asshole, but that's just his thing, you know?"

"Does he have any redeeming qualities?" Sapphire can't keep the arch skepticism from her voice.

"He's a good guy to have at your back in a fight." Boomer shrugs, an apologetic motion. "He's saved my life at least a dozen times."

His accent softens as he says it, approaching fondness, approaching humanity, approaching fear. He sounds like a man who's been to war, and come out scarred. More than just a shiny g-string and a package to match. How much is he an act, too? As soon as the thought crosses her mind, she pushes it away. Sapphire doesn't want to know whether he loves dogs, and calls his mother every Sunday. She doesn't want to know if he gives money to charity and is working on a Master's degree at night. She wants him to be pretty and empty and easily dismissed. Sudden enough she's afraid it will betray her, but too set to stop, Sapphire sweeps past him, chin held high. Startled, Starlight jumps out of her way. As she passes,

Sapphire murmurs so only Starlight can hear, though the words may as well be for herself.

"We don't have time for distractions. We have a job to do."

THIS IS THE ULTRA FABULOUS GLITTER SQUADRON, ARRAYED FOR battle—peacock feathers and sequins, green velvet and copper lamé, shimmering white seed pearls, and, of course, bunny ears. Madeline has never seen the Squadron look so fierce and so beautiful. In her sharp white suit, fedora tilted askew and domino mask over her eyes, she almost, *almost* feels like she belongs among them.

The rational side of her mind tells her she has no business playing hero. The clothes might make the woman, but she doesn't know that for sure. She can't trust that in the end she won't fall flat on her face. How will her crisp, white suit look after a battle? What happens when the cape fluttering at her shoulders catches on something?

"Everyone inside."

At Bunny's order, Silk is swept up with the rest of the Glitter Squadron. There's no more time for doubt.

Penny has one of her many weapons drawn, Bunny has her harpoon at the ready, and CeCe has her sword-cane to hand. Even the G-String Men, ridiculously under-clothed, have their boomerangs and slings. CeCe glances her way, and Silk returns the most charming smile she can: fake it till you make it.

She moves deeper into the factory, almost strutting, showing more confidence than she feels. As Silk passes one of the silent pieces of machinery, her foot comes down, and there's a sharp crack. The breath rushes out of her as the floor gives way. Silk flails for a moment, but her cry of surprise is cut short as her cape snags, arresting her fall.

"Maddy! Hang on!" CeCe's face is framed by rotten wood; dusty factory light filters in from behind her.

Madeline forces herself to take a deep breath, assess her situation. The cape isn't choking her, and for the moment, it feels like it will hold.

"I'm okay."

She looks down. It's a moment before the shadows resolve into distinct shapes—discarded machine parts, stacks of rotting storage crates, massive wooden spools holding rusted skeins of wire.

"It's a basement storage level," Madeline says. "It's not that far to the ground."

"Maddy, don't!" CeCe leans over the hole, but the wood creaks ominously, forcing her back.

It's foolish, it's risky—it's flat-out stupid and Madeline knows it. But she can't have the others trying to haul her up—the floor will collapse.

"It's not that far." Murmuring the words aloud does little to calm her, but Madeline pumps her legs, letting gravity do the rest.

The silk tears. Madeline's heart lurches, but she remembers to tuck and roll. The impact still jars, and pain spikes through her ankle. She can't help a shout—as much surprise as pain.

The world is sideways and she can't move. She's hit a piece of machinery; she's punctured something vital; only shock is keeping her alive; she'll die alone and there's no way out.

"Maddy." CeCe's voice shakes her from the endless loop of terrible scenarios running through her mind.

"I'm okay." She releases the words with a shaky breath. "I twisted my ankle, but I'm okay."

She stands, sucking in a breath, and tests her weight. Pain shoots through her ankle and she braces herself against a stack of crates. When the pain ebbs, Silk takes stock of the space.

"I see a staircase. It's in the far left corner. Is there a door up there?"

There's a murmur of voices. Footsteps retreat. Grime streaks Madeline's suit; the tatters of her cape hang uselessly from her shoulders, but she's okay. She made a choice, and she survived.

She dusts herself off, pressing her hands over her midsection. What if…? The thought is too horrible. She barely even considered it until now. What kind of mother will that make her?

"We found the stairway, but it's under a collapsed section of wall. We'll have to dig a bit to get down to you. Hang tight, doll."

Silk takes a deep breath, drawing in the scent of mildew and dust. Beyond the crates and boxes, something catches her eye, a deeper patch of darkness in the shadows. She retrieves one of the floorboards broken in her fall. It's just long enough to use as a makeshift crutch.

She hobbles closer, confirming her suspicions. An entire section of wall has been torn away, the earth scooped out to form a passageway taller than her and wider than her arms can stretch.

"There's a tunnel!" Madeline can't keep the excitement from her voice.

Fear comes close on the heels of her words. The way the earth is hollowed out—it's too irregular for machinery, but too much work for human hands. Beetles. The seismic activity the G-String Men mentioned. The beetles have been burrowing under the factory.

There's a crash behind her and Madeline's heart finds its way back to her throat. The door grinds open, then CeCe rushes to her, and a sob escapes as velvet enfolds silk.

"Shh. It's okay." CeCe strokes her hair; after a moment, Madeline pulls back, looking down into CeCe's concerned eyes.

CeCe cups her cheek, smoothes away a tear with her thumb and only then does Madeline realize she's crying. Her ankle throbs and with it comes a pulse of guilt. She can't tell CeCe she didn't even think of their baby. If the fertilization worked… She's shaking again, deepening the concern in CeCe's eyes. Madeline wipes at her tears, forcing a smile.

"I'm fine. Sorry. Everything is fine."

The crunch of footsteps approach and the room is full of glitter and g-strings, all attention turned to the hole in the wall.

"Well, I guess we know where the rest of the beetles are," Bunny says. "Now what do we do about it?"

GOLD HOOPS SWINGING FROM PENNY'S EARS CATCH THE LIGHT, winking in the dim space of the factory. She's more made-up than usual, Sapphire notes, like she's got something to prove.

"We hit them where they live." Penny draws her pistol.

"We haven't even heard from Doctor B yet," Esmeralda says.

"The whole point of this is to give him more information to work with. We're not going to get it standing here gawking." Penny's boots crunch on the grit at the tunnel entrance.

To Sapphire's surprise, Kahuna moves next, whistling and following Penny into the tunnel. Bunny unfreezes, jabbing Kahuna in the small of the back with the blunt handle of her harpoon.

"Are you trying to get us all killed?"

Kahuna shrugs, falling silent. Even as he does, something dangerous slides through his gaze. Sapphire catches her breath; she's seen that look before, in Bunny's eyes. So what is Kahuna running from? What could make him strip off so much armor, make himself so vulnerable, just to feel strong?

Boomer catches her eye. Her body tingles, and she looks away, reminding herself she doesn't want to know if he's a good guy under that floss-width of spandex. She doesn't want to think about him at all. She hurries after Penny, Bunny, and Kahuna. In her haste, her heel catches, and she nearly falls. Boomer catches her elbow, steadying her.

"Are you okay?" The concern in his eyes seems genuine; Sapphire feels worse as she yanks her arm away.

"I'm fine." It's a struggle to keep her voice low, not let it echo, announcing their presence.

The dirt-packed walls are high and wide enough that she can straighten her back. She deliberately raises her chin, not wobbling once, despite the thinness of her heels. She refuses to look back, letting the points of Bunny's ears anchor her.

"Why wouldn't you let him help you? It's obvious he likes you." Starlight moves up beside her; there's a tone of wistful resentment in her voice, faint but obvious.

Glancing back, Sapphire can barely make out the others. Starlight follows her gaze, her shoulders curling inward slightly. For a moment, everything inside Sapphire hurts. She wants to tell Starlight she's too young, that she'll understand someday. The words are trite; they taste empty, saccharine, even without saying them aloud. She shakes her head.

"Look, honey. You've known exactly who you are ever since you were seven years old. Maybe younger."

Starlight looks up in surprise; Sapphire holds up a hand to stop her.

"It takes some of us a little longer, and I'm just not ready to share who I am with someone else yet. Not like that."

Starlight presses her lips together and nods, her eyes wide. Sapphire breathes out. She'll have to deal with it someday, letting someone in, letting them see her and facing the possibility they won't like what they see. Someday she'll have to deal with the chance someone will see her and not see her; they'll see a fetish, they'll see a body and want to know who she *really* is, they'll see her but not understand this has always been her, this is who she is. But right now, it's too raw, too close.

And despite everything, despite what she knows, she can't help feeling that being herself means turning her back on her family. Her daddy wanted someone to carry on his name, and there's only her. Maybe if she'd gotten a chance to talk to him before he passed… But what would she have said? She can almost hear his voice even now—*a black man has a responsibility to his community, to his family, to act a certain way in the eyes of the world.*

The pain from the cancer was so bad at the end, even if she'd gotten up the guts to say *but I'm not a man*, he probably wouldn't have understood. With all this tangled up inside, Sapphire can't afford to think about Boomer. Not right now. Maybe not ever.

"Are you okay?" At Starlight's question, Sapphire realizes she's stopped walking.

"Yes. Thank you." She puts one foot in front of the other. Repeats it.

Then she stops, nearly colliding with Bunny and Kahuna, and all thoughts of her family and her future drop away. The tunnel opens onto a plateau. Beyond it lies an entire hollow world of façades and steps and doorways cut into the rock, all of it spiraling down like an inverted funnel.

"Holy shit."

"No kidding," Starlight says beside her.

Peering over the edge, Sapphire can just make out the shape of beetles moving in the depths. She can't tell how many there are. It looks like an entire city.

And all it would take is for one beetle to notice them and they'll be devoured by a swarm.

BUNNY CROUCHES, GETTING AS CLOSE TO THE LIP OF THE PLATEAU as possible. The drop is dizzying. Wooden bridges crisscross the space, connecting stairs and ramps and platforms. It's impossible. But they've faced impossible before. And won.

Penny crouches beside her, voice low. "There must be hundreds of them."

As Penny glances her way, Bunny catches something that's not quite remorse in her eyes. There are marks Penny hasn't bothered to hide—welts on her shoulders, the backs of her arms and her legs, just starting to fade. There's pain in her movements, too. Bunny's seen it, but Penny hasn't stopped moving. She's right where she always is, at Bunny's side.

Something twists inside Bunny, a bruise in place of her heart. She hasn't forgiven Penny. She hasn't decided whether there's anything to forgive. But for now, they're okay.

"It's your call," Penny says. "How do we handle this thing?"

"I…" Bunny says, but gets no further.

A door opens two levels below them. A man and woman in their best Buck Rogers knock-off villain costumes emerge, gaudy robes and headpieces and all.

"Victor and Helena?" Penny whispers.

"Who else?" Bunny half-smirks.

She straightens. And as she does, a terrible thing happens. The toe of one of her chunky, glittering shoes catches a tiny pebble and sends it over the edge.

The sound is minuscule. And in the echoing space it's huge. It pings, once, twice, and Bunny stops counting, breath held and heart hammering.

Everything pauses. Or maybe it's only Bunny's perception. Then the two former scientists raise their heads, and the world snaps into motion again.

At first, Bunny doesn't know what she's seeing. Parts of the ridiculous villain costumes flare wide, bright jewel-colored shields extending between their shoulder blades. When the secondary wings—delicate and glowing and veined—appear, it clicks into place. Of course they have wings. Because what self-respecting mad scientist doesn't genetically modify themselves?

Victor and Helena's external wings rattle, a sound like hail hitting a rooftop. *At least they can't fly,* Bunny thinks, but as the beetles turn their attention upward, she realizes it's much worse. They can't fly, but they can command their charges to do so.

"Move," Bunny yells. "Take out as many as you can. And stay alive!"

It's not much by way of rousing speeches, but what else can she say? They are the Glitter Squadron, and this is what they do.

Grasping her harpoon, Bunny launches into action. The beetles swarm up from the underground city. The sound of their wings is terrible and beautiful. They are a dozen colors, a shimmering mass of stained glass, shattered and brought to life.

"The dress I could make with those," Starlight says somewhere behind her.

"You can keep whatever you kill," Bunny says.

She doesn't give herself time to think as she leaps, dropping to the next platform down and running across the nearest wooden bridge. It swings under her weight but vertigo doesn't bother her. She's in her element.

She brings her harpoon up, spearing a beetle as it flies past her. Before its weight can throw her off, Bunny yanks her weapon free; the beetle tumbles into the depths. The bridge rattles, swaying with a new weight. She crouches, ready to attack, but it's Kahuna, grinning.

He's already smeared with beetle guts, holding a serrated knife almost as long as Bunny's forearm. Despite herself, despite everything and the wildness in Kahuna's eyes, Bunny returns his grin. Whatever else he may be, he's good at his job. G-string aside, there's no doubt that job is saving the world.

She throws him a mock salute, then turns, running for the far end of the bridge. More beetles swarm toward them, but if she can get to Victor and Helena maybe she can silence their call.

There's a blur of motion to Bunny's right. Sapphire and Ruby take down a beetle, barely pausing before moving on. A shot rings out. There's a crack of something striking a shell. Bunny keeps running.

She reaches the far end of the bridge, turning toward the stairs leading to the next level. With a whirring clatter of wings, a beetle launches itself from of the darkness of a doorway cut into the rock wall. Bunny hits the ground hard as the creature slams into her, driving the breath from her lungs. The edge of the platform is perilously close. Bunny rolls away, ignoring the pain in her ribs.

She forces herself to her feet as the beetle lunges again. Bunny spins her harpoon, bringing the blunt end down with a sickening crunch. The beetle twitches and she raises the harpoon, bringing it down twice more until the beetle is still. Her arms shake with the effort. She considers kicking the beetle over the edge, but there's no time for dramatic gestures.

She takes a deep breath and regrets it immediately, clutching her ribs. Another shape moves from the doorway and Bunny stops just short of running it through. The sleek blackness is leather, not beetle shell.

"M?"

M doesn't respond, only stepping aside to reveal Doctor Blood, who stares wide-eyed at the city around them.

"I never meant… I never thought…"

Bunny grabs his shoulder, shaking him. She doesn't care how M got him here, or how M even knew about this place. She doesn't care what Doctor Blood did or didn't mean to do.

"Doc. Hector." Finally Doctor Blood's eyes focus.

"This." He holds out the canister clutched to his chest.

"What is it?"

"Pheromones." It's a moment before the doctor releases his death grip. "Spray it like perfume. It should calm them down. Hopefully."

A length of rubber tubing leads from the top of the canister with a nozzle on one end.

"Doc, I could kiss you," Bunny says, and Doctor Blood's focus snaps back to her, his eyes going wider still. "But there's no time."

Bunny hands her harpoon to M, wielding the canister instead.

"Helena."

The sound of his ex-wife's name in Doctor Blood's mouth as he catches sight of her stops Bunny in her tracks. It's a broken sound, turning into a sob. Doctor Blood crashes to his knees, his scarred face a picture of misery. M touches his shoulder, then moves on. Bunny moves too. There will be time for sympathy later.

Wild, Bunny ducks and runs, letting loose with the pheromone canister along the way. Victor and Helena move down as the chaos moves upward. When she reaches the next bridge, Bunny realizes how foolish it was to leave her harpoon behind. Spraying beetles and hoping for the best is one thing, but what will she do when she reaches the scientists? Bunny catches sight of Penny, gore-covered and looking for her next target.

"Penny!" Bunny gestures, and Penny moves to converge with her.

There's a cry behind her, and Bunny whirls. A beetle larger than any she's seen yet has Doctor Blood pinned. He's holding the creature's two front legs, barely managing to keep it from decapitating him. His arms tremble, his strength giving out.

"Shit."

Esmeralda passes below her. With heart in her throat, Bunny lets the pheromone canister fly. "Es, catch! Spray everything you can!"

Bunny sprints for Doctor Blood. She's weaponless now, possibly going to her doom, but despite everything, she can't leave Hector to die.

Bunny drops her shoulder and slams into the beetle linebacker style. The beetle tips onto its back, legs working as it tries to right itself. If the situation weren't so dire, it would be hilarious.

"Come on." Bunny hauls Doctor Blood to his feet, pushing him behind her.

The beetle rights itself, turning its attention to Bunny. Her mind races. A bitter laugh rises to her lips, and she pulls off one shoe.

"It worked once before."

As the beetle charges, Bunny flings herself forward, bringing the shoe down as hard as she can. The heel connects with one of the beetle's eyes, splattering Bunny. The creature reels back, pain-maddened. She raises the shoe for another strike just as Big Kahuna—in all his barefoot, stoned, and g-stringed glory—lands on the beetle's back. The beetle bucks, shuddering, trying to throw him off.

"Just like riding a wave." Kahuna shows white teeth, toes curling to hold his balance.

He plunges his serrated blade through the beetle's head, then hops down. Bunny suppresses a shudder. Maybe Kahuna is too much in his element. But then, how does she look after a kill?

"Good teamwork," she says.

Kahuna holds up a fist. After a moment, Bunny bumps his with her clenched hand, her fingers opening wide afterward and a few sequins stuck to her palm from clutching her ribs shimmer in the air a moment.

She peels off her other shoe, drops it with the gore-covered one over the edge. Just once, she'd like to wear out a pair by walking in them.

"I'm going for Helena and Victor," Bunny says. "Gather whoever you can and meet me there."

She steers Doctor Blood toward the next bridge. "It looks like your pheromones are working. The beetles are slowing down."

Blood doesn't answer, shock setting in. Bunny rolls tension from her shoulders. One thing at a time.

Bunny reaches Victor and Helena's platform first. As she does, Doctor Blood breaks free, rushing toward his ex-wife. Recognition dawns on Helena's face, becoming a sneer.

"You're too late, Richard!" Victor says. "We've done what you never could. This is our time, and when our legions rise, you'll wish you died in that fire."

Before Bunny can move, Doctor Blood, aka Hector, aka Richard Utley Carnacki, launches himself at his former lab assistant, catching him around the waist. Shock rounds his mouth, widens his eyes, and Victor's beetle wings beat uselessly. For a moment, the two men are poised, frozen like a frame in a pulp comic book adventure. Then they vanish, tumbling together over the edge. Before Bunny can move, Helena snarls and grabs Bunny's dress, hauling her off balance.

Helena's hands hook like claws, her face a mask of mutant-beetle rage. She slashes for Bunny's face. Bunny tries to catch her wrist and misses. Helena strikes again, catching one of the long, white ears atop Bunny's head, knocking them askew. Instinct draws Bunny's fist back, snapping it into Helena's face.

"No one messes with my ears."

Helena rocks back with the blow, blood slicking her chin. Ruby is there, pinning Helena's arms to her side.

"Hold her!" Bunny shouts as Helena thrashes.

Helena's wings snap wide with a terrible rattling sound. Ruby ducks, keeping her arms around Helena as Bunny casts around for a weapon. Ruby's hold slips. She scrambles, catching hold of one Helena's wings. It rips free.

The sound is utterly inhuman, all pain and rage. Helena buckles. Behind her, Ruby is white-faced, holding the torn wing, eyes wide in shock.

"I didn't mean to. I'm sorry."

"It's okay," Bunny says. "I know."

She kneels, touching Helena's shoulder and ignoring the ruin of her back. The hard outer wing on Helena's right is awkwardly bent, the delicate wing underneath completely torn away. Helena doesn't react to Bunny's touch, shuddering and sobbing.

"Hey!" Penny's shout from below draws Bunny's attention. "A little help."

"Take care of her." Bunny addresses the platform in general, gesturing to Helena.

She's weary. Her ribs ache. She keeps an arm wrapped around her mid-section as she moves to peer over the edge. A second wave of adrenaline hits her as she does. Penny is leaning halfway over a bridge, straining to hold on to Doctor Blood. Victor is nowhere in sight.

"Ruby!" Bunny dashes for the stairs, ignoring the pain.

Ruby follows close on her heels. The rope bridge sways as they clatter to the mid-way point. Doctor Blood hangs limp in Penny's grasp, holding on by reflex alone. Bunny meets his eyes, breath tangled in her throat. He would just as soon fall, she can see it.

"Ruby." It comes out choked.

Ruby reaches past Penny, and grips the doctor's arm, hauling him onto the ominously creaking bridge.

There's another shout, this time from above, and Bunny's stomach drops. Her heart hurts, worrying about all her girls all the time. Her body aches and she wants to rest. But she can't, she won't, not until everyone is safe. She looks up.

A massive beetle dips and weaves, its flight made awkward by the bundle trapped against its body by its legs. Bunny's eyes refuse to make sense of what she's seeing. Then her pulse kicks, the image resolving. Silk twists and thrashes in the beetle's grip.

The beetle spirals lower, an erratic, weaving pattern. One of the beetle's legs slips, and Silk drops an inch. Bunny's heart lurches. Then several things happen at once.

The beetle draws even with another platform, and Esmeralda fires

Doctor Blood's pheromone spray. Her eyes widen with shock, seeing Silk in the beetle's grasp a moment too late. The beetle relaxes, and Silk drops again, dangling, clinging to the beetle for dear life. The beetle lists sideways, nearly crashing into an outcropping of stone before veering away. And from above, CeCe jumps.

Tearing her gaze away from Silk and the beetle, Bunny tracks CeCe's fall.

"No!" Bunny doesn't know who the word is for—CeCe, Esmeralda, or Silk, but it doesn't matter, because it's too late. Everything keeps happening.

Esmeralda drops the canister. It clatters against the bridge before tumbling over the edge. The beetle bounces off a rock face, caroming away, and dipping lower. Silk's grip, blood-slicked from the barbs on the beetle's leg, falters. CeCe falls.

And then, the impossible happens. CeCe hits one of the bridges, whipping out her sword cane and hacking at the ropes. Bracing her feet and one arm, she cuts the last strand free and swings over empty space. With her free arm, she catches Silk around the waist just as Silk sees her and jumps—a perfect moment of synchronicity and trust. The bridge strikes the far wall, jolting, but neither of them falls. The beetle, giving in to exhaustion, drops, spiraling down into the underground city.

Bunny lets out a breath, crashing to her knees as exhaustion hits her. For a moment, just a moment, she wants to drop over the edge after the beetle, fall like a glittering, shooting star into the depths. It finally registers that someone is shaking her shoulder. Sapphire bends close, expression drawn with concern.

"I'm okay," she says, but she has to lean on Sapphire to stand.

Something tickles Bunny's upper lip; wiping it away smears her hand with blood. She leans against the rock, closing her eyes, and concentrates on breathing shallow—in, out—against the pain in her ribs. She listens to the sound of it, timed to the beat of her heart. Voices and footsteps swirl around her as one by one the members of the Glitter Squadron and the G-String Men join her on the platform. The sound washes around her, over her, holding her. Like family. Without opening her eyes, Bunny adds her voice to the weave of sound.

"We're okay. We're all okay."

It's Thursday, which means the Ultra Fabulous Glitter Squadron goes bowling. Of course they are dressed for the occasion. Here's Bunny in strapless white with elbow-length gloves (which don't give her an advantage on the lanes, no matter what Sapphire says), her ears shimmering with ionic flare. Sapphire wears turquoise fishtail splendor, sequin train hissing with every step, while Ruby is surrounded in a froth of chiffon and feather boas. CeCe's in garnet velvet today, Silk in a slip dress the color of ice, and never mind the crutch she's leaning on.

Esmeralda put the word out, so even some of the former, auxiliary, and one-time members of the Glitter Squadron have come to join in the fun. Butch is here in all his spangled glory, his new husband Paolo in tow. The bikini girls from Doctor Blood's Martian lab are here. In honor of their supervillainous origins, they go by Bambi and Honey, but these days they're far more conservatively attired. Cherry Bomb and Licorice Whip are here to talk shop, rather than bowl. They were only with the Glitter Squadron for a few months before leaving to start their own team. The main roadblock they're facing now is the inability to agree on a catchy team name.

The G-String Men's state of undress has made the other patrons nervous enough that they have Gary's Disco Bowlarama all to themselves. They're good enough customers that Gary doesn't mind. In fact, Gary is more than happy to host. Of all the regulars who come to the Bowlarama, the Ultra Fabulous Glitter Squadron is by far the most fun. Besides, he suspects he may need their services soon. He's certain there's something moving in the walls.

Notably absent from the celebration is M. Bowling is not M's thing. Also absent is Doctor Blood, sitting by wounded Helena's bedside. Even though Sapphire counseled him against it, he's determined. He wants to say he's sorry. And besides, as he told Sapphire—no one should wake up in the hospital alone.

Ruby gets a strike. A cheer goes up around the lanes.

Bunny still doesn't trust Kahuna, not entirely, but she's willing to make peace for the sake of her girls. Starlight is trying not to look at Flash Jr., and Boomer is trying not to look at Sapphire. A waiter on roller skates brings them a round of drinks, and Starlight beams a smile.

"To friendship," Bunny says, starting the toast.

Everyone takes a drink, except Silk.

"Everything okay, doll?" CeCe leans close, her cheeks flushed with victory.

"I can't," Silk whispers. Her cheeks are redder than CeCe's. "I mean, I shouldn't. I think…"

"I'm going to be a dad?"

The shout is louder than Esmeralda's 7-10 split, the clatter of the pins drowned in the cheer as the rest of the Squadron overhears CeCe and Silk's news.

When the congratulations are done, Sapphire squeezes CeCe's arm, exchanging a look in place of words. Meanwhile, Ruby is matching Bad Kitty—whose g-string shifts from deep, midnight black to lynx grey—drink for drink. She's learned to hold her liquor much better since joining with the Glitter Squadron. Esmeralda is discussing fabric and pattern options with Kahuna. During the ninth frame, Flash Jr. approaches Silk and CeCe.

"I just wanted to offer my congratulations," he says. He shifts awkwardly from foot to foot.

"Yes?" Silk says.

A smile teases the corner of her lips at his shyness. She lets it ride as she revels in the warmth of CeCe's palm against her own, fingers entwined. It's almost as good as being up on stage. Actually, no, it's better.

"In case you're wondering, the g-string is photosynthetic. I don't have to eat while wearing it. As long as it's sunny." Flash Jr. falters.

"Are we supposed to be impressed?" Silk lightens her tone so he'll know she's only teasing him.

"Sorry. It's not like I'm even a botanist. Mom had the green thumb. I'm a graphic artist," he says, the words tumbling out in a rush. "I mean, I'm trying to be, when I'm not fighting crime or dancing. I thought maybe

I could use you two as models. Watching you during the fight gave me an idea for a new series—Velvet and Silk. You make a hell of a crime-fighting duo."

Flash Jr. allows himself a hopeful smile.

Silk grips CeCe's hand. "Tell us more," she says.

And in her rigid plastic seat, Starlight tries not to let her expression give away the flutter in her stomach. Maybe this means Flash Jr. will stick around for a while. And maybe she'll actually get up the courage to talk to him if he does.

The tenth frame ends and the Bowlarama goes dark, black light flicking on and disco strobe patterns lighting the lanes as the neon-psychedelic planets and stars on the ceilings and above the lanes glow. The G-String Men and the Ultra Fabulous Glitter Squadron take to the polished floors, turning the Bowlarama into a disco as the music kicks in.

Despite the music, Bunny still hears it when her cell phone chirps. Stepping away from the strobe of multicolored lights, she looks at the screen.

"What is it?" Penny steps up beside Bunny.

"It's from the *Bundespräsident der Bundesrepublik Deutschland. Swamp Kreaturen.*" Bunny sighs. "Attacking the Fabergé Museum in Baden-Baden."

"No rest for the fabulous." Penny grins.

Bunny drops her phone back into her beaded purse, squaring her shoulders, the familiar sense of exhilaration filling her.

The Ultra Fabulous Glitter Squadron must save the world again.

Sapphire's Summer Sangria

Take a big ole pitcher. Dump in a big ole bottle of white wine—something with a light touch, and just a little bit of sweetness. Add a bottle of apricot, peach, or mango nectar, a splash of apricot brandy, and a dash of soda water. Then grab your favorite fruits, chop 'em up, and throw them in there. Because, as I like to say, it's not a real party until you get a bunch of fruits together, and, honey, there's no wrong way to mix 'em. It's perfect for celebrating new beginnings, toasting endings, and bringing together good friends.

Acknowledgements

Writing is a solitary pursuit, but no book is created in a void containing the author alone. I owe thanks to many people for the collection you hold in your hands. First and foremost, my family - my husband, for understanding my occasional need to disappear and write, and my parents, for their encouragement and support, even though speculative fiction isn't my dad's thing, and my mom thinks everything I write is too scary. A huge amount of thanks is due to Steve Berman and Lethe Press for taking a chance on my beautiful, glittering ladies, and giving them a good home. A.T. Greenblatt for being an excellent first reader, and giving me invaluable feedback on the collection, and Sunny Moraine for the same, and for also teaching me about make up. Leah Bobet at Ideomancer for giving the Glitter Squadron their first home, and Beth Wodzinski, E. Catherine Tobler, and all the diligent badgers at Shimmer for giving Bunny her second home when she insisted her origin story needed to be told. Bernie Mojzes for inadvertently daring me to write the first Glitter Squadron story in less than twenty four hours. To all the folks who expressed excitement about this collection along the way, who acted as cheerleaders, and listened patiently. A ginormous, glittery thank you to my wonderful writing community, my chosen family (all of you, yes, you, you know who you are) - for swapping critiques, hanging out at conventions and coffeehouses, for sharing victories and defeats, for encouragement and kicks-in-the-pants. Whether I've met you in person or in the virtual world, you are all fabulous, and I couldn't do this without you. Only praise is due to all of these people; any errors, omissions, or fault in this text is solely my own. Last, but not least, thank you to you, dear reader. This collection is for you. I hope it makes your world a little more glittery.

About The Author

A.C. Wise was born and raised in Montreal, and currently lives in the Philadelphia area. Her first professionally published piece of fiction was printed on the label of a coffee can, which seems strangely fitting. Since then, her short stories have appeared in *Apex, Uncanny, Shimmer, Year's Best Weird Fiction Volume 1*, and *The Year's Best Dark Fantasy and Horror*, among other places. In addition to her fiction, she co-edits *Unlikely Story*, and contributes a monthly column to *SF Signal*. She blogs sporadically at her website, www.acwise.net, and tweets slightly more than sporadically as @ac_wise.

CPSIA information can be obtained at www.ICGtesting.com
Printed in the USA
BVOW02s0451281115

428109BV00001B/5/P